F

FAST BOYS AND PRETTY GIRLS

"Past and present intermix in this riveting story that proves, no matter how much you might want it, you can't ever really leave your past behind. Lo Patrick does a masterful job setting the stage for the gripping suspense that had me turning the pages long into the night."

—Suzanne Redfearn, #1 Amazon
bestselling author of *In an Instant*

"*Fast Boys and Pretty Girls* is a haunting and atmospheric mystery with turns as sharp as a Georgia back road."

—Jennifer Moorhead, Amazon bestselling
author of *Broken Bayou*

"Lo Patrick's latest novel, *Fast Boys and Pretty Girls*, tackles the complex and emotional difficulties that often come with first love. Never quite certain of where she stands with local bad boy Benji Law, Danielle, or Dani, an up-and-coming model with a solid future, remains on uneven footing where he's concerned. Relentless in her quest for reassurance of his feelings only creates a burgeoning friction between them as well as between Dani and her family, with devastating consequences. Dani's insecurities, willful-ness, and obsession are superbly depicted by Patrick, who turns a shrewd eye on the psychology of first love and family dynamics. Patrick's powerful writing makes this novel a standout, an absolutely riveting read."

—Donna Everhart, bestselling author
of *When the Jessamine Grows*

"*Fast Boys and Pretty Girls* is a character-driven mystery about the wounds of first love and the hunt for belonging. Lo Patrick is a compelling Southern storyteller, exploring the tension between obligation and desire."

—Audrey Ingram, author of *The Summer We Ran*

"Is there a woman alive who never, at least once, found herself obsessively drawn to a bad boy? Now that former model Danielle Greer is married with children, she hopes she has left that destructive obsession far behind her. But author Lo Patrick is not going to let her off that easily. Patrick's skillful writing will keep the reader turning the pages as Dani's past crashes head on into her present."

—Diane Chamberlain, *New York Times* bestselling
author of *The Last House on the Street*

Praise for
The Night the River Wept

"Haunting and unputdownable, *The Night the River Wept* is a gritty rendering of small-town tragedy and the far-reaching shadows it casts. Lo Patrick writes a stubbornly resilient heroine determined to untangle the secrets of a forgotten past and skillfully leads the reader along a twisty path to an unexpected yet satisfying ending!"

—Laura Barrow, author of *Call the Canaries Home*

"Lo Patrick introduces us to vivid characters populating an authentic small Georgia town, their lives tangled like kudzu vines. *The Night the River Wept* is an intriguing mystery that will have you turning pages until the wee hours of the morning."

—Beth Duke, bestselling author of *It All Comes Back to You*, *Tapestry*, and *Dark Enough to See the Stars*

"*The Night the River Wept* is a page-turning exploration of small-town secrets and the far-reaching effects of tragedy. With wit and wisdom, Lo Patrick weaves an unforgettable story of heartbreak, love, and second chances—and proves herself as a compelling new voice in Southern fiction."

—Kristy Woodson Harvey, *New York Times* bestselling author of *The Summer of Songbirds*

"Lo Patrick's sophomore novel, set in a small Southern town, explores what drives us to murder and how solving the mysteries of the past can captivate and even unite strangers. The tragic killing of three boys has repercussions that resonate through the town of Faber and in the heart of Arlene. On a journey of personal growth and redemption that pulls the reader along, Arlene becomes obsessed with solving the long cold case and with her neighbors and coworkers who still live with the trauma of it. This is a gripping portrayal of a small town where everyone has their secrets and the lines between guilty and innocent blur."

—Quinn Connor, author of *Cicadas Sing of Summer Graves*

"Smart, sassy, and utterly heartbreaking, this seductive Southern novel has to be my favorite mystery of the year. I rooted for Arlene as, struggling with her own loss, she becomes obsessed with the Broderick boys and their story. *The Night the River Wept* is a brave book that explores how difficult it can be to escape the past."

—Emily Critchley, author of *One Puzzling Afternoon*

"In *The Night the River Wept*, Arlene is a frustrated, lonely housewife until she finds a job at the local police station bagging evidence. There she immerses herself in a decades old murder, determined to solve the crime. Lo Patrick writes an original and moving tale brimming with mystery, heartache, and wit. Sure to be a Southern fiction favorite, Arlene's journey pulls the reader in and doesn't let go."

—Rochelle Weinstein, *USA Today* bestselling author
of *This Is Not How It Ends* and *What You Do to Me*

"An increasingly gripping Southern-crime tale. Patrick (*The Floating Girls*, 2022) interweaves themes of addiction, loss, and poverty alongside those of resilience and community bonds, especially those bonds held sacred between women. Readers who enjoyed the mysterious, character-driven plot of *Where the Crawdads Sing* or the atmospheric Georgia setting of *Midnight in the Garden of Good and Evil* will find an enjoyable page-turner here. In Arlene, Patrick has created a determined, likable, and charismatic heroine fit for a series of Southern-crime novels."

—*Booklist*, STARRED review

PRAISE FOR
THE FLOATING GIRLS

"[A] compelling mystery...Kay is the smartest, funniest, most curious young narrator I have come across in some time. Her voice stuck with me long after I finished reading."

—Tiffany Quay Tyson, award-winning author of *The Past Is Never*

"*The Floating Girls* is a powerhouse of a Southern novel... This lush and mesmerizing debut has a beating heart of its own. Lo Patrick is a standout new Southern voice."

—Andrea Bobotis, author of *The Last List of Miss Judith Kratt*

"Fans of *Where the Crawdads Sing* will love this immersive mystery set against the salty air of Georgia's marshes. In Patrick's atmospheric prose, the water and its characters come to life."

—Lindsey Rogers Cook, author of *Learning to Speak Southern*

"To read *The Floating Girls* is to feel a small-town slowness seep into your bones. The book's narrator, Kay Whitaker, is a stubborn young girl you'll never forget. A cracking story that unfolds in gorgeous prose in the stultifying heat of the American South."

—Hayley Scrivenor, author of *Dirt Creek*

"Superb debut… The crackling energy of Kay's narration—a winning mixture of insight and naiveté, humor and pathos, vulnerability and strength—provides a welcome counterbalance to the oppressive setting and the pain the characters try to suppress. It's a masterly achievement."

—*Publishers Weekly*, STARRED review

"Many readers are looking for the next *Where the Crawdads Sing* and will find *The Floating Girls*…is a close cousin… It has its own unique charms, featuring a winning young protagonist that will remind readers of Scout in *To Kill a Mockingbird*."

—*Augusta Chronicle*

"Readers will be unable to peel their eyes and hearts away from Lo Patrick's *The Floating Girls* as secrets are revealed in the span of a Georgia summer."

—*Deep South Magazine*

"Don't sleep on Lo Patrick's powerful coming-of-age and family drama set in the humid backwaters of Georgia… *The Floating Girls* has been compared to *To Kill a Mockingbird*, thanks to its child narrator, exploration of heartbreaking family secrets, and highlighting of social issues."

—*Reader's Digest* Editor's Pick

ALSO BY LO PATRICK

The Floating Girls
The Night the River Wept

fast boys
and
pretty
girls

a novel

LO PATRICK

sourcebooks
landmark

Published by Sourcebooks Landmark, an imprint of Sourcebooks
P.O. Box 4410, Naperville, Illinois 60567-4410
(630) 961-3900
sourcebooks.com

Cataloging-in-Publication Data is on file with the Library of Congress.

Printed and bound in the United States of America.
VP 10 9 8 7 6 5 4 3 2 1

For Nyima

1

It was likely to happen in Pressville. In any town up that way. The trees obscure vision; the roads are a puzzle, winding and steep. Exposed limestone and kudzu on the shoulder, the green blanket heavy and wide. One corner leads to another; one bend in the road is only an introduction to a longer, starker curve. When a hard rain comes down on a hot day, the fog makes a wall up the dizzy valley. I'd duck sometimes on the back of his bike. My head wasn't near a thing, but the roads were so swallowed by the laurel and the bent limbs that it would feel like trying to tunnel out. Pressville was the kind of place I wanted to tunnel out of, with a chisel. The winding and weaving, the dipping and lolling. My stomach turns and I grip tighter when I remember.

We lived on Bell Road. We were the one nice house in at least a mile's stretch—if you didn't look too close. Our home needed work too, but like with the rest, you had to be standing right next to it if you wanted to know which repairs were required. There were other houses with stained latticework under their porches and discarded belongings cluttering their carports, but ours was bigger, older, grander. It had once been lovely and was now just a reminder of what we weren't able to maintain.

Pressville, Georgia—somewhere between Atlanta and North Carolina—is a place filled with long lives lived on hills or in ditches. Generations of green, mud, tops, and bottoms. The Greer house—my house—stood out because of its ornate woodwork and size. No clutter on the porch, just clutter inside. The clutter of minds fractured, thoughts on parallel highways; no intersections, no crossing paths, until just the one. The one impact. The one moment of descent, magnetic and foretold.

There's no room for error with the shoulder so small, so insignificant compared to the curve of the road, the angle of the mountain. You have to go slow on Bell Road. Everyone knows that. Everyone knows you can't drive like that on Bell Road.

2

2019

It was thirteen years after the accident. I was living in the family house—again, still. My parents didn't want to take care of it anymore. They'd never really taken care of it to begin with, a lot of excuses about expense and other commitments, and then ultimately all the bad memories they associated with what happened there. They did not stay long. It sat empty for some time, and then I sat emptily in it while Jasper and my girls came along.

What no one else in my family wanted, I took without outstretched, grasping hands. I was going to move back home—not just to Georgia or even just to Pressville but to the house on Bell Road where I'd grown up. This was a comfort. No one else was comforted by the idea of living there. My parents weren't going to sell it, but no one wanted to see the marks on the road day after day. There was always the chance they'd repave, but my mother reminded us that the marks were not only on the road but in our minds too—where they couldn't be covered with new asphalt.

I'd married Jasper and had our four girls. We lived in the house on Bell Road together. Sometimes it felt as though I woke up there with twenty years of my life gone, most of which I'd spent trying to recover from that single year. One year lasts a lifetime when it's the year that changes everything.

Our girls—Tessa, Leigh, Pamela, and Rose—were slight and wandering, much like I was when I had each of them. Like a vapor meant to represent the water it came from, I lingered around existence, theirs and mine, in a fog of uncertainty. I never grew up; I never changed. I only appeared to justify my milky, drifting existence. I had to be somewhere, doing something. Such is the requirement for those of us who didn't die in an accident when we were sixteen.

It was Tessa who found them. The bones. "There's bones down there!" Her face was pale except for her cheeks, flushed under her wide, shocked eyes. "Mama!"

"There, there," I said, wishing Jasper were home and not at a sales conference. In almost all memories of significant moments in my children's lives, Jasper is at a sales conference. "Where?" I was woozy from day sleeping and the chocolates I'd eaten for lunch.

"In the ditch!" Leigh, Pamela, and Rose were behind her. We'd misnamed Rose. She was olive colored, with blond hair and angry brown eyes. She'd been an unexpected and difficult baby. I thought

I'd done her a disservice with such a precious name. Everyone would be surprised once they got to know her.

"It's bones," Leigh said. She scowled. She never trusted the way Tessa told stories. Pamela remained quietly concerned, always contemplating the ways in which I could fail them.

"Okay. We'll call Daddy." I'd fallen asleep in the front room with the window unit going at full blast. In the afternoons, I liked to go in there and lie on the tiny couch with my feet under a blanket. I almost always fell asleep. The girls were old enough now to give me a reprieve—ten, eight, seven, and five-almost-six. It seemed they'd all come at once, the way I woke up one day with four sets of nostrils sniffing out my inauthenticity. I always felt they already knew who I was.

They also knew not to play in the road. There was only the small eyebrow drive and a little patch of grass out front. Instead, they ventured to the back—where the woods began, and the ditch. The woods and the house had been in my mother's family for a hundred years. My mother had refused to sell them to a number of developers numerous times, even when money was tight, which it always was.

I heard a crack of thunder outside as the window unit cut off, having reached sixty-six degrees. We were supposed to get rain much later. Storms moved on odd paths, zigzagging their way around mountains and over lakes. A storm would introduce itself hours before dumping its load with a stark fury. All I saw was sun out the window. It would be a while before we got hit.

I shuddered and tried to refocus on the girls and what they were telling me. It was cold in the room, and there was this news of bones, and thunder. "I'll go out and take a look." I stood up; I had chill bumps on my legs. We were all in shorts and T-shirts. The girls, as Jasper liked to call us. We all dressed the same, surviving the muggy summer heat in small rags. Our skin exposed and our feet bare; I'd trained them to muscle through by being hardly dressed. I didn't know my motivations half the time. I was left at home with four girls, so many feet and bottoms and long, tangled hair. I did what I had to do to get through the years.

"Ragamuffins," Jasper would say. He was not endeared. He preferred crisp. The breadth of what he was willing to accept was very narrow. He would have liked us more neatly cropped. Being from the southern half of the state, he had never understood the mountains. It was like he couldn't get a good look at anything once we went north. He was used to flat, unobscured nothingness and a family with perfectly arranged judgments.

Tessa and Leigh led the way while Pamela hung back a little. She blocked Rose, who both wanted to see the bones again but who was terrified and angry at her weakness in the face of them.

"Girls, it might be a raccoon or something," I said. I didn't go back in the woods anymore. I had as a child, but the interest faded—and then the accident. I never set foot back there again after the accident.

The angle of the land was dramatic. We had to walk sideways, one leg down and one leg bent at an extreme, with a lot of space between our feet. Pamela was in flip-flops, which kept sliding to the side so as to lose their point entirely. I wasn't wearing underwear or a very supportive bra. I felt loose and uncoordinated.

"No, it's a head," Leigh said eagerly. "It's a human head."

"How would you know?" Tessa wanted to be the one to know everything. She was the oldest, but not by enough. She had to assert her authority often and at inappropriate times. "We don't know anything about raccoons, Leigh."

We got closer. I hadn't known exactly where the girls found their bones, but I could see a pile of leaves, most damp underneath, about fifty yards down the hill. The colors went from pale brown to almost black because of dirt and hidden moisture. "I don't want you going this far. You won't be able to get back up." I was talking about myself. "I didn't know you girls were going down this far. I don't like this."

"But she went down." It was Pamela.

"Who?" I took the opportunity to stop my descent.

"The girl who died."

"How do you know it's a girl?" I was sweating down my back and having to swat gnats away from my face in order to see clearly.

"Her shoes." Pamela looked sorry to have to tell me this. "Her shoes are still there too."

I was going to have to call Cady Benson.

3

My name is Danielle, but I went by Dani as a model. I'd always hated that before—Dani—but as soon as my booker said it was going to be all the rage, I was committed.

Claudia, my agent, said I was such a "country bumpkin" that I had to be something "really southern and hickish. You know, like honky-tonk town." I took some offense at her suggestions, but perhaps not enough.

Claudia was from France, allegedly, so she may not have known the difference. She claimed Parisian origins, but no accent could be detected. We had French models with the agency, and when they greeted her in what was apparently her native tongue, she acted like she couldn't hear them and then immediately started speaking loud English with affectations on the open syllables. Someone told me she was really from Ohio. Thanks to Claudia, French or not, I was a one-name model. Dani. My mother made the strangest face when I told her. I was only seventeen and thought I was making brilliant sense.

"I'm going by Dani. Just Dani."

"What's wrong with Danielle Greer?" my mother said. She was in New York with me at the time but was leaving after only two weeks. She'd come to set me up in the model apartment and take in some sights. I had about eleven appointments, or castings as I learned they were called, a day and didn't get to spend hardly any time with her at all. I also didn't book any of the jobs, and thought maybe they'd been wrong and that my cowgirl look was not that popular. Or maybe I just wasn't that pretty or my butt wasn't the right shape. I knew one girl had been released from a runway show because her calf muscles were too flat.

"Her legs look like triangles," I heard one of the fashion people say. "Long triangles." I didn't want to have long-triangle legs, so I did fifty calf raises that night before I went to bed.

My mother failed to comfort me after this day of endless rejection and stayed focused on what was most important to her. "I almost didn't name you Danielle because I hate Dani so much—and what do you mean *lingerie*? You're seventeen." I also hadn't booked a bra ad. I was skipped over in the waiting room and not even asked in to model the underwires.

"You can go," a man told me without even looking at the little stack of Polaroids of myself in my underwear that I'd brought with me.

"My agent says Dani is cool," I said to my mother. "It's country, and people like that right now." I bit my lip, not so sure that was true. Either that or I wasn't country enough.

"You tell that pale-ass poser she wouldn't last a day on the ridge!"

I didn't tell Claudia anything. Not then and not ever, really. I was never in the position to tell people something. My mother was good at it no matter her position. She was certain that I was headed in the wrong direction, given the bras and the way I had to go half-naked into every room, but was secretly impressed by the money—I'd gone to a couple of castings for jobs that paid over twenty grand a pop. She wouldn't let on for years that she couldn't believe how much money models made. Money is the best way to win an argument; no one can disagree with it.

And money had been my selling point when a model scout approached me in the Pressville Mall. "Please let me try! I can't do nothin' here," I had said to my parents. "We don't even have the money for ballet." It wasn't all true. I'd quit ballet at fifteen because, my God, was I bored with the positions and the small foot movements. Even if it had been my decision, it was helpful to my parents that they no longer had to pay for it. "Maybe I'll make enough to be able to take ballet again," I'd said, pleading. I may have dropped to my knees at one point. I did beg. It was like it was the only thing I'd ever wanted—to be a model—even though I had never even considered the idea until precisely that afternoon in front of Abercrombie & Fitch.

I was seventeen and a day when a man with a mustache came up to me and said, "Have you ever considered modeling?" He explained that everyone in fashion wanted that rural farm-girl look. "You know—very country." It was Frank Dabney. He's the coauthor of my story, as all disruptors are. It didn't have to be this way. That's what I would have said to Frank Dabney years later, every year later.

"Oh, okay." I wasn't sure what he was saying. I did not grow up on a farm and hated the smell of all animal feces. I made a comment about cow shit and how much I hated plows. Frank Dabney put his hand on my arm and said not to worry about cow shit or plows anymore. I'd actually never seen a plow anyway. My mother stood next to me, shocked at this sudden transformation... I wanted to take ballet again AND I hated plows? She glowered at me, but even more so at Frank Dabney. He inspired much glowering where my mother was concerned.

To try to assuage her fears, my mother manhandled Mr. Dabney—her specialty, in addition to glowering, has always been manhandling—by immediately asking him a whole assortment of arguably irrelevant questions.

"How the hell did you get to Pressville?"

"What kind of car do you drive?"

"What is your wife's middle name?"

"Do you call your mother?"

"What does she think of you prowling local malls and talking to teenage girls?"

"What did you eat for breakfast?"

He answered that last one with a smirk. "Buttermilk biscuits, in fact."

"Oh, so you think you'll make friends by poking fun at the southern way of life? You gonna ask if my dog's name is Skillet next? If I married my cousin or if we live in a double-wide and take welfare?"

Our dog's name was Skillet. He'd died when I was thirteen, but his name was indeed Skillet when he'd been alive, so I think that part was just her losing her train of thought. Dabney remained composed and assured my mother that he was originally from Tennessee and knew more about the southern way of life than anyone who'd ever made fun of her. "I said buttermilk biscuits because that's what I ate."

My mother softened a little. "Where in Tennessee?" she asked.

"Memphis."

She grunted in slight disapproval. He might as well have said Atlanta, a place riddled with wicked traffic and criminals. People from Pressville and beyond avoided Atlanta and all the freeways that lead to and from it. Nothing but trouble in a place with all those people. We liked trees and nature where we were from. Like Walt Whitman, it was us and the leaves of grass.

4

Cady Benson. Her significance cannot be overstated. No matter how hard I tried, I couldn't get her off my back—or rather, I couldn't get my mother's insistence off my back. This insistence seemed to come out of nowhere, then proceeded to follow me for the rest of my life, a lot like Cady Benson. I'm sure my mother had her regrets later, involving the Bensons in our affairs, pulling Cady inside the circle with such enthusiasm. It's when I think very deeply about this that I am the sorriest. It was from a good place that my mother wished for Cady to know me. We couldn't have foreseen the irony.

The Bensons owned a restaurant in Pressville. Not far from the mall. I knew the Bensons—everyone did. Benson's Restaurant had been around for at least thirty years. We never ate there. My parents thought it was overpriced and "only chicken." We could eat chicken at home. Humble birds were for humble meals with

Rice-A-Roni and canned green beans. "Who goes out to eat so they can have chicken?" my mother asked time and time again. I always had the feeling that it really had nothing to do with the chicken.

I knew that Cady, the eldest of the Benson children, lived in New York. She was practically famous for it. She was a detective there. People said she'd run into the Twin Towers on 9/11 but my mother said that wasn't true. "Making things up so they can brag on one of their own. A lot of good that did, anyway. If it's true. Doesn't sound like she got anybody out. Just ran in so she could say she was a hero. No thank you." That chicken really left a bad taste in my mother's mouth. She never had anything nice to say about a Benson—at least at first.

"Cady went to New York to work for the police," my mother corrected me whenever I used the Bensons as an excuse for my upcoming move. "Not to run around in a thong." We typically argued about my future modeling career over dinner; we needed nourishment if we were really going to be able to get into it. The six of us sat around a long plank table with our elbows propped up, usually eating chicken.

"She might wear a thong under her uniform," I said.

"Sounds serious!" My dad chuckled. He did always laugh at the word *thong*. He was surrounded by women, drowning in thongs. I'm surprised he didn't get one wrapped around his throat, with all the girls' panties in the house. There were five of us, including my mother.

If I'd been asked to go to New York to play soccer or build something with logs, my mother would have been pleased and encouraging. Soccer was a good enough reason to do anything. As was working with your hands. She referenced logs whenever she wanted to prove we were hearty people. "This table's made of logs!" she shouted over my protestations more than once, as if log tables would change my mind. I never liked that table; it was uneven because of all the logs.

Soccer and logs were everything to my mother. She had one good foot—her left. She'd played soccer at Pressville Community College for three years while getting her nursing degree and was a staunch advocate for women's rights because she said she hadn't been able to play soccer when she was little due to the organs between her legs.

"Sounds serious," my father always said when she got on her soapbox about gender equality in sports.

Then I went and made money posing in my underwear, and she wasn't sure what to say about it, because the girls made a lot more money than the boys when it came to modeling. "Hmm," she mused. "Same in porn."

I had three sisters: one on her own and the others a set of twins. Chantel is older than I am, and then Raquel and Janelle are three years younger—and of course, I'm Danielle. My mother made sure all our names ended in the same sound, which to an unknowing audience might make her seem like the kind of woman who wears fake eyelashes or platform shoes, but she isn't—not entirely. She's two people: that woman, and someone else I feel like I've never met. From my mother I learned how to be whoever I wanted to be without explanation and that it was perfectly okay to switch between my selves anytime I pleased.

Frank Dabney tried to outwit my mother, unsuccessfully. I think he sensed she would be in the way in New York, and he was right. He initially suggested that my father accompany me during my first trip there. Frank came to our house for dinner after the fortuitous meeting at the mall. He was wearing a leather jacket and white trainers. "He looks so cool," I told Chantel, who was wearing a baseball cap but then immediately took it off and brushed her hair. My mother said maybe I shouldn't model, because Chantel might get jealous. I frowned, and then my mom said frowning was not my "look."

Chantel was jealous, but she was only five foot five, so she got over it when Frank Dabney said models had to be five eight minimum. Chantel had my mother's height and not much else from either of my parents. She looked like Clara, a distant relative who had gotten pregnant with a married man's baby and run off to South Carolina, where she died jumping into an empty swimming pool with a bucket over her head. There was lengthy debate about whether she knew the pool was empty or not. "The bucket!" my mother shouted at her own mother whenever they discussed "Clara's incident," as it was called. "She had a bucket on her head!"

Clara was my cousin's much younger sister from her father's third marriage. Too confusing and scandalous for us to keep up with, but Chantel reminded everyone in the family of Clara with her tight little body and wavy black hair. When Chantel was moody, we usually blamed Clara.

Raquel and Janelle laughed at Frank Dabney because he ate with both a knife and a fork and didn't cut his chicken with only his fork. I caught my mother watching him and his utensils closely—studying this foreign behavior. My father tried to make small talk, mentioning sports and weather and the drive from New York. My mother made a photocopy of Dabney's ID and taped it to the front door. "In case they find the bodies and wonder what happened," she told me specifically.

Frank laid out the plan for New York. He said he would send me there to meet with two agencies for whom he scouted, and then we'd have a trial run to see if I was able to book any jobs. "If that goes well, then I'd like her to go to Paris for Fashion Week."

My father stopped eating and made a lurching noise. We all looked at him and waited for him to breathe. "Sounds serious," he said.

"She has school," my mother reminded Frank like she'd heard this was something you were supposed to say.

"School can wait," he said flatly. "She has the opportunity right now—and I mean right now—to see the world, make a lot of money, and have experiences that most people can only dream about."

"Yeah, well, nightmares are dreams too." My mother had now raised her voice and was pointing a carrot at Frank Dabney, who did not look intimidated by our small family in our small town with our small ways and even smaller carrots.

"Listen, Deb," he said, "I do this all day, every day. I know the fears, I know the concerns, I know the way it sounds—but it's a legitimate business, and the window of opportunity is very narrow. I think Danielle has a very, very, very in look right now and that she's going to do really well in New York. Claudia Brasche at Lawton is going to flip out, so all I can say is—give it a chance. She could make a lot of money in a short time. College paid for. Dance lessons. Whatever she wants."

"Yes, well, we have a police officer friend in New York, Miss Cady Rae Benson. And believe you me, if Danielle goes there to do her 'in look' stuff, Cady will be right next to her, armed and prepared to defend our family at all costs."

"Cady Benson?" I asked. "I didn't think you liked the Bensons."

"Hush," my mother said. "I like 'em now."

5

It was my father who talked my mother into the idea. Frank Dabney left after dinner, refusing to join us for Mayfield strawberry ice cream—for my mother, the final insult.

"What? He's too good for Mayfield? I thought he said he was from Tennessee! Mayfield Dairy is the pride of the south. You don't turn down a scoop unless you're a godless Yankee. Or a serial killer!"

"He said he was lactose intolerant, Deb," my father said. My mother was not persuaded.

We all watched Frank Dabney drive away in his black rental car from the front porch. Ours was one of a hundred houses on a mountain road north of downtown Pressville. It was an old Victorian that needed a lot of work. That's what we told people when they came over. "Place needs a lot of work." I heard myself making similar claims when it became my house. It ran in our blood to make apologies for things no one else noticed. I think southerners are naturally sorry; it's probably mostly about the war.

The Victorian that needed a lot of work sat behind a gravel roundabout about five feet off the road. There were steps that led to the wraparound porch and then on to the front door. We had a steep, winding staircase inside. It had been my grandparents' house before they died and left it to my mother, their only child. It was a beautiful home, on the Historical Registry. Cavernous and sturdy, it reminded me of the kinds of people who didn't live in Pressville anymore. For a time, it had been a sort of destination for wealthy outdoor enthusiasts or old mountain money—ladies with petticoats and decorative umbrellas. But that changed. The Pressville I grew up in was good for fishing, decent schools, and nice views from small, run-down houses.

It was a Pressville I was immediately willing to abandon when I found out I could live in New York City. My mother and I left as soon as school got out at the end of May; I had just finished my junior year. This was to be the only time one of my parents escorted me. My friends asked me at least six thousand questions about modeling in New York, none of which I knew how to answer. I showed them the pictures Frank Dabney took of me in my bikini, and everyone agreed that I looked like a model. I'd always been too skinny but had quite a chest, so there was that. My hair was long and stringy, a dark-reddish color that I hated until everyone in New York said it was perfect. I had a smattering of freckles over the bridge of my small nose and eyebrows that were steep over my dark-brown eyes.

"Perfect," Frank Dabney said when he took a close-up shot of my face with his Polaroid camera.

"Don't listen to him," my mother said loudly. "Nothing's perfect."

When we got to New York, we met Frank and Claudia Brasche at the Lawton Agency, which sat on the eighteenth floor of a twenty-six-story building. When the elevator door opened, we were promptly greeted by a sneering young woman with a bleached-white mohawk. The offices were sea green and completely glass—fake glass, according to my mother.

"It's all fake… You know that kind they use in hotels?" she whispered to me. "It looks like a dentist office."

"No it doesn't," I snapped back. Our dentist in Pressville had ancient paisley wallpaper and plastic maroon countertops in his office. "It's awesome."

My mother looked worried and angry as I walked around the office in a pink two-piece and made pouting faces for the lens. Hardly anyone spoke to her. Everyone was done wooing Deb Greer and now only cared about getting me in front of as many photographers and designers as possible. They knew my mother would leave New York and cease to matter. They were right.

"I want you to get in touch with Cady Benson." My mother was now almost yelling. "She's a cop here! A police officer."

My mother had been near obsessed with Cady Benson since the inception of the New York plan. We went from thinking her family's chicken was beneath us to making Cady the center of our universe—my universe.

"I want you to be in touch with her. She's another Pressville girl, alone in this city. Working in LAW ENFORCEMENT!" My mother directed her voice and her gaze at Frank Dabney, who had a tape measure around my hip bones. "Oh, how convenient. Touching asses is part of the job." She rolled her eyes. "Next you'll tell me you do breast-cancer exams too."

"I'll call her," I said.

"I've already reached out to her mother. She said Cady would love to see you. She claims she did some babysitting for you girls back when Cady was in high school, but I don't remember that. I've never used a babysitter in my life, and certainly not a Benson. Anyway—" My mother scooted her chair forward. It made a loud ripping sound on the polished concrete floor. "It's a good idea, though. For you to see her. Regularly. She can keep an eye on things. For me." She was rattling on absently. Neither myself nor Frank Dabney were very concerned. Not with my mother or Cady Benson.

Claudia said she was going to ask for a "top tier" rate for me right away. She seemed very pleased with both me and herself to announce this. "Top tier. We won't mess around." I beamed while my mother sneered. She must have known it was all smoke and mirrors from the start. I had to give it to her later; she knew I wasn't that special.

6

When we finally made it far enough for me to really see the bones, I was feeling sick to my stomach and was concerned about making it back up the ravine. "Okay," I said to no one in particular. "That's close enough."

"But you gotta see her shoes," Leigh said. "She has an anklet."

I closed my eyes and swallowed.

"It's silver," Leigh added.

"Okay." It seemed it was the only thing I could say.

"You gotta call the cop lady."

"I know, but first we have to get back up the ridge." I wasn't as close as the girls. "Get away, please." I muttered to myself, again wishing Jasper was home, but he wasn't expected back from the conference until the morning.

"Call the police, Mom!" Tessa wanted action.

"Yes, honey! We have to get back to the house first." I turned to head back up, still winded and trembling.

"She's so small," I heard Pamela say.

"I wonder if she was pretty." That was Rose.

7

The first months in New York were magnetic; no one could have guessed how I would take to the place. Since I'd grown up in complete tree-filled silence in the apple capitol of North Georgia, one might have assumed I'd be intimidated by New York. Not so. I felt at home there, instantly.

My mother did not, however, align with the city and spent the two weeks she was accompanying me to my castings and meetings with my agency scowling at everyone we met. She was only cynical and skeptical—nothing else.

"You'll be staying in Room 402," the woman at the hotel told us.

"Why? Is that the room they just fumigated? Can I ask why the carpets needed to be replaced? Was it blood or fecal matter?"

"I'm sorry," the woman at the front desk said nervously.

"Yeah, that's what I thought..." my mother started to say, her determination to spoil the fun verging on sociopathic.

Later, at the ninth Italian restaurant we'd visited that trip, our server asked, "Would you like crushed red pepper or Parmesan?"

"You taste them first," my mother said, pushing the small canisters back toward him, "so I'll know you're not trying to poison us."

Her accent—our accents, though I was trying desperately to hide mine—was obnoxious and outspoken. She yelled at all the cab drivers, even the mild-mannered ones who calmly drove us. She told Claudia that she was watching her. "Best sleep with one eye open," I heard her say one day at the agency while Claudia was giving me a list of appointments. Claudia pretended not to hear. My mother wore hiking boots to a runway casting where she called the artistic director "son" and told me to mind my manners when I pulled on the gum in my mouth and blew a bubble while talking to a fitter. "Act like I raised you right, please," she said over the hum of hurried voices in the room. "I won't put up with New York nonsense. No ma'am..." She shuffled her feet in her boots loudly. "Act like a lady or I'll shove a boot up your ass!"

"Amen!" a young man in skintight white leather trousers said. "I love southern mamas." He laughed and shook his head in admiration.

"Watch your mouth!" she snapped back. I was both proud and mortified. Some people seemed to really like the way she was acting. It was how she'd always acted. I was used to it, but Debbie Greer was a sore thumb in New York. I kept hearing that she was "so cool," so I went with it. Maybe it was great that my mother was such an overdone redneck, and even better that she didn't want to change herself the second she got to New York City. Even Claudia smiled in approbation when my mother told her that the Greers didn't pay for water.

"Bottle a water'll cost you five dollars here," she said to the rapt Claudia. "No thank you. I'd rather drink outta a toilet."

"Probably the same water," Claudia said with a nod, and I knew my mother finally approved.

I did not, however, hold on to the Danielle Greer who left Pressville. I morphed into Dani and left Danielle in the closet of my tiny bedroom at the model apartments every time I went out. I didn't want to be from a small town in Georgia, but more importantly, I didn't want anyone to think I was.

I was to remain in New York until the end of the summer and then go home and back to high school. That didn't happen. Before I could head home, Claudia sent me to London, after what she called a "great run" at New York Fashion Week. She kept telling me everyone was "dying" over my look. "London calling!" she sang. "You'll do even better there." I hoped so because I hadn't really been booking much. No matter how much smoke Claudia blew up my rear, I wasn't landing things the way she seemed to think I would. People acted interested but I wasn't selected, over and over again. I did start to wonder if this was just how agents talked to new girls to get them to forget about home and everything else—this promise of superstardom. Teenagers like to hear how important and fabulous they are and don't need much of a reason for it.

Right before I left town for my first trip abroad, I got a call from Cady Benson asking if I wanted to meet for lunch. I was caught off guard and immediately felt overwhelmingly busy. Claudia had helped me get a rushed passport, and I'd been told to buy an adapter for my phone cord. I didn't know what anything meant and had been embarrassed that I didn't know how any of this worked. The business-affairs woman at the agency had asked me if I had "documents," to which I'd responded, "I have my learner's permit." She'd laughed, and I remember hearing her tell other people in the office the story like we would all share a chuckle over how stupid I was. I'd felt like I was being interrogated at the passport office and almost admitted to smoking pot in tenth grade when the man behind the plastic partition asked me if I swore the statements in my paperwork were true. My mother had had to Express Mail me my birth certificate and complained about the cost. I'd never had to do any of these things before and was worried about going on an airplane overnight. My mother kept telling me that was when planes crashed the most. Cady's call was immeasurably irritating because of how ill-timed it was. She had no idea how important and scared I felt.

Instead of responding to her right away, I called my mother and blamed her for "setting me up with homegirl Benson. I'm trying to get ready to go to London!" My mother and I argued about my priorities for about twenty-five minutes on the phone before she hung up on me. She'd said I was tarnishing her good name by ignoring our "old friends." I reminded her that she never liked the Bensons. She said I needed to get my facts straight.

"And don't come back with a British accent... We won't be able to understand you!"

My flight to London was to leave at nine at night, so I had the whole day to sit around wringing my hands and thinking about how cool I was going to look with a stamp in my new passport and about all the things that could go wrong. The lead-up to my departure had been so frantic that an entire afternoon to wait was like torture. Out of boredom and a desire to brag, I decided to call Cady Benson back while I was killing time before heading to the airport. The only thing I knew about her was that her parents owned the chicken restaurant, she was about eight years older than me, and she worked for the police in New York. My mom had said she'd gotten her criminal justice degree from some community college in Georgia but always wanted to be a cop in New York City. Like I cared.

"Cady," she said when she answered. I was sitting on my bed in the model apartment I shared with a few other girls. It was like summer camp, or maybe a college dorm—not that I'd ever lived in one.

"This is Danielle Greer. From Pressville."

"Hey, girl! How's New York treating you?"

"Oh, good. I'm actually leaving for London in a few hours." I thought to tell her London was in England in case she didn't know.

"Wow! Isn't that something? My parents tell me you're a big-time model here. That is so cool! I just wanted to get in touch; I hoped we could maybe get together—two Pressville girls in NYC! I know you've been here a while now. Sorry I didn't get a hold of you sooner. Have you been keeping yourself busy? Are you seeing all the sights?"

"Ummm," I said slowly. "I'm modeling, so you know—"

"Have you seen a show on Broadway yet? I'm sure you've been to Central Park. Maybe we could go to Ellis Island or to Rockefeller Center. It's not Christmas yet—duh, but it's still really cool. And it's a heck of a line, but the Empire State Building is totally worth it. I've only been to Tavern on the Green once 'cause it costs an arm and a leg, but anyway—those are just some ideas. I love exploring the city. I've got a whole list of things I want to do, just striking them off one by one. I just saw *Chicago* with my friend from work. That was such a hoot! And next week, we're going to a Yankees game!"

I rolled my eyes, thinking this was an incredibly annoying conversation and that her accent was ridiculous. Somewhere in the back of my mind, though, I felt a pinch of sadness. I'd done none of these things. All I did was go to appointments and parties with the other models and the old men who paid for us to drink. When my mom was there, we'd gone to Central Park and walked down Fifth

Avenue and then back up Park, but that was pretty much it. I went into Bloomingdale's and bought some makeup, trying to act like a snob who can afford a sixty-dollar tube of lip gloss. My mother had shuffled around the store looking frantic and repeatedly asking me where the bathroom and fire exits were.

I was just about to tell Cady that I hadn't had time to sight-see, given my schedule, when she interjected, "And there's Ground Zero. That's a really somber place, but I'd love to take you if you haven't been. I cry every time, just a warning."

"No," I said abruptly. "No, I haven't been to Ground Zero."

"It's not going anywhere," she said sadly. "So that's that. Do you want to get together? I'm sure you don't really remember me. I babysat for you girls a couple of times when you were little, but I know I've been gone from Pressville for a while. I was in Douglas getting my associate's before I came here, so…anyway."

"When I get back from London," I said like I was in a hurry. "I usually go to places in the East Village and Lower East Side to hang out, so… Or Brooklyn. A lot of my friends live in the Village, so we could meet up there."

"Okay," she said. "It sounds like you can show me around!"

"Some places are kind of…you know, like there are a lot of celebrities there, so 'normal' people don't really go. You have to know someone."

"That right? Well, that sounds cool!"

"Yeah. Anyway, I'll call you when I get back from London."

"Have a great trip!"

"It's work," I said, trying to figure out why I was being so rude.

"That is so neat, Danielle."

"Yeah, thanks."

I grabbed my cigarettes and went to smoke out the living room window. We weren't supposed to do that, but all the girls did. I leaned over the rusted frame and looked down at Sixth Avenue. This was such an ugly part of the city. I tried to feel better by imagining all the great parties I'd go to in London. Some of the girls who'd worked there said it was a wild town. I thought maybe I would ask one of my roommates if they wanted to see *Chicago* when I got back to New York. I didn't even know where a person went to see *Chicago*. I thought that was another city.

8

Claudia showed up in London to shepherd me and some other girls. I think she liked pretending we needed her and that she had to help us. A couple of the girls said Claudia needed a dog. "Or a kid."

She gazed at me lovingly over dinner one night while simultaneously watching everything I ate. "I told you they wanted the farmer look!" she said of my hair. "That's not very 'farmer.'"

"Riga did it," I said. I'd been sent to Riga, a stylist, before a shoot for a British department store. I had a bob now—shaggy, but a bob nonetheless.

"Well, that's fine, then," Claudia said before telling me I was her star. We went to a club after dinner, where she told me that I could always throw up my food if I ate too much. "You know that, right?" She had a glass of champagne in her hand and tried her best to look understanding. Apparently, according to one of my model friends at the agency, Claudia had told some people at the office she thought I ate too much and that it was going to catch up with me.

I did eat too much, especially for a model, but we ate in Pressville, and I found that I was hungrier in New York and beyond than I'd ever been. Most of the girls split granola bars, shared a carton of soup, or drank part of a smoothie before tossing the cup. This was not enough for me, so I ate alone. I had one friend, Judith, who also liked to eat, but she ended up going home to California because Claudia said her stomach jiggled when she walked.

I came back from London after a few weeks having booked only two jobs. I couldn't figure out the math, but it didn't seem like I'd made money while I was there. Still, Claudia insisted it had been a successful trip. "Everyone loved you!"

My parents were outrageously upset when I said that I was not returning to finish my senior year of high school. Claudia called to tell them I was going to stay in New York. I couldn't do it myself. I solicited Claudia's help, then sat silently while she told my parents what I was doing with my life and tapped her fingernails on the top of her desk. She promised them she would arrange tutors. "She will have her degree in normal time, no troubles." She suddenly sounded Russian, which prompted my father to speak slower and louder when communicating with her. "She very smart girl—a little fighter," she went on. "We make sure she gets education."

I didn't really understand why Claudia wanted me to stick

around. I wasn't booking all that much. Things came in spurts, and just when I thought I was getting some traction, I'd go a week or two without a single job. I got turned down for little stuff that I was almost embarrassed to admit I didn't book, like a runway show at a mall in Yonkers. Claudia laughed off my failures and told me I was on the verge. She said it all the time: "On the verge!" She said that to some other girls, too, though—girls who'd been in New York a while. I just pretended it was because they were doing their hair different or had a different style. I could talk myself into or out of anything, especially with Claudia acting so desperate to keep me around. I would find out later that the more girls she could send to a client, the better she looked; she needed me for her pile. I guess it was a compliment to be part of her pile, but she made it sound more important than that, like it actually meant something for me to be there.

———

"Are you on drugs?" my mom asked the second I walked in the door for my first visit to Pressville since leaving the June before. It was March. I'd been gone for almost eight months.

"No," I sneered. "I don't have time to do drugs." I played the exhausted-from-extremely-demanding-work-conditions card the entire time I was home. I even showed my father an article in the Atlanta paper that detailed sweatshop horror and said I could relate.

My parents needed help in the yard: "I'm too tired; besides, all I do is work."

The trash needed to be taken out: "Chantel will have to do it. I can't feel my legs from all the walking. The runway, you know."

Mom wanted someone to set the table: "Ask the twins, I have to rest. I'll be working sixty hours a week when I get back to New York." I hadn't worked sixty hours since I got to New York, probably not even sixteen. Every single time I got turned down for something, there was a little chink in my armor—and for every poke at my self-esteem, my personality got worse. I could hear how I sounded when I talked to people, how full of myself and vapid, but it was like I was playing a part. I thought if I acted that way, then Claudia and Frank and the rest were right. I was a star only if I acted like I was.

Being away from New York wasn't good for my psyche either. All I could think about was getting back to the city so I could keep trying to live up to the reputation I was giving myself at home. I emailed Claudia at least three times a day to "check in," always asking her what I was missing and assuring her I was returning. She only wrote back twice and told me to chill myself. I called my friends from the agency regularly, chattering like a penguin at ninety miles an hour and making sure to be heard throughout the house when we got into hourly rates and the celebrities we'd met at parties. None of my sisters were as impressed as I wanted them to be—not even the twins, who were at least superficial enough to find it interesting. They were too young, and I was too desperate. They were cheering for the middle school football team and had little boyfriends with hair on their upper lips and cracking voices. They looked at my portfolio, oohing and aahing, before turning on the television and forgetting I was in the room.

Chantel was in college at the local community school. She was studying library science and playing intramural tennis. I wanted her to feel small and insignificant compared to me, but she didn't, not even at five foot five. And some part of me was a little jealous that she didn't. I didn't think I could go back to not caring about modeling. Once this idea of myself got planted in my brain, there was no uprooting it.

I practiced my model walk in the hallway between our bedrooms. There was a mirror at one end and plenty of room to sway my arms and lean back the way I'd been taught. Claudia gave weekly runway classes at the agency. She posed and pranced in front of us, always with a cigarette dangling from her heavily injected lips. I caught on to the walk very quickly and wanted everyone in my house on Bell Road to know it.

I don't know what I expected—maybe unbridled awe. I didn't get it. My parents ambled around the house absorbed in their daily lives, unaware of what a privilege it was to have me staying with them. My father drove a truck for FedEx like he always had, while my mother complained and read house-decorating magazines, keeping a close eye on me and my sisters in her passive-aggressive way. She ran the carpool for cheerleading and still had to take Chantel everywhere. She was almost twenty but without a license and no car of her own. Life had gone on in Pressville—the same life I'd been living for almost eighteen years. There were a few moments when I felt like I'd missed something, but mostly I was worried I was becoming them again. I'd convinced myself I'd never belonged there. I went back to New York after eight days, thinking it was all about to take off for me, that it was just a matter of time before I was on top of the world.

9

Jasper," I said softly into the phone. I had a way of dragging out the second syllable of his name: Jasperrrr.

"Yeah." He was always so curt with me when he was on the road, traveling salesman that he was.

"Can you get home?"

"No. I'm in Mobile."

"I know that, but something's happened."

"What? What happened? Danielle, I'm at a drinks thing. I can't really talk."

"The girls found a body."

"What? Jesus Christ." He was shuffling about, heavy breaths hitting the receiver as he made his way out of wherever he was. "What do you mean, 'a body'? A person? Where?" It was suddenly quieter.

"Down the ravine. It's human bones, obviously been there a long time."

"The girls found it?"

"Yes, I was napping."

"Danielle, you can't just fall asleep in the middle of the day with them wandering around the woods."

"Please—with the lectures, Jasper. It's always a lecture with you. And it was the afternoon, anyway." As if that made any difference.

We'd fought before he left; we usually did. I would never have described Jasper and me as really getting along. From the beginning, there'd been this agitation that rattled between us like a can we couldn't stop kicking back and forth—neither of us wanting to keep it but also not wanting to give it to the other. I was trying to talk softly. The girls were in the next room, watching TV. I hadn't known what to tell them, so I flicked the remote and gave them some popcorn I'd burned in the microwave while trying to figure out what to do.

"Have you called the police?"

"No," I said. "Are you in the bathroom? How did it get so quiet?"

"No one's here," he said angrily. "I'm outside the bar. It's like two hundred degrees."

It started to rain outside. "We're gonna get a storm here."

"You should call the police. Have them come get the body. We don't want a body on our property, Danielle. Get the police over there. When did they find it?"

"I don't know—an hour ago, maybe."

"And you still haven't called the police? Come on. Get someone over there. Now!"

"Stop yelling at me."

"Fine, but you're making me nervous."

"No, I'm just… I don't want to traumatize the kids." I was back in the front room with my eyes on the wall unit. I did so love the rattle and hum of its slowly dying motor. I had a clementine in my hand; I pressed its skin, then dug my fingernails in, breaking through with my index finger. I had juice on my nail.

"They're probably already traumatized if they were out playing alone, with their mother asleep, and they found a body."

"It's bones."

"Fine. Call the police, then let me know what they're gonna do about it."

I hung up without saying anything more. I could hear a commercial for fabric softener coming from the den. The girls laughed. It was that one with the bear.

10

U p to this point, I'd been living in the model apartments with large groups of girls from every country in the world. I figured out early on to avoid the Russians and everyone who talked like them—and who might be from a country nearby. The Brazilian girls were the most fun but also had the worst luck with men. The Australians partied almost as hard as the Canadians, and the English girls all thought they would be the next Kate Moss and cared too deeply about fashion. Every Russian I met was named Anna and wore too much mascara. I was frightened of Anna K. and didn't look at her when we ended up at the same appointments. Her eyes cast a glare that spoke of witchcraft or worse—Communism. She ate only Subway and saved all her money, declaring the rest of us "iy-jots" for wasting our fortunes. She said she was not going to be poor when she got older. Later, I would think her wise.

Most of my best friends were the other American girls plucked from the heartland, like daisies that hadn't yet had a chance to wilt and crumple. Like me, I'm not sure what would have become of them if they hadn't been ripped from their roots just as they'd started to bloom. I wasn't the only one who was trying not to say things like "doohickey" and "fixin'" in public. A lot of them eventually went home and didn't come back. Judith was one of the first to leave. When she told me she didn't really want to be a model anyway, it was like she'd cut her head off right in front of me and was talking out of her neck.

Claudia got sick, very sick and could not be my agent for a while. According to some of the other girls, she'd been sick for a long time, although no one was sure with what, exactly. She was replaced by a man named Dillard, whose only speaking voice was a high-pitched scream. However grating his voice was, he was kind and well liked. He also loved me and got me my two highest-paying jobs. I was the face for a perfume made by a French designer whom no one had ever heard of and then for a clothing line based in LA. I made more money in a month than I had the entire year before. I also found out, after bragging about my paychecks to Chantel while I was home, that I made more money than my dad. She should never have told me that. I couldn't stop talking about my six-hundred-dollar sunglasses and the leather jacket I got at Saks in front of my parents after—like I was mad at them because they didn't understand how important these things were to me and that they would never be able to do the same. It made me mean. I didn't know to see people as unworthy until I realized how much everyone else didn't have.

After I took a trip to Saint Bart's with a few of the other girls—and some older men who paid for it but whom we barely spoke to while boating around the Caribbean, drinking expensive bourbons and smoking cigarettes, wearing hats someone bought in Italy—I went home for an extended visit. I planned to stay for the entire month of August. I didn't tell anyone, but I thought I was becoming an alcoholic or a drug addict or both. People popped pills and smoked weed at shoots and shows, and I'd taken to joining in whenever I felt like it, and I mostly felt like it. I drank all the time and had stopped eating in secret. I just didn't really eat at all. No longer as hungry, I was thinner and more worn looking. Dillard told me so, but he said it in a nice way. "You need to go home to Hicksville and get your hearty cowgirl look back, sister friend." He pulled me close to him and said, "Casting directors are talking—you look tore up from the floor up." I was tanned from the trip to Saint Bart's and wearing my hair long again. I thought I looked fine but took his advice. I went home and said I would rest for the next month.

Chantel had driven down to the Atlanta airport to pick me up in her new, hideous car. It was an enormous family wagon that I had a hard time believing could make it up and down all the hills in Pressville. She and I didn't talk much during the car ride back home. She had a country station playing on the radio and her hands at precisely ten and two on the steering wheel. She looked even dowdier than normal and had bangs that stopped right at her eyelashes. They were clearly bothering her, because she couldn't stop messing with them during breaks from her perfect driving. She was wearing light-pink lip gloss and a high-cut purple shirt that was somewhere between a tank top and a neck brace.

"It's good to be home," I said during a moment of prolonged and uncomfortable silence.

"I'm never leaving," Chantel said proudly. It was a comment made to provoke me. I didn't respond and reached for the pack of cigarettes in my bag. "You can't smoke in my car," she said angrily. "That's so gross, anyway."

The first thing my mother asked me when I walked in the front door to the house was "Did you ever meet up with Cady Benson? And why do you smell like smoke?"

"She tried to smoke in my car," Chantel said with a flick of her bangs.

"It's a station wagon," I said. "And no. We talked before I went to London, but I forgot to call her back."

My mother exhaled heavily. "That was months ago, Danielle. I really wanted you to talk to her. That was important to me. You are up there all alone, and I know them. I want you to get in touch with her."

"I did talk to her," I said, tossing my bag on the ground.

"Just haven't hung out yet." I was annoyed but didn't sound it. I'd promised myself I was going to make an effort to be pleasant while home.

"Everything smells like smoke," she said.

"They all smoke in the apartment," I said of the models. "One of the reasons I'm getting my own place." I'd signed a lease before leaving the city—a studio in Tribeca.

"I think you should have stayed there. It was so much cheaper." My mother wiped her hands mindlessly on the front of her pants. She was clearly making dinner in the kitchen, given the aroma of chicken broth and garlic in the house, but she'd walked to the front door to greet me. The house didn't have a garage; we all parked in the roundabout in front. It necessitated a lot of car shuffling and driving over grass, especially now that Chantel had her Volvo. "You don't even have a roommate now, do you? I think you should have a roommate."

"No roommate," I said. "But I can afford it."

"She smokes," Chantel said, annoyed that her previous comment about me lighting up in her car had been ignored.

"I think they all do" was my mother's vacant reply as she walked back to the kitchen. "Dinner's almost ready."

"You're such a snitch," I said, punching Chantel lightly on her arm.

"And you think you're God's gift," she said. It was going to be hard for me to be pleasant.

Cady came up again over dinner. I tried my best not to roll my eyes as my parents got into a long conversation about how nice it would be if I had a "friend" in New York.

"I have a friend," I said. "Plenty of them." I was picking at my food, oddly self-conscious in front of my own family about what I was eating.

"Don't you like the food?" my mother asked. It was her homemade chicken noodle soup, with double-wide egg noodles and garlic bread from the freezer pack.

"I love it," I said. "I ate on the plane."

"That was hours ago." My mother was nervously moving her napkin about. It was either nerves or hostility. She didn't approve; this had been the theme of our relationship ever since Frank Dabney descended like a lurking vulture at the Pressville Mall. Disapproval. I wasn't sure I approved of her either.

"So this Cady person," my father said, as if this were the only thing anyone could think to talk about.

"You know I was in London, right?" I said. "I got to go to Spain too."

"You didn't drive, did you?" my mother asked.

"No. I took cabs and the train."

"You could have taken a cab here," Chantel offered. "From the airport."

"So Cady's father has been ill. Very ill," my mother said. "She's been coming home to see him. There's talk she may move back."

"That's too bad," I said impatiently.

"Yes, battling cancer. Very aggressive."

"Okay." I put my spoon down. "I've never even met her. Claudia has cancer too."

"Who's Claudia?" my father asked. "And you have met her!" he added enthusiastically. "She worked at the restaurant, and your mother says she babysat for us a couple of times after school. I don't remember it, but that doesn't mean anything… Half the time, I don't even remember my own name!" He laughed jovially. It was actually from my dad whom I think I got my looks. He had the same auburn hair and upturned eyes. His chin came to a perfect point like mine, and he was tall and gangly—something I had actually found embarrassing when we were younger, before modeling. He'd had a ridiculous mustache since the day I was born. It was thick and well-groomed, lying on his upper lip like a lazy caterpillar, too fat and complacent to provoke metamorphosis. Joe. Joe and Deborah. It was like I'd made them up.

"She may even be home now," my mother said. "She visits a lot."

"Dying dad, and all," I said before licking a crumb from the corner of my mouth.

"You look tired," Chantel said. "And older. With your hair cut short like that."

"They did it in London for Top Shop," I said. "And anyway, it's not that short anymore. I'm growing it out."

"Do they cut hair the same way in England? Like with the shampoo bowl and all that?" my dad asked.

"Yes." I pushed myself back from the table abruptly, rattling the stained glass chandelier that had hung in that exact spot for at least fifty years. It was one of my grandmother's prized possessions, purchased on credit and hung with delight and care. When they gave my parents the house, she specifically instructed my mother on how to clean it. I thought it looked like a light fixture in a chain restaurant, and my mother's cleaning attempts always left smudges on the small panes of glass. "Sorry," I said. "I'm really tired."

"I'll find out if Cady is in town!" my mother called out to me as I walked over to the stairs.

"You do that!" I snapped back.

11

It was during this visit home that I met Benji. Benji Law. If I had known how much this single event would affect everything, I think I would still choose it. I would still get out of Chantel's car that afternoon.

Benji and his brother, Blake, rode motorcycles, mostly shirtless and barefoot on little Japanese crotch rockets that made a racket when they really got going—like a supercharged lawn mower. You could hear them coming and then see them going, glowing young bodies and sandy hair being whipped by the southern wind. If I close my eyes today, it is all I see or hear. Still.

Benji was barely sixteen when we met, and Blake, my age. I knew who they were, of course—it was Pressville; you couldn't live there without knowing who everyone was. But I'd never really paid much attention to them. When I look back, I see myself like a bulldozer just tearing through life without regard, churning dirt while I press on, trying to be special, trying to matter. And then I did matter to some random middle-aged man at the mall, and it all made sense. It was like I'd always known I was going to be told great things about myself and that I was going to believe them. I had to have walked past Benji a hundred times at Pressville High School and never paid him any mind. It could have been so different, but it wasn't.

Because Benji was younger—two grades below me, and just out of the span of my concern—he'd only been on the periphery of my attention. His brother I knew when we were kids, but he'd since dropped out of school altogether, and I can't say I'd cared when I heard. I was also a high school dropout—something that made my mother's stomach turn—but I felt my reasons were worthier. Blake Law left because he was up to no good and needed more time to be up to it. I was a model.

I'd been passed by a motorcycle on one of the steep, thin, swirling roads in Pressville every day of my life. It wasn't unusual to hear the racket of a small engine on the road. You could really get a good lean in on Bell, where we lived, and Duckett, and especially over on West Street, which was a short road but one hell of a bend. I'd never paid them or anyone else on a motorcycle any attention until that day. It was like I banged my head real hard and never got the vibrating to stop. I was locked in a shuffle for the rest of my life. I was eighteen and ready.

The reason we were going to the Shell station that afternoon was so Chantel could refuel after the long drive to the airport. She told me rather proudly that she'd bought the old yellow station wagon herself—and also that it had been close to a full tank of gas to come get me the afternoon before. "Good job!" was all I said in response, although I did slip her a twenty for the gas.

The Shell was at the bottom of a winding hill—Delk Pass. It was old as dirt, with pumps that didn't have catches and a convenience store that had more dust and expired snacks than customers. The lot was mostly cracked asphalt and weeds, and the sign had been sliding off its post for a decade. It was the closest gas station to our house; I imagine I would have seen Benji sooner or later based on that fact alone. That day was insignificant in all respects but one: the timing must have been significant. God moving his pieces around on the board, curing his boredom and the dullness of heaven and eternity to watch us squirm, to see if his pawns would make it to the other side.

"Who are they?" I asked Chantel when Blake and Benji tore past us on their bikes as we drove to the Shell. They swerved into the opposite lane to take the turn around Chantel, who was going at a snail's pace. I'd noticed she went even slower downhill than up. I'd already asked her if the wagon even had a gas pedal. She scoffed and said of course, like I might not know. I had a license but was honestly too scared to drive, so out of practice and with hardly any experience to begin with. The boys slid to the side of their bike tires and then upright before gunning it up the road in front of us, their tanned backs reflecting the sun. They rode right next to each other like they were connected by an invisible string. No helmets, no shoes—just bodies and sun. I felt the vibrations then; they just got louder over time. So loud I was never really able to hear over them again.

"Law boys," she said, not convinced of the gravity of the situation. "You know Blake."

"Not anymore," I said. "What are they even doing?" I asked the question like we suddenly had electricity after years of darkness.

"They work at the gas station." We pulled into the Shell and saw them parking their bikes on kickstands.

I looked at both Blake and Benji, but only really at Benji. I could see the difference between us. He hadn't been pulled from the earth yet like I had. In full bloom, I'd been yanked from the soil, roots and all. He was still stuck in Pressville dirt. He was not for me, and because of that, he was the only thing that ever was for me. I was summoning the flames from hell, right there in the passenger seat of Chantel's yellow Volvo. When he looked at me, I felt the slide from solid ground, gone wobbly and ridiculous in a station wagon. I would have done anything. I did.

"Oh my God," I said to myself as I got out of the car. He gave me an innocent smirk that I returned. Chantel noticed me leaning on the car and looked confused.

"That's Blake's brother."

"I know," I said. I couldn't figure why that mattered. Blake could have as many brothers as he wanted if they looked like this. "He's hot as hell."

"No way," Chantel said. Her biggest celebrity crush was Dan Aykroyd. I thought that spoke volumes.

"He looks like a model," I said.

"Oh Lord—you and the models. He looks like he models chewing tobacco...or WD-40 or something. Give me a break."

I ignored Chantel and went into the Shell to buy a Coke and some cigarettes, knowing Benji was already inside. He'd given me a nod and followed his brother into the store as I walked away from the pump where Chantel was wrestling with the gas gun. He was standing at the counter, getting cash from the gentleman tending the register; I had to guess he was getting paid since Chantel had said the boys worked there. He turned around to face me, still shirtless and glowing. His dark hair was tousled and longer by the ears. He ran his hand over his head; it was like an invitation.

I walked over to the counter and leaned in, never having sincerely done anything like this in my life. "I'm Dani," I said.

"Hey, Dani," he said. Blake was standing nearby but hardly paying attention to us. We'd never been friends. I'd always thought of Blake Law as a troublemaker, somebody who'd end up in jail soon enough.

"Do you want to come over?" I asked him quietly. I was provoked, and I couldn't stop responding.

He laughed a little before glancing over his shoulder to where his brother was standing. "Okay? I don't know you or nothin.'"

"I went to P-High," I said. That's what we called the high school.

"Well, I know that, but like…we never hang out or whatever." He couldn't stop smiling, and I couldn't stop leaning. If I had to say what it was between us, this smoke-and-mirrors, drug-like feeling taking over, it was probably me shedding my skin. I was so uncomfortable all the time—painfully uncomfortable. My new world was like living in the clutches of a hawk. I was looking down on everyone, but I was terrified—terrified that I didn't fit in, that I didn't know what anyone was talking about…because I didn't. Terrified I couldn't keep up or would never be sophisticated enough. Terrified that it really, really showed that I hadn't finished high school and was from the sticks and was clueless about the world, art, films…all these things people were talking about around me but never with me. I wasn't included in these conversations, just glanced over like one of the articles of clothing they were pinning to my body. I didn't even know about fashion, which was supposed to be my world. I'd shopped at the Pressville Mall for my entire life, never owning anything that didn't come from Penny's or, at best, the Gap. I wasn't like the people I wanted to impress and who seemed so impressed by me, but only one part of me. I was like the Law boys. I was like Benji, and man, did I want to be. It was the one honest thing I'd said to myself since Frank Dabney told me I had the look.

"I'm home from New York," I said, never able to stop myself from trying to outdo everyone at home.

"You don't look like you're from New York," he said, squinting.

"How would you know, anyway?" Now we were both smiling. I'm not sure what look had been on my face before that moment. It was the first thing we shared, that smile. Then the secret, then the undoing. Then the accident.

My family went to see a movie at the new theater in town that afternoon. We'd made our plan earlier. I was originally going to join them but then changed my mind when Chantel and I returned from our errands. After we left the Shell, I told Chantel I wanted to get a coffee somewhere. She said okay and took me to the 7-Eleven. "This isn't really what I meant," I said when we pulled in the parking lot.

"Then what do you mean?"

I got a cup anyway and then complained of being very tired when we arrived home.

"You just had coffee," Chantel said loudly.

"Yeah, jet lag or something," I told her, even though Georgia and New York are in the same time zone and the flight's as quick as a whip. "Anyway, I drink coffee for the taste." I smiled nervously and waited. My dad was disappointed I wasn't joining them, but no one else seemed to care. It was a Saturday, and he had the afternoon off. "Sorry," I said and went up to my room until they left.

Benji was on his motorcycle, circling our road, waiting for my mother's van to disappear from the front of the house. I'd told him what to do at the gas station. I'll never know how I knew or how I managed to communicate it to him so clearly. There was another side to me; we'd had only brief encounters so far, but when I met Benji, this other self enveloped me like a strangling grasp. I just went along with her, with this bad self, this interloper. She was the one who allowed me to do exactly what I wanted, but she went away after the accident. I'm not sure I've done exactly what I wanted ever again.

My mother's van had been gone less than five minutes when Benji knocked on the door. I ran down the front steps to open it. I was about to crack from excitement. Part of it was the sneaking around, but it was mostly the throbbing I felt in my low abdomen. I'd been so caught up in myself and my effect on other people that I hadn't allowed myself to be affected by anyone else. I was now affected, pulsing with it. I was wearing jean shorts and a tank top, not the green peasant blouse I'd been wearing earlier at the gas station, which I thought in some unfortunate positions made me look flat chested.

"How old are you?" I asked, pulling him inside while giving a furtive glance at Bell Road. It was only a minor character at the time—the house too. There was nothing significant about anything without a pulse. I would later yearn to be an inanimate, innocent bystander, though I had my suspicions about motive. Even asphalt and plank board can have it, if you ask me. There is intention in everything.

"Sixteen," he said. He smelled like gas and was wearing a red T-shirt.

"Cool," I said. He smiled; then we went up to my room, and after an hour I had to help him out the window, where he ran to his bike, which was parked on the side of the house. I really don't know why we pretended everything was so dire, so secret, so needing to be so hidden. I could have just told my parents I was seeing a local boy. They sure were proud of Pressville; they probably would have supported it—except I knew they wouldn't. I knew he wasn't what they had in mind for me. None of what I was doing was what they had in mind. Benji was from the other side of Pressville—not in a geography sense, because it really wasn't big enough to have a lot of sides, but the part of it that was ugly, hushed up, ignored, shameful. There were a lot of poor people who didn't finish school and who were in and out of trouble all the time in Pressville and any of the towns up north, near the mountains. There were drugs and pregnant teenagers and kids without good homes. My mother was always ragging on Atlanta for all the things I saw just down the road. I guess she thought if people were doing drugs and abandoning their kids and breaking into cars, it was worse if they were doing it from a city apartment and not some derelict hovel off Chambliss Road—unequivocally the worst part of town. Modeling or no, my parents wouldn't have wanted Benji Law in our house. I told myself it was because they were hypocrites. I always had to say something nasty about them in my head to justify how I was acting.

Benji walked his motorcycle silently through the bit of woods there behind the house—the threshold to the ravine that made up the whole downward slope of our property—and out to the street about a mile down the road.

When my family came home a couple of hours later, my mother made a comment about those "Law kids ridin' all over the place like a buncha hellions." I could hardly breathe. I should have just told her then. It was the secret part of it that turned it sour, like a bad brine.

12

Because it was Pressville and there was only one detective, the girl at the station connected me to Cady Benson's cell phone. I could hear water running in the background when she answered. "Cady Benson."

"It's Danielle Striker," I said.

The water stopped. "Who?"

"Danielle Greer."

"Right." She waited. "Is everything okay?"

"No, not really." I exhaled. The girls were staring at me from the kitchen. I'd separated myself from them all evening, putting small barriers of space between us. Wherever they were, I was in the other room, past a threshold of my history that they were never going to know. "The girls… My daughter, my daughter Tessa found some remains in the woods. Down the hill…" I trailed off.

"It was me who found it!" Leigh was cross and sitting on a

barstool at the counter. They were waiting for dinner. The popcorn had done nothing to curb their appetites.

I held up my hand and closed my eyes, indicating I would deal with this detail later.

"Remains?"

"Yes. Yes. Human remains. They're down a ways. The girls were playing and just…sorta came upon them."

"Have you touched anything?"

"No!" I startled myself with the volume of my voice. "No, I didn't touch anything."

"Well, I guess I mean, did the kids touch anything?"

"They might have at first. It's really far down. I didn't know they ever went down that far. I was inside. It's the ravine, you know."

"I know. I'll come over. I'm going to send some forensics people—they may get there before me. Just please don't touch anything, keep your kids inside the house, don't let anyone near it."

"It's a girl," I said.

"Okay." We were both quiet for a while. I could hear her thinking. I was sure she could hear my heart trying to break through my rib cage.

"Do you think it's…?" I stopped myself.

"I don't think anything—yet," she said.

"You can see where they pulled the leaves up—my kids. There's a big wet pile right in front of it."

"Poor soul," Cady said.

I looked up at my girls, with their elbows on the kitchen countertop and their powder-pink faces pinched in muddled intrigue, and wondered how they could exist in the same world as this thing, this piece of the past, this crumbling bit of my infrastructure on which nothing good could be built. I was reckless. I was always so reckless. I was not a person you could put anything on. I would tilt at the last second, just when you thought you were safe. I'd tilt and crush your precious baubles.

13

W hy are all the men so old?" my mother asked me after looking through the photos on my phone one afternoon. "I mean, really."

"I don't know," I said. I thought I would need to start locking my phone. "Probably because they're rich."

"You're rich. Do a bunch of working girls—not that kind of working girl but girls with a job"—she cleared her throat—"need men to pay for things?"

"I think that's just the way it's always been. The boys our age are only after one thing."

"They're all after one thing, Danielle."

I tried to smile.

Before I initially moved to New York, my mother had insisted we sit down and have a long talk. My father was at the table and did a lot of grunting and moving about, but the gist of our conversation was that I was to keep my legs closed and do what I went there to do. "We're allowing this—and you're seventeen, so we do or do not allow it still—for a few more months," she said. "We're allowing this because you want to try to be a model. Now, I was a soccer player and have my nursing degree, so I don't understand it one bit, but I'm willing to support you. But if I find out you're up there dating every Tom, Dick, and Harry you meet and going around drunk and partying—because believe me, I've seen the E! channel—then you'll come home and we won't help you financially. Partying and dating every guy in town is not modeling. You will be financially cut off if you don't stick to the plan."

"You aren't helping me financially," I said, because this was always my point, even before I started making any money. "The agency is paying for me to go."

"We may have to help you, though," my father said sympathetically. "Things may not go well. You may need our help, so all your mother is saying is to keep your top on and be a good girl. Once you start acting a certain way, it's really hard to stop. Doesn't take long for a bad habit to become your personality."

He was right, because once I rolled around on my twin mattress and purple sheets with Benji Law, I changed personalities. Turns out I got turned out right there in Pressville. Maybe New York had something to do with it, maybe not. I'll never really understand the urgency I felt to act on every impulse. First it was the modeling; then it was Benji. I thought I was powerful, being that I seemed to be making things happen that I wanted to happen, but I suppose a drug addict could say the same every time they scored a hit.

I saw Benji every day. I made excuses to be alone at home so he could sneak over, started asking to borrow my mom's minivan so I could drive to the Shell station, made arrangements to meet him behind the bathroom at Dix Park, and anything else I could think of to get him next to me even if just for a few minutes. I dreamed about him, thought about him all day, and heard his voice in my head when I was alone. I called the agency after a month and said I was going to stay home for a little longer. Dillard asked me if I could drive to Atlanta for castings, and I said sure, thinking that Benji and I could go together and I could get us a hotel room. No more sneaking around; our meetings could be more than five minutes, we could sleep in the same bed, we could hold hands in public, and I could pretend I wasn't doing anything wrong for a night or two.

And I wasn't doing anything wrong, but the Romeo and Juliet element that I'd added to the story took on a whole new meaning the more I lied about it. It was like that stupid song they teach you in preschool—one white lie leads to another, even if there's no reason for the first one. Of course I knew what everyone would say about him, about his family—trash—but there was no reason for me to hide the way I did. Benji was easy to judge, out there on the bike with his shirt off and a cigarette hanging out of his mouth, and the fistfights I heard about, and the pot plants in the bathroom, and all the time in detention at school. When you mentioned a Law, that was what you heard. I figured everyone was talking about Blake, not Benji, but even if it was Benji, I didn't care. I decided I already knew what kind of reaction I was going to get. He wasn't good enough for me—that was what my parents would say. It's funny to ask myself why I would think that; I was just like Benji, only I was doing all that in New York, where we didn't have to hide pot in the bathroom.

The job in Atlanta was for a soap commercial, something where I had to spin around in the shower with lather all over my shoulders and make faces like someone was giving me a massage. Dillard set up my appointment and told me where to be. My father drew a detailed map of the Atlanta neighborhood where I'd be going. "I know this area well," he told me, smiling like he'd finally found a way to be useful. I thanked him for his help and put the map in my bag. "Let me know when you get there. I want to know if the directions were right." He put his hand on my shoulder and closed his eyes, satisfied.

"Well, I hope they're right!" my mother bellowed from her place in the kitchen. "Atlanta traffic is like the seventh level of hell!"

My father raised his eyelids. "Sounds serious."

"Anyway, she lives in New York, for God's sake. She knows how to get around—certainly a lot better than I do." My mother had a tendency to brag about my life in a backhanded way, like she was both thrilled for and dismayed by me all at the same time. I think that is a fairly accurate description of our relationship for most of my life.

I asked Benji to come with me, then booked a room at a swanky place in town. I told him he'd have to wear a shirt and that we couldn't take the motorcycle. He asked why, and I said, "Because you don't have a driver's license." He didn't. The Laws weren't concerned with things like driver's licenses. They got along just fine without them in Pressville.

"You drive it, then," he said, so I did.

I'd gotten my license since coming home. Claudia had said it was stupid not to have it, because I needed ID for everything. "You need it to get paid, for God's sake!"

We wore helmets and boots, and I wore a Hervé Léger leather jacket. We tore down Highway 85 at ninety-five miles an hour, the whole way. My hair was so knotted when we arrived at the hotel that I thought I might have to cut it off. The valet gave me a sideways glance, but I figured Atlanta people were used to rich kids, so I didn't care. Later, I would learn that Benji's motorcycle was a hunk of cheap junk and that no one thought we were rich. The valet must have just thought we were trashy rednecks or plain stupid—but probably both. We checked into our room, and I immediately called down to room service. I did all the things that people had been doing for me for the past year. I treated Benji like a pretty girl. He looked out the window and said he didn't like the city—any city. I told him he'd have to change his mind, because I was taking him back to New York with me. His face was suspicious and steely; I knew to change the subject.

I pretended we were married while we were in Atlanta—like a little girl with her tea set, dress-up clothes, and baby buggy. We went out to eat for every meal, and I bought him a suit that I really couldn't afford. He smiled a lot and talked about his parents, whom he seemed to think were great people doing a great job raising him and his brother. They thought he was camping.

"Camping in your suit, right?" I said, laughing as we walked out of Nordstrom.

He sneered a little. "I'd rather be camping than wear a suit. I don't need one 'cept to go to a funeral, and I ain't plannin' on that anytime soon."

"Whatever," I said, failing, as always, to appreciate the significance.

I was only really aware of how young we looked once, when a waiter at a Thai restaurant brought one glass for the wine and refused to give us a second. Neither of us was of age, but apparently I was an easier sell. I drank from the bottle and gave Benji sips when no one was looking. "I don't even like that," he told me, grinning with his crooked teeth. Around different types of people, I became more self-conscious for him.

Benji came with me to my job but stayed outside the building where the shoot took place. He told me he was going to go for a walk, but every time I peeked out the warehouse door or walked outside to smoke a cigarette, he was leaning on the bike with one foot up under him. I heard a couple of the set girls talking about him, which I tried to ignore. Someone said he was my brother, but I didn't correct them. They'd made a shower in the middle of a huge empty hall in what must have been an abandoned building. I did about twelve takes, lathering my hair while closing my eyes. We wrapped after three hours. I could tell Benji was anxious to get out of there. We rode back to the hotel in what I thought was satisfied silence.

"So do you even like modeling? And why do they call you Dani at these things? Everyone else calls you Danielle." We were in our room, lying on top of the duvet. We had to check out in a matter of minutes. I'd told my parents I was going to take a cab to and from the hotel. They were shocked, asking how much that was going to cost me, so I lied and said the agency was covering it.

"The Ritz-Carlton and free cabs all the way to Atlanta," my mother said. "A person'd think you were maybe more than a model..." She trailed off, perhaps talking herself out of something. My father's only concern was whether I would show the cab driver the map he'd made.

I rolled onto my side to answer Benji's question, feeling very important that he'd noticed I had a different name for work. "My booker is this crazy lady who thinks she's French, and she thought Dani was a redneck name, and bein' that I'm from the sticks, she wanted me to have it. I don't know..." I trailed off because of the look on his face.

"Pressville ain't the sticks," he said loudly. If Claudia had been there, she would have said he proved her point.

"Well, no…" I knew I'd misspoken. "But you asked—that's just what she thinks."

"And you're not a redneck. Your family has more money than mine. Y'all are, like, ritzy or whatever."

"No," I said. "No, we're not rednecks, Benji. Claudia's an idiot. Forget her. She's dead to me."

I laughed and then stopped abruptly, remembering that Claudia was sick and was having chemo treatments. She'd emailed me and said she wore a hot wig, and by hot I mean my head sweats.

I wrote her back and said I'd bring her some southern air-conditioning, because it's the best, and that I'd met a nice boy at home and I wasn't sure I wanted to leave. She responded almost immediately and told me to leave the boy in Georgia.

You're too old for boys anyway. Get a man here in New York, darling. You'll thank me for it when you're forty and can't get paid to smile in your underwear anymore.

"She sounds like an idiot," Benji said.

"She is." I ran my hand over his forehead. "She's a total idiot."

Later that same day, Claudia called me, effusive. The director who'd done the shampoo commercial wanted me to do a shoot in New York for waterproof mascara. Same massage faces and twirling around under a stream of water, just a different product. She'd also booked me a six-page layout in a fashion magazine that she sounded particularly excited about. "It's more model-y than the shampoo shit," she assured me. "It will be good for you."

Both were to pay well, and I was running a little low on funds, having not worked for a month while still paying for my apartment in New York. I was itching to live on my own again, but the thought of leaving Benji was like scratching my face off with hot coals.

"You could come with me," I told him after I'd explained that I needed to go back to New York. We were at his house, lying on his bed in the room he shared with Blake. The place was in constant disarray, and I couldn't really figure out if his mother knew who I was. She was friendly but dazed and sleepy. Benji said she was sick, but I think what he meant was that she was an alcoholic. His father too. When they were home, they were kind of like the house—all the lights on, but nobody there. Other than old, tattered furniture, there were bath mats being used as rugs in the kitchen and some childhood photos on the walls of Benji and Blake and the older sisters. It seemed interest in documenting their growth had waned around the time Benji was six. I had the sense that everyone there had given up. Benji and Blake were the remnants of something that had been going well, at some distant point in time that no one could quite recapture or clearly remember.

It wasn't just the way the house looked—derelict and unkempt— or even that Benji's parents were definitely having some mental health struggles that prevented them from getting off the couch or holding down a job; I knew the police were over at the Laws' sometimes. I knew Blake had been in trouble with drugs before and had already been to juvie at least once. I knew that both Law boys were only in and out of school and that Blake had been officially expelled the year before, even if I told myself he'd just dropped out. I knew they had drugs in the house and that their older sister stole some of their mom's medication when she came by to visit. I think her name was Tina, and she'd be over borrowing something with her boyfriend, who had a bunch of tattoos on his neck, then go into the hall bathroom and come out with her hand in a clench and leave right away. Benji had said the cops had been by a lot the year before because of fighting; I didn't know if he meant his parents or Blake or the sister. I never asked him to elaborate. I hadn't seen him do anything wrong other than riding the motorcycle without a helmet...or a license, and maybe a few times I'd noticed him and Blake shoving something in their pockets at the Shell station and walking out without paying for it, but that was all. I can't say that I didn't know there were problems or that I didn't think the problems were serious. What I can say is that I didn't care. I would have cared at one time in my life, but I didn't care then. I'd learned to overlook anything in New York.

"Yeah," Benji said absently. He was messing with the TV remote and focused on wrestling. "But I don't know about me in New York."

"Or I can come back here, and we can just go to Atlanta all the time so we don't have to hide."

He looked at me like he wondered what I was talking about, this confused, vacant stare indicating we did not feel the same about something very significant.

14

Most of the time when I was talking to my parents, I was not only giving just half the story but also paying them only half my attention. I could look at them, nod, speak, answer questions, and appear engaged, but my mind was always on Benji. I could feel the throttle of the bike when sitting at the dinner table. I could smell him when I sat next to my sisters on the couch in the evening. I thought about his back when I ran errands with my mother. If we ever passed him, which we occasionally did, my mother would stop speaking or turn the radio up, trying her damnedest to act like she didn't notice. It pained her to ignore them, the Law boys, but she knew better than to say something. It was like introducing the cancer but asking it not to spread. I wouldn't say a word when they passed, either, but my stomach would sink to the seat of my pants and sit there twisting, churning, and quickening my breath by pulling down on a thin thread of insistence. They stood, they leaned, they jutted one knee out on sharp turns. Neither of them ever had a helmet, so you could see their faces in a tight squint. Benji would pop wheelies and gun it past Blake, followed by Blake taking his turn. They were racing to their doom, seemingly unaware of the privilege they had to live so close to the edge of their mortality. The hair on my arms stood up every time I thought about it. When I was on the back of the bike, the visor of my helmet down—Benji's sister's old one—I'd lean in tight on Benji, making myself form to him. We'd shirk the limestone edges and kudzu-covered shoulders that dropped off into fields of wildflowers and deep grass. It would have been okay with me to roll over the edge with him, landing in a bed of flowers. We could die right there in a meadow. I might have considered it a favor from God to go doing what I loved.

If the Law boys were on their bikes, everyone knew it. My mother could pretend she didn't see them all she wanted. I couldn't see anything else. And anyway, we were both pretending. She was pretending I wasn't who I was, and I was pretending I knew why I had to be this way. Some people just can't stop running toward the fire.

My mother also pretended she didn't notice that I had a tank top tan line and scrapes, healing bruises, nicks, cuts, and scabs all over my arms. Chantel had commented that she didn't think I'd be able to model looking "like a farmhand."

"That's why I got to model in the first place," I said. "Because I look like a farmer."

I even had Benji take a few photos of me in front of the motorcycle wearing ripped jeans and a loose top that accentuated my tan lines and wounds. He was uncomfortable and refused to let me take any pictures of him.

"Why are you making that face?" he asked, laughing meanly as I lifted an eyebrow.

"That's just the face I make." I sent Claudia the photos. She wrote back an hour later.

Get your ass back to New York. Hammond just booked you for Antilly. I need you here next week.

"I gotta stop riding the bike," I told Benji after our photo shoot. "I'm getting beat up. They won't like it when I go back to New York." I ran my hand over his buzz cut. We were lying on his bed again. I could hear the sound of a radio coming from the kitchen. His parents hadn't been concerned with me in the least. I don't think either of them ever spoke directly to me.

"Gonna be sad when you go," he said, looking up at me, a slight crinkle in his forehead.

"I want you to come with me."

"Why?"

"So we can be together."

"I mean, whatever," he said, reaching up to kiss me.

That evening, when I got home from Benji's, I heard my father ask my mother while she was making dinner—they thought they were alone—if she'd heard that I was dating one of the Law boys, "that kid who rides the motorcycle all over the place." I was in the living room, sprawled on the couch, listening but undetected.

"I heard something like that from Bonnie Blalock, but she gets her information from Rita Ellenhart at the post office, and our darling Danielle doesn't go to the post office, so I don't know how Rita would know anything about Danielle or that Law boy, who most likely couldn't write a letter to save his life."

I flinched.

"I don't really get why she'd want to go around with some kid from here when she's got her whole thing with the 'six-hundred-dollar sunglasses' going on back in New York," my father said. He was making fun of me about the sunglasses; it was so unlike him, and here I thought they'd been impressed.

"She's just like them," my mother said. "No schooling, no direction, just thrill-seeking. Low-hanging-fruit kind of people." My mother reminded everyone that I was "uneducated" at least ten times a day.

"Here's the butter, my uneducated daughter."

"Please don't put that there. It will leave a mark. Uneducated people don't use coasters."

She was joking, but she was also making a point. I'd tried to tell her that I was actually more educated, more enlightened, more worldly, and also that I knew how to earn a buck.

"That's what strippers say" was her only reply.

"She's young, Deb," my father said.

"She's not that young. She could serve in the military. She can vote! That's what I don't get… It's like she's all grown up with her career and all that, but then we're supposed to excuse everything because she's young. Some career—you don't have to have a lick of good sense to be successful."

"I'm not even sure she's all that successful," my dad said. "I have a feeling she'll be done with the modeling sooner than later. Or it'll be done with her."

I felt my jaw go slack as all the air went out of me. He was right, of course. It was true that it wasn't going all that well for me, but I hadn't thought he'd know that. I'd been so pushy with how great I was doing. It was like he'd talked to Claudia and found out I was barely booking and that I kept getting passed over for even the lower-level stuff. My dad had never seemed to have a lot of opinions or much say in what was going on in our family. He let my mother take the wheel. He was a bit like Chantel: no personality of his own, just contrasts—my mother's foil. But I guess I was wrong; he sure seemed to have a personality tonight, and one that didn't think I was all that great. I would never have guessed.

"Anyway," my dad said. "He's awfully young, though—the Law kid. And aren't they always in trouble? I know the older boy already went to jail. Danielle's not a troublemaker." He wasn't trying to convince himself of anything. I wasn't a troublemaker. I played it pretty straight growing up. I made decent grades, did what I was told, and minded my manners. Benji and his family were a departure. I knew it and so did my parents.

"I swear if we'd never let her go to New York, she wouldn't even care about those kids," my mother said, stirring something in a pot and putting the wooden spoon down on the counter. Neither of them said anything for a while, and from my perch on the stairs and their shared, needling silence, I knew nothing would ever be the same. They knew it too. "She never cared about the Law kids before, but now that it's anything-goes-Danielle, she's smitten. You mark my words, we're going to live to regret talking to that idiot at the mall."

15

2019

Cady hadn't aged a dime, while I'd gotten older by a hundred bucks. When she came to my house, still in her pinch-waisted pants and slim button-up shirt, I thought we'd gone back in time. Meanwhile, I was heavier throughout the middle, sagging around my eyes and mouth. There was a laziness to my gait now, an overall clumsiness and lack of agility. I seemed to have gotten stringier and less connected over time. Cady was still neatly packed into her tiny frame with her pert, expectant face—unchanged by the experiences that had marked me. They coursed through my veins and left me fallow, unreachable, distant, and abandoned.

"Hi, Danielle," Cady said when I opened the door. She was holding her phone in one hand and a small notepad in the other.

"Sorry to bother you with this," I apologized from my perch above her. My height had never made me feel so small.

"With a dead body? I would dare say that's my job." She smiled dispassionately.

"Right."

"I'm going to walk down there. I have a team coming. Nobody's here yet…" She looked over her shoulder. "Of course."

"Do you want me to come down there with you?" I pulled at my bra strap before folding my hands in front of my waist after realizing how inappropriate that had been. I was used to being alone or only with my daughters, who were not old enough to realize that I was so often an unkempt mess without a shred of decorum. The bra strap was still twisted and showing from the neckline of my shirt.

"No. No, you can't go down there."

"Okay. I don't think I'm like a detective or something… I just meant because it's steep or whatever."

"Right." She turned away from me. There was a car approaching. "Okay, they're here. I don't know how long we're going to be back there, so…we might even have to put up some lights. It's getting a little late." She glanced at her watch. "Yeah, I don't know how long this is going to take."

"It's just one body," I offered.

She snickered. "You don't know what it is, Dani." No one had called me Dani in a long time. "I'm going to have to talk to your daughters too."

"Yes," I said. She hadn't asked me a question.

"Since they found it."

"Yes."

"You never found anything back there before?" she asked, looking at me directly. I pressed my lips together.

"I don't go back there," I said.

"But you used to."

"When I was a kid." It felt like we were arguing. I could hear footsteps behind me.

"Mama?"

"Yes?" I turned around. It was Pamela.

"My stomach hurts."

"Okay."

"I'll let you get back to it." Cady patted the doorframe. "Y'all don't leave town, now."

"We're not going anywhere," I said, turning back to her.

"Good." A van pulled in the driveway with the state logo on the side. "Real good."

16

I had quite a fantasy going about myself back in Pressville with Benji. I was convinced he was the real me, the one who grew up in Georgia. I made every excuse for my attraction to him. He was the summer mosquitoes, dirty feet, the stickiness of July after a long day on the lake, the disintegrating freedom of those last few days in August before school started again. I was spinning yarns left and right about how he was my homecoming—even with so much evidence to the contrary. I wasn't licking Bomb Pops at the playground or kicking around my mother's old soccer ball one dull afternoon after another. I wasn't even partying with old friends or drinking Mr. Pibb in the gas-station parking lot while waiting for a carload of boys to drive by and tell us where to go for a good time. I didn't see any old friends. I said it was because I didn't want to—both my parents had asked me if I was going to catch up with Wendy, Lauren, Kate, Allie, any of my "old crew." I hadn't heard from any of them. I figured it was because I'd dropped the ball after my first year in New York. I tried, initially. I called, returned emails, laughed at photos they sent. It just didn't last, this enthusiasm to find what they were doing interesting, comforting, meaningful at all.

To add insult to injury, no one had really sought me out when I came home. Everyone knew I was in Pressville, but I suppose they'd been ignored one too many times. I'm sure if I'd made the effort, shown up at one of their jobs—Wendy's, the pet-supply store in Lincoln, Allie's dad's real estate office on Baker—I would have been welcomed. It was up to me, and I couldn't be bothered. A lot of them were almost off to school somewhere, studying to be teachers or psychologists or other things I'd never wanted to be.

"They never call anyway," I said of them after my mother's third inquiry. "We don't have anything in common anymore."

I could remember my friend Allie telling me that I was too serious one time when we did try to catch up over the phone while I was in New York. It was a busy day: I had a fitting and two castings on opposite ends of town. I'd called her while walking between the train and the second of my appointments, trying to impart both how excited I was to talk to her *and* how busy and important I was.

"You're so serious all the time," she said after being reminded for the fourth time that I was in a rush.

I could almost hear my father. "Sounds serious!" He was right. So was she. "I mean, serious about modeling," she corrected herself. "That's all you ever want to talk about, and it's really not… that serious."

I told her I had to go, because I did. I booked both jobs that day. That was one of the last times I called Allie. She never called me again, either, which was a relief once I started running around with Benji. No one was going to understand that, least of all any of the kids I grew up with, who'd only heard about how awesome it was for me to get out of Pressville. And they wouldn't have understood what I was doing with one of the Law boys; that would have been an even greater mystery.

"See, in the beginning you were acting like a prisoner here, and now you're running around in the woods, soaking up the local color like you wanna move home," my mother said to me one afternoon near the end of my stay. She was smiling, but it was a loaded smile that meant she knew what she was saying was only half-true, just like the way she dressed with her tight jeans and bouffant hairstyle was only half the story. Never trust a woman with acrylic nails. If she feels she has to hide her nail beds from view, then there's other, more important stuff that she doesn't want you to see.

"Just nice to be around nature," I lied. "Not a lot of nature in New York."

"All kinds a nature here." She pursed her lips and stared at me.

Benji didn't seem to understand what me going back to New York meant. When we said goodbye—at his house, while his parents were napping in the living room—he hugged me like one would hug a nice aunt who'd brought muffins. He said, "Well then," and patted my shoulder. Later, I would realize that he didn't think I was coming back and that he didn't really care. It wasn't his fault. It was mine.

My family was less ambiguous. "You should stay here," my mother said urgently on the final day. "Something's happened to you there. I don't think it's a good idea to go back. It might be the water."

"Actually, New York has the cleanest public-water supply in the country," my father said. He'd started combing his hair straight down his forehead, I suppose in an attempt to avoid looking like his hairline was receding. My mother nearly gasped every time he walked in the room. Her face couldn't hide her disapproval.

"Thank you," my mother said. "Thank you very much for that information, Joe. But you know what I mean, Danielle. One bad decision after another. I just don't have a good feeling." She was staring at me a little too directly, just like when we'd been talking about all the nature I was loving in Georgia. I couldn't figure it out, though—it seemed like they would hate me running around with Benji more than they hated me being in New York, or maybe they hadn't decided which was worse yet.

All my friends in New York were gone when I returned. A lot of them were working abroad, or trying to, while others had gone home for the summer and either weren't coming back or weren't back yet. I was suddenly new in town again and feeling like I'd forgotten everything I'd learned. My apartment felt eerily empty, like something significant had been removed, and there was a faint odor that was not unpleasant but made me think someone else had been there while I was gone. I felt like I was being watched and had trouble sleeping for several days. I was exhausted, frequently napping restlessly in the afternoons and waking up startled and nervous.

Claudia told me to beware of "camera installations... You know, the owner might have gone in there while you were home to make sure he could get a look at Dani any time he wanted. Can't say I haven't seen it before." Thanks to this conversation, I did start feeling like I was being watched in a government-surveillance sort of way. My English friend, Todd, who lived in New York in hopes of Broadway stardom, came over and told me the place was haunted. I told him to stop talking like that.

"But it is. You'll be tormented here."

"Why? I love it here. I'm just not sleeping well. That's why I feel bugged."

"I wouldn't live here," Todd said. "I'd get a roommate or something. I can't live alone, anyway. I hate it so much. Oh my God—"

I thought he might be about to suggest I take him in, so I changed the subject and asked him if he thought wool was itchy.

"Yes!" He was equally as enthusiastic to discuss wool, and with that, it seemed I was off the hook.

A few of the promoters who always took care of us at clubs in the city heard I was back and invited me to a restaurant opening. Sometimes I couldn't understand why they were making a fuss over me; if I were really a big-time model, I'd be working, not hanging out at their stupid parties.

I went by myself, wearing a black catsuit with my hair in a severe ponytail. I was photographed while on the red carpet and tried to imagine Benji beside me, with his dirty ankles and shaggy hair flopping over one eye in the sun like a visor. All night I kept trying to see him in the other people I was talking to, but he was not in New York, and the Danielle who loved him felt very abruptly out of place there. Oren, the promoter who'd invited me to the party, gave me a strange look when he welcomed me. "You're so down and out, Dani! This ain't Beverly Hills." I had no idea what he meant and figured I really hadn't known what anyone meant the entire time I'd been modeling. I drank whiskey until two a.m. and took a cab home. I think I cried in the back seat, but I don't really remember. I know I called Benji's house, but no one answered. They were all asleep. It was nearly three a.m.

We did speak on the phone—infrequently, because Benji didn't like to talk on the phone, or really at all. For some reason I was comforted by this and liked the way the silence sounded between us. I called him in the evenings; I'd lie on my bed in a T-shirt and boxers and pretend he was next to me. I did so much pretending then, another remnant of childhood I'd warped and made into an adult behavior. If something wasn't panning out, I made believe.

I was always relieved when he said he missed me and asked when I was coming back. That was kind of all he said. He'd drag it out like he was whining. "Awwww, can't you come home and be my girl?" I would giggle and play at something more serious than was warranted. Then one day he surprised me.

"Just move up here," I said, not really thinking he would. "You don't have to stay forever, but since you're not in school, I guess, what does it matter? It'll be just like Pressville, only it's New York."

"Okay," he said. "I'll come up for a while."

"Wait, what?"

"I'll come up to New York."

"You will?"

"But it's not Georgia. Don't say it's Georgia."

"Oh my God, Benji." I curled my toes and leaned over, thrusting my fist into my stomach. There was a change in my breath. I kept swallowing to try to sound calm.

"I'm not gonna like…live there or something, just stay for a while."

"Okay!" I was close to squealing.

It took almost an hour of conversation for him to understand that I could not pick him up from the airport and that he would have to take a cab. We finally decided that I would be the one to take a cab to the airport and then escort him back to my apartment, which suddenly seemed dark and cramped now that I imagined someone unfamiliar with New York real estate seeing it. I didn't think Benji was going to be all that impressed, even though the bathroom was nice and I had a full-size refrigerator—two things he would barely notice. Everyone had a full-size refrigerator in Georgia. That was hardly something to brag about.

I booked Benji's ticket for him—he would arrive in four days. After helping me bring a few loads of my stuff from the storage space in the Bronx, Todd told me he was taking a vow of silence and would be "difficult to reach." I said okay. I didn't want to talk to him anyway, and I certainly didn't want to introduce Benji to Todd or vice versa. It seemed all the stars had aligned. It was going to be just me and Benji in New York for as long as I could keep him there.

Benji was a nervous wreck upon arriving, visibly uncomfortable and intimidated in a way he had not been in Atlanta. It endeared him to me and made me feel responsible for his well-being. New York was like another planet for a kid from Pressville. I remembered.

The city baffled him, mostly because he couldn't understand why anyone wanted to live there. "Place smells like an armpit," he told me after his first day on his own. I had a runway show and had my fitting, followed by a casting for a leather company's ad for a line of pants with lace-up crotches. Claudia told me to wear leather pants to the appointment. I had a pair, and so I did. Benji liked the pants and said I should "wear shit like that more often…like with boots or something."

I bought him a video game console his second day in New York, to which he was glued when I left for my casting. He called me about two hours later while I was waiting for a fitter to take my inseam and said he was bored out of his head. I told him to go for a walk.

"There's nowhere to walk."

"This is New York. There is everywhere to walk."

He was unconvinced and said he missed his motorcycle too.

"I don't!" I said, thinking this was somehow funny.

"Well, I do." He sounded angry. We held on to the silence we'd created over the line, and for a moment I felt guilty. Benji was miserable, and here I was, in leather pants, smoking a cigarette with a guy named Garth who had his hand between my legs, holding a tape measure.

When I got home that afternoon, it looked to me like he hadn't left the apartment. He was in a sore mood, with his arms crossed over his chest, sighing heavily every few minutes as if trying to make a point about something. Instead of trying to actually talk to him, I said we should go get a drink.

"Someplace fun!" I said too cheerfully.

He said okay, but more like he thought I was trying to pull a fast one. He wore soccer shoes with his ripped jeans and a black hooded sweatshirt. He fit right in, as far as I was concerned.

We held hands, which we hadn't had much occasion to do in Pressville, being that we didn't walk anywhere. We were either in bed or on his motorcycle. I was beaming and hoping people passing us would notice that I was taken, loved, someone's. He didn't seem to be feeling the same way about things and dropped my hand. I reminded myself to give him time to warm up. "New York is a place that grows on you," I said. "I promise. It will get easier." He didn't respond and kept walking. I caught him in a frustrated squint right as an ambulance came barreling by, its sirens shrieking. A man walking opposite us told whoever he was talking to on his phone to get dog food, and a girl dropped her purse in gum.

"I'm not, like, moving here or something," he said after a minute. "I'm not gonna live in New York."

I ignored his comment as we continued walking.

Benji kept ordering Coors Light everywhere we went, which embarrassed me because half the time they wouldn't serve him, and the other half they gave him the beer like it was redneck charity. I tried to talk over him when bartenders approached us, but he'd get even louder: "Coors!" Sometimes people around us would look at him funny, and a lot of the time they didn't even have it. I couldn't understand why he was holding on to home so much. It hadn't held on to him. From what I understood, no one in his family was worried about him or demanding he come back. He'd been in New York for almost ten days, and he hadn't mentioned his parents once. The only thing he'd said was that his brother told him he was missing out on some "pretty sweet rides" that he could have been fixing at the Shell.

"You know there's other beer besides Coors Light," I said.

"I don't really care about beer, Danielle. I'm not tryin' to become like some beer expert."

"Right, I know."

"So just leave me alone."

"Ouch." I was serious but made it sound like we had an inside joke about him telling me to leave him alone. I was most concerned about the girls sitting next to us at the bar hearing him say that to me. "Kinda hard for me to leave you alone when you're living with me." I was leaning over, my head dipped down like a flamingo. I can remember smiling patronizingly, like Benji was my dog that I'd just had to discipline but who I was about to reward with a treat. Something was offtrack, and I couldn't get it right again. I thought it was New York; it just didn't suit him. "We don't have to live here forever," I said. He sneered, then went silent for a bit. He seemed to say something to himself that got his mood in balance and was more pleasant after the reset. We ate chicken wings and made fun of Chantel. Benji got a kick out of Chantel because of her seriousness and the way she was always pouting. We walked home arm in arm, and I'd never been so grateful. I was certain we'd moved on, gotten over the hump, busted the hurdle to pieces. We would no longer have to jump over anything. We could stroll now. The whole beginning of our relationship had felt like strolling, and then it had been a furious, sweaty sprint.

Just like I couldn't stop trying to decide for him what kind of beer Benji should drink, I couldn't stop lying to my family. I could tell they'd heard that Benji was in New York with me. Pressville was small enough that even teenage gossip got some traction. My mother would make odd comments about kids living in New York on their own.

"I mean…I let you do it, but you were seventeen…"

"Not sure what a kid from Pressville would want with living up there; everything's so expensive, even the water, and there's all the people doing farmers' blows on the sidewalk like it's a cattle ranch or something."

"I didn't think you were making enough money to support two people…not with six-hundred-dollar sunglasses to pay for all the time."

I skirted the issue, purposefully finding her difficult to hear when she made her remarks. "Huh?" I'd say, then start talking over her response. I made some bold proclamations about being lonely and hating living on my own, to which she'd laugh in a snide, judgmental sort of way.

"Oh, I'm sure."

When Benji heard my end of these conversations, he'd slink down farther on the couch and pull his hood over his face—full well knowing that I was lying to my mother. I didn't explain myself when I hung up. I usually pretended to be in a fantastic mood, only further heightened by the exchange. A couple of times, I did make a comment or two about how annoying my parents were, to which Benji would sneer.

"Moms are the best thing in the world. You can't be mean to your mama." So much of what he said made me uncomfortable with myself. I'd find I was questioning my behavior based on Benji's philosophies. I felt like an idiot around him, which was hard to explain. I'd put myself in the position of being the one slumming it, because that was what I thought everyone else would say. I thought maybe Benji thought he was lowering himself by running around with some pretty-faced, empty-headed girl from his high school who didn't graduate, couldn't fix a motorcycle, and was mean to her mom.

It might have been because I was already feeling insecure—nothing about Benji coming to New York was working out the way I'd hoped—but I didn't book a few jobs in a row. I'd been on a bit of a hot streak, but it abruptly ended. Claudia said I needed to wear my hair differently. "Or dress different or carry a different bag, I really don't know, but something isn't working, so let's nip it in the bud. Just be different." It was an awkward conversation that had me nervous and fumbling at auditions, something I thought I was over.

One of the girls I met at a casting told me she'd made a bundle doing an ad for AT&T. She was bragging, but all I could think was that she wasn't that cute and maybe AT&T liked girls who weren't that pretty. I called Claudia and asked her if I could do some cell phone stuff.

"What?" she asked. "Cell phones? We do fashion. I know

you're not booking, but you're not going to do cell phone print. I don't book cell phone ads. I said that you shouldn't leave town for so long, and you did, and you look different for some reason now. Your face is more like a moon. No one is biting. You look too sad. Everyone says you look sad, and I know it's because of your boyfriend and how he's so country and out of place in New York. No one will let you fuck him in peace, but I can't very well tell Dave Boyd at Gucci that I've got the girl for him except her face looks like a crying dinner plate. I can't do that, now can I?" Claudia had to take medicine as part of recovery, and it made her grouchy. We all told her that. Her response was that she looked good grouchy. "Bitch is my best look—makes my face look thin."

That was another thing: Benji came along with me to a few appointments at the agency. I don't know what I'd expected, but most people tried not to stare and gave the same fake smile I always saw at the open calls when girls who were five five and wearing weird tube tops came in hoping to get signed. In the beginning, I'd quietly mocked those people, thinking they didn't know how it worked and that you had to get picked up somewhere just looking fabulous like I had. But the longer I went without really hitting it big, I started to feel bad for them and was then embarrassed, because of course they wouldn't think I was a famous model, and maybe they thought my face looked huge too. Benji would barely set foot in the agency and always—after the first time he actually came in—said he'd wait downstairs, in the hall, or out on the street.

"Not my kinda people," he said. He was right. I don't think they were ever my kind of people, either, but I hadn't bothered to notice. "Too weird." And they were weird. I don't know why I wouldn't let myself think that until he said something.

After Claudia's comments about my face, I told Benji I needed to start running, and no more beer. He said my life was ridiculous. He also said he was tired of playing video games, and then almost immediately, he got a job at an auto mechanic's in Brooklyn. One day I came home from an appointment and he was gone. His things were still in the apartment, so I knew he hadn't left for good, but I had no idea where he was. He came back about an hour later and said he'd met some guy at a gas station on Broadway who told him his brother needed help at his garage in Brooklyn. He said it took him thirty minutes and three trains to get there, and after a couple of weeks, he was making more money than I was. He suggested I go get a waitressing job and that we forget all about this modeling thing. "I like Brooklyn, anyway," he said. It was a few days later that I found out he was actually working in Queens, nowhere near the Brooklyn line, and that he'd been confused this whole time. The shop was called Queens Mechanics. I don't think he had any idea that the first half of the place's name indicated location.

It was the way Benji would absently look away from me sometimes when I was plotting, scheming, writing the rest of our story together that had me believing he did not necessarily feel the same way about me that I did about him. He didn't make dramatic proclamations or grand gestures the way I did. Every sentence out of my mouth was this urgent assurance that this was only the beginning. My mother would later accuse me of hiding the relationship because I didn't want to take it seriously. All I could think was that I'd never taken anything so seriously.

"Right, but in your mind. It's different when you have to take something seriously in front of everyone else. The modeling was the same…" She'd wander off. "How can anyone do that with a straight face, you know?"

Benji was biding his time. I think maybe he didn't want to hurt me, or maybe I'm getting him confused with someone older, someone with more experience, someone I couldn't toy like a cat batting a hooked fish on a line. I tell myself he cared about me and that was why he was there. It might have also been that he didn't have anything else to do and that Blake was getting into a whole lot of trouble at home, so he figured it would be better not to be there. He didn't tell me about Blake; my sisters mentioned things occasionally about him being arrested or getting caught with a gun or having to go to court because he'd sold some kids acid at the middle school. I would barely listen. I thought everyone was jealous of me and wanted to ruin my happiness. Just like Chantel shouldn't have told me that I made more money than my dad—once, that one month that I did—she shouldn't have told me she thought my mother was jealous of my looks. I believed it and made it my reason for assuming that my mother—and everyone else—was not only jealous of the modeling but of my grand love affair as well.

"I wouldn't let someone live off me like that," my mother said once. My days were punctuated by her sly remarks. Every time we talked, she added a little dash of disapproval. I did wonder why I continued to call. "When the coffers run dry, those types of people always move on. They aren't making the same kind of decisions you're making…if you know what I mean."

"You don't know what kind of decisions I'm making." I tried adding my own sly remarks in the same vicious tone I seemed to be saying everything else to her. I ignored her insinuations, and she ignored my disrespect. Perhaps she thought it was what she had to do to keep me. I'd been slipping away from her since we went to the mall that day. A mother, I learned, tries to keep her grasp even when the other hand is making a fist.

"Well, I know when I was your age, I'd already met your father and we were already talking kids. I knew exactly what my future was going to look like because of the choices I was making. No nursing, no trying out for the Olympic soccer team, no meeting a guy from California, even though I always wanted to go to California. I wanted to go to San Diego. I saw pictures of it in a magazine and I was smitten, I tell you. I was going to meet and marry a man from San Diego, and we were going to jet off to California, and I was going to finally say I'd been somewhere. But I met your father, and he was too good to pass up, so we got married and had a baby, and I don't regret a minute of it, but that's the kind of decisions I was makin' then, and you are thinking like an adult because I let you move away and think you're an adult—and you aren't, and he's thinkin' like a kid, and there is no meeting in the middle. There's no middle."

"Who's a kid?" I'd always pretend I didn't know what she was talking about.

We mostly talked when I was going from thing to thing, not in the apartment, where Benji could hear me. He really didn't like the way I talked to my mother; maybe he was sensing that was how I'd start acting if he stuck around long enough.

When I think back on this period of time, it is like there was the low hum of an air-conditioning unit or a distant leaf blower in the background of my life. I don't know exactly what I was doing, but by God, I was doing it, and I couldn't really hear clearly because of all the noise.

"So tell me your impressions of New York," I said to Benji one evening. We were eating banh mi in the Village. Benji was initially reluctant and uninterested, but I convinced him to keep an open mind and try the food. He polished off seven sandwiches and a Vietnamese coffee before leaving, which he said made him "Wired!"

"I don't know—filthy. It's a filthy place, but I can see why people think it's cool to live here. You don't have to go very far to see a crazy person or somebody with fashion sense, and people are fit and move real fast; you know, not like at home, where everybody's kinda lazy and slow like. And I guess it seems worldly to live here, like you'd know about politics and all that. I mean, it is cool—I get it—but it's not for me. I like Queens, though."

"So you like it? You could live there?" I was hopeful.

"No," he said, shrugging. "I'm glad I'm here. I can always say I did it. But no, I don't want to live in Queens."

"Well, I'm not going back to Pressville," I said sternly. He looked at me closely but didn't speak. "So that's it?" I said to his silence.

"So what's it?" We'd left the restaurant and were almost back to the apartment.

"You're leaving?"

"Jesus H. Christ, Danielle! I don't know if I'm leaving. What do you want from me? I love you. I love being with you. I came up here like a fool with a heart for a brain, and you just want so many answers. I don't have 'em. I'm sore trying to figure it out for you. I miss my family. I miss home. No, I don't want to live out my days here. There aren't any trees! How do these people live? The air's like spoiled milk. I don't hate it, necessarily. I'm happy I'm here, 'cause I'm with you, but you're acting like we're getting married or something. I'm sixteen."

I looked around quickly, praying no one had heard that last part. "But you talk like you've got one foot out the door all the time," I said, reaching for his hand.

"That's 'cause I do! I don't know what to tell you. Are you really gonna latch on to some wannabe auto mechanic from Pressville?

You're really gonna set your sights on that? I just can't give you answers. Not the answers you want. I miss my mama." He looked like he was about to cry.

———

The summer ended but then popped back up in early October. There were biblical rains and thunderstorms almost every day, and then a heat wave that cooked the streets. And Benji said he wanted to go home, very definitively. We were eating cereal on the floor of my apartment. "I wanna go home," he said—again, I suppose, thinking I might not have heard him the first time.

"For how long?" I asked. He looked at me the way a person who is about to jump off a cliff might look at the person trying to stop them.

"I don't know, Danielle. I just want to go home." He put his spoon down in the bowl. I saw that there were a few bites of Cinnamon Toast Crunch left there. I reached over with my own spoon and a sly grin. He moved his bowl away from me and said, "Gross." I'm not sure my feelings had ever been more hurt, not in my entire life.

———

Cady Benson called me the following day while I was walking to the store. I answered my phone without really looking at the number—local, Pressville. "Hello?"

"Hey, Danielle. It's Cady."

I was confused for a second. I knew another Katie from the agency. I looked at the screen on my phone and sighed heavily. "Hey, Cady."

"Did you want to get lunch?" She was talking like we'd already made these plans and she was only calling to confirm.

"Oh. No, I can't. I have to work today." It was true enough. I was supposed to get my hair cut at Todd's friend's salon. The stylist had said he would do my hair for free if I'd pose for some photos with him for his website.

She was persistent. "All day?"

"I'm on my way there right now, and I don't know what time I'll be done." I was smoking with one hand and holding the phone against my head with the other. I took a pull from my cigarette and waited for her to give up and go hang out with her lady-cop friends. I figured they were all short and wore button-up shirts that were too tight around their bra line. That, and pants that showed their underwear—right down the middle of each flat butt cheek. I had no idea why I hated her so much. I didn't know her. She meant nothing to me, but the irritation was suffocating. "Sorry," I said meaninglessly.

"How about I come by your place tonight. We can grab a quick dinner."

"I moved."

"Okay, where are you now?"

"I really can't. Sorry." I sounded angry now. "I can't today."

She was silent for a moment. "Danielle, I told your mother I would see you. I know I'm bugging you. I had hoped we could be friends, but that's okay. Really, it is. But I don't want to let your mama down. She helped us a lot while my dad was sick."

"Is he better now?" I'd stopped walking at a busy intersection. I was bumped a few times on the shoulder and elbow. I glared at the sidewalk.

"No, he passed away at the end of May."

"Oh." A cop car roared up the street and paused right in front of where I was standing. "I'm really sorry!" I shouted, thinking it necessary to be heard.

She said something else that I couldn't hear.

I shouted again, "I'm so sorry!"

Suddenly, we were disconnected. The line went dead. I shook my phone, knocking my cigarette ash all over my pants.

"Watch it, bitch!" a teenage girl sneered at me as she dusted her own leg.

I started to walk again, not sure if I was actually going the right way. I tried to call Cady's number back a few frantic times. Either my phone wouldn't connect or she'd ventured into a dead zone, but I couldn't get through. I couldn't even get the phone to ring. I stood in the path of aggressive foot traffic and texted her. I'm really sorry about your dad. I am late for work now. My phone isn't working right.

I walked the rest of the way to the salon feeling rushed and irritated. I tried calling Benji to calm my nerves, but he didn't answer. Cady did not call me back and did not respond to my text.

17

Claudia called me one evening, frothy and almost panting, when I was in the midst of yet another argument with Benji about moving home. For the past week, that was all we had talked about. That, and Cady Benson and why wouldn't I be nice to someone from Pressville. It had been strained, to say the least, not to mention Todd kept texting me to ask if I'd used sage on the apartment yet, and did I have a leopard-print leotard he could borrow?

Benji was going to finish the month at the mechanic's place in Queens because he didn't want to leave them hanging; then he was going to head home. He kept telling me, almost like he was asking for permission while being defiant. The end of the month was nearly three weeks away, so I thought I had time to fix things. I refused to accept what he kept telling me was about to happen.

Claudia's voice was scratchy and urgent. "There's a new girl in town from the south—not Georgia, I don't think, but next door… Kentucky, wherever that is. Louisa Radcliffe. Very *Gone with the Wind*. I need you to help her, get her situated—you know, welcome her to New York and find her a place to stay."

"Find her a place to stay? I barely found myself a place to stay." I'd started talking to Claudia a little like I talked to my mother. The strain was always with me, finding different directions to flow depending on who was in my way. "And *Gone with the Wind* was in Georgia, not Kentucky." My mother would have blown her lid. No one got to claim Margaret Mitchell but us. No one.

"Yes, but you did, and you're good at that type of thing. She's young. She's going to need help getting set up, and all I could think when I talked to her was that she sounded just like you. Identical. Twinsies. So I need you to kind of take her under your wing. Can you do that for me, *mon petit bisou*?"

"She can't stay in the model apartments?"

"Her parents don't approve of that," Claudia said sharply. "They've heard stories about diseases and poor morals and all the rest. They want her in her own place or with someone they can trust."

"Oh," I said, a little miffed. The model apartments were good enough for me and the other girls. This Louisa Radcliffe better watch her step, awfully big for her Kentucky britches. "I can't really help her out. It was murder for me to get my own place."

"Well, don't kill anybody," Claudia said. "But I've kind of made some promises here. I told her parents that if they let her come for a few months, I'd find her somewhere suitable to live…and that I had a good Georgia girl who could look after her. So…do your best. Can't she stay with you? Split the rent or whatever. I'm sure it wouldn't hurt to have some help." Suddenly, I knew what the call was really about. Claudia had gone from telling me I'd be making ten thousand dollars a day to suggesting I'd need help covering rent.

"No," I said. "No, I don't want a roommate—or I mean, I already have one…"

"Yeah, but one who can pay. Anyway, she's kind of a needy little thing. Only fifteen, and the mother's high-strung. They have money, you can tell, and they want her to be a model, but they don't know a damn thing about it—lots of questions, a hundred concerns every time we talk. I've about had it with all the emails, but you know, I think she's special. So anyway, you're a southern girl and she's a southern girl, and I need your help."

"Kentucky isn't real southern," I said, about to explain my position.

"Sure sounds like it is. Think about yourself when you were her age and how much you needed someone to take care of you. How nice would it have been to have a Dani on your side? Come on now, don't let me down."

"I don't know if I'm a good influence or—"

She cut me off by making a kissing noise and hanging up abruptly.

I stood with the phone still pressed to my ear for a few more seconds before putting it down.

It must have been God's timing—Louisa's God, not mine—because within a week of Claudia asking me to help Louisa, I saw a sign in the lobby of my building: STUDIO AVAILABLE FOR SUBLET. SIX MONTHS LEASE. GOING TO SEATTLE. I took the number and called it immediately. The ad was for a place on the second floor. "It's really small," a young man with a meek, trembling voice on the other end of the line told me.

I called Claudia and said I'd found Louisa a place and would make the deposit, but I was going to need to be paid back.

I told Benji about it when he got home that day, and all he said in response was, "You didn't have any jobs today?"

"No," I answered flatly.

I shook my head as if trying to clear the room of his stupidity. "Anyway, you'll have a new playmate. Louisa—that's her name—gets here next week, and she's about your age. No more babysitting."

He didn't really say anything to me for the rest of the night, glued to his game controller on the couch and immune to distraction. We ate cereal for dinner again and went to bed next to one another but disconnected. I wasn't babysitting him, and we both knew it. He worked more than I did and had had to cover the power and water bills that month.

Louisa arrived a week later with her dingy mother in tow. The two of them made more noise moving in than the entire building combined on a Saturday night during the summer. Louisa was clearly spoiled, clueless, and insufferably beautiful. She was a lot more special than I'd ever been, but she wasn't really aware. She smiled too much—in a pageantry sort of way, so much that it appeared disingenuous—and had piercing eyes that even in their youthful wandering made a person feel understood or judged or both, each sensation taking its turn. Her mother carried herself like a snobbish, suburban idiot, but there was clearly a lot more there, and we found out after a time that she'd been a very successful criminal defense attorney before having Louisa.

Louisa's mother did not appear to understand what the hell was going on in my apartment and either thought Benji was my little brother or God's gift to Louisa, because she said, at least a dozen times, that she was "so happy there's a nice southern boy here!" Me being a nice southern girl was entirely irrelevant.

Then, just as quickly as things had slowed down, I booked three jobs in a row and could breathe a sigh of relief. Claudia took me to lunch and told me the reason I was working more was because I had lost weight. She then ordered the gnocchi while I ate a salad with the dressing on the side. She wouldn't know it, but I hit McDonald's on the way home.

When I arrived back at the apartment after my lunch with Claudia, I found Louisa and Benji sitting on my couch, watching *The O.C.* Benji jumped up when I came in and smiled too broadly, like he'd been taking cues from Louisa. She smiled, too, with her wide, tanned face and upturned alien eyes all framed by her stick-straight blond hair. Her neck was especially long and her collarbone especially jutting—no wonder everyone had been in raptures over her. I had a bit of an outburst at the sight of them, although at the time I'm not sure what I thought was going on; I guess I was just upset that they could sit around watching TV together while I had to eat salad with dressing on the side. I called Benji a dickhead, started crying, and then locked myself in the bathroom. It was the second time that week I'd sat fully clothed on the toilet to cry. Only this time I locked the door, which I expected to be a clear sign that I was on the ledge. Benji knocked lightly and tried to comfort me.

"She left," he said softly.

"I'm going to bite her if she comes back," I said before emerging.

"Okay, vampire," Benji said, smiling. We hugged, and I decided not to feel like he was making up for something. I thought maybe I was crying because I'd just eaten a Big Mac in a putrid walkway between two buildings, terrified that Claudia might find me and make me spit it out. I had a few reasons to cry that day, only one of which was finding Louisa Radcliffe in my apartment.

18

2019

Jasper drove back that night. He had called me again from his work function and said he was checking out of the hotel. "I don't want to leave you there alone. With the girls."

Jasper had taken a job that required travel because I hardly ever left the house. He had no reservations about whether or not I would be there when he returned, and the girls were too little to go anywhere without me. He had pride of ownership over someone who just wanted to be owned. I failed to see how that could satisfy anything, but it did.

"We're fine. We're not even supposed to go outside, and the driveway's all blocked."

"But the police are back there, right?"

"Yeah, Cady is...and some other people I don't know..." I'd never really told Jasper the part about Cady. He knew about the accident and that I'd known Benji, but that was about it. It was a local tragedy. Everyone knew about the accident.

"Okay, well, I'd feel better if I was home."

"I'm sure." We talked some more, although I wasn't really paying attention. The girls had had their bath—we could still fit them all in the claw-foot tub in the hall bath. Tessa thought it was embarrassing and nasty for them all to be together in there, but it was so precious an experience for me that I ignored her protests and said something about saving money or water or the planet. They got so dirty during the day that there was a ring around the tub each night when they got out. I took to it with the sponge and the Comet. My mother had done the same in that tub a thousand times, even though my sisters and I had rarely used it. We preferred the shower in the primary bathroom. My mother hadn't been sentimental; we bathed the dog in the claw-foot and then later my dad when he'd had shoulder surgery and couldn't take a shower.

I combed each of their hair in turn, using coconut oil to make it shiny. I left their hair long; I couldn't even remember if I'd ever had Rose's cut. Their narrow, bony shoulders looked similar from behind—a token of their innocence, this lack of broadness, lack of heavy experience, lack of weight. Their backs looked like models' backs, so thin and angular, lithe and unencumbered by flesh. My mother told me never to let any of the girls model. The thought hadn't even crossed my mind, although all I could think about on some days was the way life had once been and all the attention I'd gotten because my shoulder blades looked like those of a nine-year-old.

"Daddy's on his way," I said. I was letting them stay up. Cady and her team—whoever they were—from the state had set lights up down the hill. We couldn't see their glare from the house, but there was a distant, unsettling urgency about their presence that was going to make it hard for me to sleep. A discomfort I assumed for the girls. We put on *The Mighty Ducks*, which they deemed old-fashioned, and sat on the couch together.

Everyone fell asleep but me and Pamela. "Who do you think it is?" she asked me during the final game scene. She was as disinterested as I was distracted.

"Look," I said. "She does a spin there."

"Who's in the woods?"

"I don't know, Pamela." I reached out and jostled her small thigh. "It seems like she's been there a long time, whoever she is."

"Do you think you knew her?"

"Oh, no. No, no, no, pumpkin. I didn't know her." I turned away and pulled my hand off her thigh. I wasn't worthy to touch her.

19

In spite of her stifling, near-constant presence in my building, I barely talked to Louisa, preferring to give her monosyllabic greetings if we passed on the stairs or in the hall. It didn't appear to me that Benji was really seeing that much of her either. She was too busy being fabulous and sought after, just as Claudia had predicted. We were down to a week left before the end of the month. I hadn't asked Benji a single question about how he was getting home or if he was still going.

The guy who owned the apartment where Louisa was staying called me every other day to tell me something about the place or some utility that was still in his name or some stupid thing about the recycling. I didn't think any of it was my responsibility, and during the sixth call, I walked down the stairs to her apartment— still on the phone with him—and knocked on Louisa's door. She opened the door, bug-eyed and wearing pajamas.

"Here, you can talk to her yourself. I'm not her mother," I said into the phone before shoving it in Louisa's face.

"Can you please give him your mom's number? I don't want to be in charge of your lease anymore." I stood in front of her with my arms crossed over my chest while she nodded and said "okay, okay" over and over again into the phone.

I was watching the calendar like a hawk—there were four more days until Benji was to leave. Halloween was going to be his departure date if he stuck to his guns about going at the end of the month. Work was slow, and with Benji gone all day at his mechanic's gig in Queens—where I'd never visited him, not once—I found myself with a lot of agitated time on my hands. I was calling Claudia too much and taking my own measurements with the seamstress tape, pulling just a little too tight to get my waist where I knew it was supposed to be. During one of my unnecessary "check in" calls to the agency, Claudia told me she'd heard that Louisa had some boyfriend from Georgia.

"What?" I said.

"You didn't hear me?"

"I heard you, Claudia—but what do you mean?"

"I assumed you knew him. You're all from Georgia. All y'all." She laughed in her husky put-on French accent, which sounded more and more fake the more time I spent with people who were actually from France.

"I don't know her boyfriend or anything else. My boyfriend is from home," I told her, like she didn't know.

"Yes, dear," Claudia snipped. "Go see Rory at Li West tomorrow. Let's get this job, please."

"I'm not, like, desperate or something," I said defensively.

"No one said you were desperate. Maybe I am."

I did not book Li West; Louisa did. I had to hear about it from Claudia and then, strangely, from Benji, who said Louisa had told him.

"Why is she telling you about her jobs?" I asked when I got home that day to his greeting that he was sorry Louisa took my big job.

"She said she saw you at the…place, whatever it's called."

"So she was bragging at my expense. Stop talking to her…"

Benji drew his eyebrows together. "No."

"Okay. Don't." I put my hair in a messy ponytail and stuffed my feet in my running shoes. "I'm going running." Benji didn't say anything more and I left, seething.

I ran oddly fast for about two minutes, then stopped, exhausted, and pretended to stretch. I had to pee and hadn't brought headphones or my phone. I wasn't sure what to do with myself and started running again, although this time not as fast. I might have been trying to smack something out of the bottom half of my body. I returned to the apartment an hour and a half later; during most of that time, I'd wandered aimlessly at either a slow trot or directionless stroll, getting close to but never actually reaching Central Park before sneaking into a bathroom at a sushi restaurant while the host wasn't looking.

When I came inside, I saw that Benji had collected a lot of his things. There were two duffel bags sitting by the front door. I could hear but not see him, so I stomped into the bedroom, where he was folding a white T-shirt.

"What are you doing?"

"I'm going home," he said without looking at me. "My flight leaves in a few hours."

"You have a ticket?" I was sweating and trying to catch my breath. All the people I'd passed on my way back to the apartment had looked either terribly lonely or terribly determined. The longer I was in New York, the more I didn't think there was much difference between the two. I felt both in that moment.

"I booked it last week."

I stomped my foot. "With what money?"

Benji tilted his head to the side and squinted angrily. "That's another thing. I don't need your money. You don't even have that much money, if you ask me, and I don't need it either way."

"You could have told me you booked your flight." I was seething and on the verge of cracking my teeth, such was the grinding.

"I tried! You don't listen to me. You're pissed off all the time and don't hear a word I say."

"Then why don't you pay the rent, if you're so rich and can go get plane tickets behind my back?" I was shaking and could feel my face getting wet, though the sensation of crying was distant and somehow foreign. I couldn't stop my lip from trembling either.

I knew I was a wreck, but it was as though it was happening to someone else—this upheaval.

Benji rolled his eyes. "I'll leave you some cash. Okay, I'm outta here, Dani." He sneered that last bit out.

"Why are you doing this to me?" I wiped my face.

"Doing what to you? Can I ask the same question? Why are you doing this to me? My life can't be chasing you around and...I don't know. I'm really homesick, and I need to go home and hug my mama."

"Okay." I shrugged impatiently. "What if I come too?"

He closed his eyes in annoyed consideration. "Yeah, that would be awesome."

I knew he didn't mean it. "Fine. I won't come at all." I sniffled, then looked in the mirror hanging over my dresser and saw what Claudia was talking about when she said my face looked like a crying dinner plate.

20

With Benji gone, I found myself chumming up, rather quickly and too intimately, with a girl from California who'd just returned from Australia, where she "didn't work once...at all. Such a waste of money." Her name was Dana. I really don't know if I liked her, but we decided (without any evidence to support our theory) that we were as thick as thieves and therefore did almost everything together. We were getting older, which is a strange determination to make at the age of eighteen, but there were so many younger girls everywhere we went—castings, dinners, the agency, all the parties and events. "Everyone is sixteen again," Dana said. "I'm thinking of moving to LA."

I thought I might cry and told her it would break my heart. "Yeah, well, we're not married," she answered.

Dana was taller than me and a little thick for fashion. I knew she was rejected for a lot of jobs because she was heavier set, with broad shoulders and more athletic legs. I was a terrible influence on her; I relentlessly suggested late-night snacking and round-the-clock iced-coffee beverages. "Can't get these where I'm from," I told her.

"God, it's that country?" She had a snobbish way about her that I couldn't reconcile with her Sacramento upbringing, mostly because I'd never even heard of Sacramento.

I decided after weeks of excessively close bonding with Dana, wherein I learned that she'd suffered from constipation and had a threesome with her sister's boyfriend and her sister's best friend while in high school—"Don't ever tell Jackie!" she said, swearing me to secrecy, and I assured her that her words were safe in my vault-like head—that I would confess that my boyfriend from Georgia had been living with me in New York and that he'd left. Up to this point, I'd told myself and anyone who would listen that the reason Benji had gone home was because of his mother. I said she was sick and that he was coming back.

"I'm heartbroken," I said, fully embracing Dana's dramatic and immature outlook. I think I even said, "Oh my God, I'm so heart-broken. He totally left me. It's over!"

Instead of comforting me or encouraging me to do everything in my power to win my young boyfriend back, she said, "Get a grip."

Undeterred by this response, I told her I was in love.

"With some hillbilly guy from Georgia? Listen, Dani, you're not going to be Dani forever, making all this money and living in Chelsea with furs and Whole Foods and a twelve-dollar-a-day coffee habit."

"I live in Tribeca," I told her. "And I don't wear fur."

"Right, so you really won't be living there forever."

"What? No. I want to move back home."

"Oh my God, no you don't. What about your iced coffee? Anyway, I don't know what's going on, but it's totally unacceptable, and I really think you need to cut it out. The kid's in high school, and you live in New York. It's just weird." I decided I didn't like Dana and felt a compulsive urge to remind her that I knew about Jackie's boyfriend and the girl, Kylie, out in the boat on spring break. Dana wrote me an email a few weeks after I'd confessed my heartache and said she could tell I was mad, but couldn't we hang out again? I didn't respond. I was too embarrassed to be around her after the way she'd reacted.

Benji hadn't called me once since he got on the plane. He always answered when I called him, but he didn't return the favor. I assumed him leaving was permanent while pretending it was temporary. He hadn't told me he was coming back, and he'd never told me he was going to stay. He was an empty box that had never really been full of promises anyway, but I had yet to be honest with myself about it.

New York was cold, blowing, and crisp. I wore scarves every day and had to keep a tissue handy because of the way my nose reacted to the heat in the buildings and then the suddenly whipping frozen air outside. I trekked from Grand Central all the way down and over to Madison Square Park one afternoon when the sun was out. People were glowing with optimism that winter was not going to be so bad that year. I sometimes called Benji while walking around the city. He said it was too loud to talk, and he didn't sound all that interested in me calling him back from somewhere quieter. When we hung up, I found that I was crying and staring at the Flatiron Building. Someone thought I was an architecture student and moved to tears. "I know. It's amazing, isn't it?"

All I said was "What?" and ran away, humiliated.

Todd was a little more understanding and, in a way, uplifting when I finally told him about Benji. We'd had margaritas, which Claudia told me never to drink because they were "belly-fat factories." Claudia said that about everything fun, and here she was, the one who was so sick.

"He sounds divine," Todd said, "but he also sounds gone… I'm sorry." I'd shown him a picture of Benji sitting by Fisher Lake, and when I looked at it after allowing Todd a glimpse, my stomach twisted, and I went hard of hearing for a few seconds. "He certainly doesn't look sixteen. God, I'm living in the wrong place if that's what the boys look like in Georgia."

"Well, not all of them," I corrected. "Let's not get carried away."

"I definitely think you've changed since you came back and

found love," Todd told me. "Love and heartache—because let's be honest, you can't have one without the other. You're so much wiser or...I don't really know, quieter. I mean, I'm not sure it's because you got dumped, but you're really deep now. I like it on you. Loss is a look for you. It really is."

"Thanks, Todd," I said. I hadn't even finished high school and had no skills to speak of. I felt about as useful as a blank pair of dice, but I was used to taking compliments from strange men and pumping myself up with them, even if they were mostly backhanded.

I called Claudia one especially bleak afternoon, having avoided the agency a little since Benji left. Claudia actually looked sick now and was using a cane. It wasn't that I hadn't taken her illness seriously before; it was that she very clearly didn't want to talk about it. I didn't even really know what kind of cancer she had—the type and severity were never discussed. The rumors were that she'd had three rounds of chemotherapy so far and was going to have to have another. Claudia tersely answered questions about her health and usually very quickly changed the subject when anyone mentioned the cane. She was still wearing wigs, and that was singularly acceptable conversation because she could make jokes about wigs. It was harder to laugh at a cane. Normally, I just made sad, very concerned faces when people told me she was out again for treatment and then went on asking about my castings or if I could get a free haircut at Belle Vie in the Village.

"I'm thinking about going back to Atlanta for the winter," I said.

"It's November," she replied flatly. I'd called her cell phone and could tell she wasn't in the office. It was too quiet in the background.

"Right, but it's getting really cold."

Claudia went on to tell me that Atlanta had some work. "But why are you even asking that? You're not moving to Atlanta. You'll make no money there. Modeling is a hobby in places like that. You're working here. You're making money, I'm making money—no one is going anywhere."

"No, no, I'm not moving," I said. "Just don't want to spend winter here."

"So I'll send you to Miami, but not Atlanta. God help us, you'll have to get a job at the 7-Eleven." There was something with Claudia and 7-Elevens. She talked about them all the time. One of the receptionists told me Claudia had worked at a 7-Eleven in Ohio before she became a famous model booker and started pretending she was from France.

"It's cheaper there," I argued.

"You can't give up your place here, Dani. You can't. It's a death sentence." We both went quiet. Everyone tried to avoid talking about death around Claudia too. I couldn't think of anything to say. "Just… ride it out," she said after a long pause. "Sometimes you have to ride it out." She must have known why Benji left, that it had nothing to do with a sick mother and that we both knew he wasn't coming back.

Cady Benson showed up at my building the following day. I'd taken the stairs down three at a time, practically jumping. Even though Claudia wasn't amenable to me leaving—a boon to my confidence—I was also riding high on this idea of going home and reuniting with Benji in Pressville for good. I decided to enjoy what little time I thought I had in New York and then be done with it.

I stumbled out onto the blustery New York street with an unlit cigarette already in my mouth and my lighter in my hand. I had my headphones on and was determined and eager. I always appreciated the curious stares I got while jetting to a fitting or job. People knew who we were, the models. There was no mistaking it, especially in certain parts of town. I was going to miss that sort of thing for sure; that was what kept girls there for so much longer than they should have stayed.

"Dani?" a small, tight young woman with long, light-brown hair said to me as soon as my feet hit the sidewalk.

I stopped, pulled the cigarette out of my mouth, and said, "Yeah?"

"Cady Benson." She extended her hand. She couldn't have been an inch over five four and had a round, bright face with wide-set eyes and a pinkness to her light complexion that made her seem very young and timid.

"Oh," I said, thinking I must have scheduled something that I didn't remember. "Hi."

"Your mom asked me to track you down!" She laughed for no reason and spoke too loudly. "She gave me your address. I was going to buzz you, but you beat me to the punch!" Her accent was distinct, pronounced, embarrassing. I thought I noticed people turning toward us—her—in cynical curiosity.

"Right."

"You goin' somewhere? I can walk with ya. I just didn't want to ignore your mama's request. She's been wantin' us to meet for a long time now."

"Yeah, sorry about that," I said nervously. "I was in London, and then I went back home." It was ridiculous to mention London. That had been months ago.

"So I heard."

"I have to walk to Chelsea," I said.

"Okay, then. Have you been to the pier there? I also heard there's like a mall or something that's got a lot of cool stores."

"It's not a mall," I said, turning toward her with my face in a knot. "It's—"

"Or whatever," she said. She put her hands in her pockets. We were walking, but very slowly and like we didn't know where we were going. I'd shoved my cigarette in the pocket of my jacket—a long, oversize pea coat in a dark-colored plaid pattern. I'd found it in SoHo at a street market. It had smelled like cumin when I bought it, but Todd told me he had a fix for that. He used lavender oil and a hanger, and we went to the roof of his building on a mild day. It worked and didn't smell a bit like the marijuana Todd and I had been smoking up there while the jacket aired.

"I thought you worked for the police or something," I said, nodding at her clothes while trying not to pay too much attention to her.

"Yeah, I work for the NYPD, but I'm off today. No uniform." She pointed at her pink oxford shirt tucked into gray slacks, which were tight at the waist, causing the shirt to make a kangaroo pouch under her bra line. I was going to say she looked like she was wearing office clothes, but I didn't want to be mean. Actually, I did, but my attitude came from some undesirable, small place inside me that only did the talking when I felt threatened. My dad always said of the wildlife around Pressville that if we didn't confront it or make it nervous, it wouldn't bother us. I was being confronted and made nervous. I bit my tongue, though, and said nothing about her clothes.

"That sounds cool," I said instead.

"Yeah, they're moving me to Homicide, so this will be my uniform." She shrugged and looked down at her clothes, pleased and justified.

"Yeah, okay," I said, thinking she must have read my mind.

"Street clothes, but proper, you know? Like business."

"Right." We walked with slightly more urgency. "I have a job today," I said. "That's where I'm headed."

"Yeah, what's it for?" She was smiling cheerily and having to take rather large leaps to keep up with me. I felt infinitely superior to her, as I usually did around regular people. Such is the world of fashion and beauty. Feelings of superiority are like makeup: They can be put on for any occasion. When necessary. When required.

"Print work. For a magazine. It's eight pages." That was a lie. I was to be in the background of a three-page layout for some magazine I'd never heard of. The cigarette had broken in my pocket. Its innards were all over my hand. I was annoyed that I felt I couldn't smoke in front of her.

"Cool. So anyway, I don't want to bother you when you're working. I just hate to let your mom down."

"Why?" I asked insolently. "She's not very nice to your family." I paused. "Sorry. I guess I just don't get it or something."

Cady's face was briefly drawn and thoughtful. "She is nice to us. She came and cleaned for us when my daddy was sick. Made us dinner a few times. She was wonderful. She's worried about you, is all. That's how mamas are."

"She went to clean?" I said. "Doesn't sound like her." We waited for the light to change so we could cross Seventh Avenue. Cady watched me closely but didn't flinch.

"Yeah, she's been cleaning and went and picked up some groceries. Nice woman." There was an edge now. "I was just supposed to lay my eyes on you. I'd still like to get together if you want. Or see some sights—or anything, really." I decided to screw it and lit a cigarette while she was talking. I couldn't look her in the eye, feeling she was less friendly than I remembered from our first conversation. I had been excited about this job; I knew and liked one of the other girls. The mood had been ruined.

"Yeah, we can go to the park or something," I said.

"I run there every day," Cady said. "Oh." She looked at my cigarette. "Maybe you don't…"

"I run," I said, blowing a stream of smoke in her direction.

"I go at six. We could meet by the—"

"But I'm not supposed to run," I lied. "Makes my legs too big."

"Okay, then. So much pressure," Cady said, not really pointing at anything.

"I'm naturally thin," I explained. "So it's okay for me. But yeah, some girls—"

"Oh, no, I was talking about the steam," she said, turning to face a vent. "All these buildings on this land. Pressing down." She laughed a little. "They should call it Pressville!"

I tried not to roll my eyes. "Why are you here, in New York?" I asked, trying unsuccessfully to sound friendly, to restart the conversation in a more agreeable way. We'd stopped walking for no reason that either of us could appear to define. She was as confused and uncomfortable as I was.

"I always wanted to do it. It's been my dream to be NYPD my whole life."

"Right."

"There's not so much crime in Pressville. I went to school for it, so I thought I'd come up here and give it a go."

"But...do you even like it?" I put my cigarette out on the ground and stepped on it with my cinnamon-colored moccasin.

"I love it, but I see it for what it is." She looked at me closely. Even though she was a good head shorter, I didn't feel like she looked up at me. I was on her level whether I wanted to be or not. "But now I got an eye on you, so I can report back to Deb that you're alive and kickin'," she said with a light smile.

"We'll hang out," I said like I was doing her a favor. "I promise."

"Keep your head on your shoulders, Danielle. Don't miss home so much you do somethin' silly."

"I don't miss home," I said defensively. "Not at all."

"Okay." We looked at one another for a second too long, and I knew that I had been unceremoniously judged.

Cady thought she had me pegged, but she didn't understand me one bit. I was a mystery to her. She could run in the park every morning, but she'd never be as strong as me. I had endurance to spare, and everyone was going to figure that out. We said goodbye. I called her a cunt under my breath after I turned to go. I had no idea why I was so angry.

Late autumn remained brisk and moody for me, like an undetected edge I kept tripping over. I couldn't get to the right temperature—either too hot because of all my layers or freezing because of the wind sliding down the faces of the tall, austere buildings. As soon as I'd get out on one of the avenues, all the swirls of air that had been trying to find some place to go would swoop into the gap of metal and glass and sideswipe my face, stealing my comfort, my composure, my fortitude.

I was still walking aimlessly for hours a day—Claudia was pleased because I was "thin and firm." I worked quite a bit, turning down jobs overseas; however, those trips never worked out for me. I'd get skipped over at appointments or sent to second- or third-tier jobs that didn't pay very well. It all seemed like such a hassle to make just a little bit of money.

I called Benji during one of my post-wandering, lonely evenings where I pretended he was at home longing for me and wishing he could come back much in the same way I was longing for him. I was lying on the bed in my apartment, feeling especially sorry for myself, which I'd strangely come to enjoy. The way he answered the phone was a little odd, like he'd been expecting me to call but was then disappointed to hear my voice.

"Oh, hey," he said. I had the feeling he wasn't alone.

"Whaddya doin'?"

"Oh, I don't know. Thinkin' 'bout you," he said.

"It's Danielle," I had the urge to confirm.

He laughed. "I know!"

"I can't believe you left me up here." We hadn't really talked about him leaving since he left, just little passing conversations with snide, sideways remarks about being ditched or men who run out on their ladies, but the gravity of my fit had not been given its due. He chuckled but didn't say anything. "I'm gonna come for Christmas," I told him. That was over a month away, but I felt like mentioning it, to see if I could get a rise, to see if maybe he'd say he was going to come to New York before then.

"Well, that's good. So listen…"

I let my breath catch. "Yeah?"

"Blake and I got picked up the other day, so like…kind of a bad scene, if you know what I mean."

That hadn't been what I'd expected. "What do you mean, you 'got picked up'?"

"We were just messin' with some stuff, and some kids like, I don't know… It don't even matter, but I gotta go to court and be on good behavior and all that. I'mma go to Weatherby for a while so my parents don't stress out."

"I don't understand what you're saying."

"Whatever, Danielle—I'm just tellin' you we got arrested, so I'm just gonna be layin' low and bein' good, is all."

"How did you get arrested?" I was sitting up in my bed now. I'd almost bought a couch the week before; Todd's friend was getting rid of a sleeper that I thought would look great in my place, but I had this urge to keep my load light. I kept thinking I would be leaving New York soon—because I was wanted at home, because I had a reason to go back to Georgia.

"We were sellin' some shit at the store. Dan said it was okay, but I guess it got around. But whatever. It's fine. I'm just tellin' you so you don't hear it first from someone else."

That had been why Cady showed up at my place. I was sure of it now. My mother wanted to see if Benji was there, or maybe to make sure I wasn't home with him. She'd heard about him getting arrested. If there was one thing Deb Greer despised, it was drugs, and then second on her list of most hateable things was people who got arrested for drugs. She and my dad didn't even drink—no light beer, no wine coolers, nothing. She thought pot was a one-way ticket to a homeless shelter, and she wouldn't stand for making light of it. "Gateway to hell!" she'd say. The harder stuff was the work of the devil, and every Greer knew it. I'd done some experimenting, but I was careful. My mother wouldn't help if we got hooked on drugs. Anything else, but not that.

"So you spent the night in jail?" I asked. "Was it drugs?" I'd just assumed, but in case I had to argue with my mom about it, I wanted to be sure.

"Juvie," he said. "And it was longer than a night." He was laughing slightly. "And yeah, we had some pills and shit… Whatever, it doesn't matter…"

"I definitely think it matters, Benji. What about Blake?"

"Well, see, that's the thing. He's eighteen, so he's still inside 'cause he's not a kid by the law."

"'Inside'? What are you? Mafia or something? Benji, this is serious."

"I know, Danielle! That's why I'm tellin' you. I gotta go to Weatherby now 'cause part of my plan or whatever is that I go to school."

Weatherby was the alternative high school in Houton for kids who either got kicked out of Pressville High or who needed to go to school on nights and weekends for whatever reason. My mother had always referred to it as "the scum school." She really could be unrelenting.

"Sounds serious," I said without smiling. "I guess it's good I'm not coming home for Thanksgiving, then."

"Why?"

"If you're in trouble, then we probably can't hang out or whatever."

"Right."

"So do you want me to come home or what?" I was fishing.

I could hear how I sounded, this pleading desperation slamming into the walls of my studio apartment like glass. The needs I felt at this time in my life were clots in my veins that kept me from moving anything properly through my body. It was like once something got stuck up near my head, there was nothing I could do to get it to pass through. People should be allowed to grow up before they have strong feelings about someone. If I could rework our nature, that would be the first thing I would fix. No more kids being pulled by chains made of their stupidity and want. That was all I had—this want. To work, to be liked, to be enough. Poor Benji didn't realize he'd put a choke collar on just by showing up that first afternoon.

He was quiet. I could hear noise from the house beyond him. There was water running and muffled voices I assumed belonged to his parents.

"Well, if you don't want to see me…" I said to his silence.

"I do wanna see you, Danielle, but I don't want you to go crazy out of your way or spend all your money coming down here. And like I said, I gotta get myself together. Like I gotta meet with people checkin' on my progress."

"Has this happened before?" I asked. Of course I'd heard all the stories about Blake, but I did wonder if Benji had ever gotten in real trouble like this. "Do you do drugs?" I added when he didn't immediately answer me.

"Not really," he said.

"Not really?" I sounded angry, though I wasn't. I guess I just thought I knew everything about him. Chantel had told me the last time she called that Benji had gotten arrested when he was in middle school for stealing a motorcycle. I'd told her that was ridiculous because kids that young don't get arrested. She said I was an idiot. "Did you get arrested before?"

"Oh, like you're one to talk with all those freaks in New York and the people at your modeling jobs. Holy shit, those people are a mess. And I can guaran-fucking-tee you that those people do drugs and have been arrested before."

"But seriously, though, are you into drugs?"

"No! Danielle." He stopped talking, palpably frustrated. "No, I'm not into drugs. I'm into money." He chuckled again.

"This is so not funny."

"What's funny is you yellin' at me."

"I'm not yelling… Sorry, it just scares me that you could go to jail or something."

"Naw, I'm good. I'm gonna be a good boy from now on."

"Okay, well, I'm coming home for Christmas. And you don't need to worry about money, Benji. I make lots of money, and I can pay for stuff. I don't want you thinking—"

"Oh, come on, man. I'm not worrying about money. I said I like money—and anyway, you don't… Never mind. I'll see you when you get here for Christmas, okay?" I could hear call waiting clicking on the line. He hung up without another word.

I sat on my bed with my phone in my hand, wondering what I was doing. It had been such a strange conversation. I thought maybe I didn't even like him, but I couldn't stop trying to win him over. I was like one of the rich men we hung out with, with their desperate need for affirmation. I never got the impression they really liked me; they just wanted to be seen with me and the other girls. They paid for things and had us swarming around them for free drinks, food, access—whatever it was we seemed to think they could offer that we couldn't do for ourselves. They wanted to be seen a certain way, and we wanted things for pretending to find them fascinating. I'd given my affirmation freely. Benji was more reluctant to do the same for me—the juvie-hall druggy kid with the junked-up crotch rocket had more character than I did.

22

I was hanging out with Dana again. I'd developed a blister the size of a quarter on the back of my heel, so I couldn't walk aimlessly anymore and was tired of lying on the bed in my apartment. She was the only one who wanted to get coffee and complain with me for hours on end. Even Todd had said I was being a bit of a downer—one he needed to avoid because he had an audition for the part of a happy crab in a children's production off Broadway.

"I just can't have bad vibes," he explained over the phone. "After this, I'm trying to get into this Tennessee Williams thing, so we can definitely roll when I'm prepping for that. It's super depressing."

Dana still couldn't believe, with all the excessively rich people we knew, that I was all torn up over a boy without a shirt who lived in a condemned (her word, not mine) house with his drunkard parents in some Podunk town in Georgia.

"Did I tell you about his house and his parents?" I asked, having no memory of sharing any of that with her. "And anyway, I don't think I like rich people."

She rolled her eyes and said, "Oh, please."

But I wondered if I did like rich people after all. I certainly was impressed by them. Money seemed to be the thing I valued most; my whole family was that way. All my parents had ever talked about was money. We didn't have it, and boy, did we know that from the get-go. Talking poor was my parents' defense against expectations. We shouldn't get our hopes up because here we were, living hand to mouth after all this time. My father played along, forgoing household improvements he could have done on the cheap because money was tight. It was too tight for a lot of things, and we heard all about it. I wondered later if maybe my obsession with modeling had been more an obsession with not having to think of myself as poor the way my parents did. They didn't get to brag; they complained. It didn't dawn on me that there might have been other things to brag about than being thin and pretty.

Occasionally, girls would tell me that they were enrolling in school—Hunter College or moving to LA to go to Cal State this or that. I always nodded and said, "That sounds awesome," but really I had no idea what to think. I was supposed to use tutors so I could pass my high-school graduation exams, but that never happened. Now it seemed awkward to ask about it, so I didn't.

"I guess I'll just be stupid," I'd told Benji one night when we were in Pressville, before he'd come to New York and left me there. We were both having a laugh about not finishing school, so I thought we were on the same page. "That, or go to college when I'm thirty."

"I'm not stupid, and I'm not goin' to college," he'd said back. "I wanna work on cars, and I don't need a degree for that. School's boring as hell. I don't care."

I imagined myself as a local auto mechanic's wife in Pressville and was strangely comforted. I could go barefoot and listen to Pearl Jam in the kitchen of our ramshackle house, set on cinder blocks with a small vegetable garden out to the side. I'd ride a motorcycle because now I knew how after practicing on an eight-lane highway when Benji and I went to Atlanta. The vision of me without hope or purpose but living with Benji in my hometown gave me a feeling of happy boredom that I wanted to hold on to, dearly.

"I guess I always thought I was supposed to go to college," I'd said.

"You don't do anything you're supposed to do," he had answered, and again, I assumed it was because he knew better, somehow both my minion and my mentor.

Claudia, because she was strangely intuitive on the one hand—deeply entangled in our lives like a mother we weren't afraid to talk to about all the things we were doing wrong and the bad decisions we were making—and also because I wasn't able to hide my dismay, was kinder to me than she had been in a long time.

"How is my sweet little Danielle with the boy from the sticks?"

"He went back home."

I went in to Lawton to pick up a check. I'd been quiet lately, failing to tell anyone but Dana and Todd what had happened. Louisa clearly knew that Benji was gone, but we didn't talk about it, and she did her best not to speak to me if we ran into one another.

"Oh my," Claudia said when I told her. "Well—and there he'll stay. Anyway, he can't be out of school yet. Let him finish school so he can make lots of money and take care of you." She set about adjusting her wig. "Thing is so ridiculous," she said, pointing to her head. "I'm going without it starting next week. I'll wear scarves or something. Everyone can tell it's a wig, anyway. What do I care?"

"Do you feel okay?" I asked. She looked at me with vaguely wet eyes. It might have been the first time I asked about her illness in all this time she'd been sick. I didn't know how to care about her like that. The relationship was not sewn that way.

"I feel the same as I've always felt," she said.

"I'm sorry."

"I am too." I wasn't sure if she meant about herself or about me. "But we press on, don't we? We're not in charge."

"No," I agreed.

"But you are young, Dani. Young people never realize how big the 'in front' is. It's like the ocean. At my age, what's in front is more like a puddle or something. Not much can happen in a puddle. You have the sea, my little fish. There's so much time for things to happen, so much space for them to happen in. It's all possibilities." She pulled at her wig again. "All possibilities."

She was being kind, but I was so rattled with insecurity that all I could think was that she was telling me I should try to find another job because clearly the modeling wasn't working out. The check I'd gone in to get was for a hundred and forty dollars. It had been a long time since anyone had told me I was going to make thousands of dollars a day. I smiled at her weakly and said something about Benji being a mechanic and me wanting to make my own money. My only defense was to take everything literally, to home in on the one thing people said that might offend me.

"You can make your own money," she said, agreeing dismissively. She was done talking about Benji. Everyone was.

Later that night I called my mom to tell her I was thinking of moving home. She inhaled and exhaled loudly during the entire conversation, exhibiting patience but wanting me to be sure that she felt strained in doing so.

"Is this because that kid is in jail?" she finally asked while I was talking about my dreams of opening my own ballet studio in Pressville. She had tried not to laugh when I first said it. I claimed that all the runway modeling I'd done had rekindled my love of ballet and that I thought I'd be a good dance teacher now.

"Oh, he's not in jail," I said to her comment about Benji. "So, because of all the high heels, I think I could do the pointe shoes and show the girls—"

"He was very much in jail, Danielle," she interrupted me. "He is not a reason to come home. I don't even really understand all of this, and I'm not going to pretend to. I don't want to understand it, but he and his brother went to jail. It's not the first time for either of them, and I... Let's just leave it at that. He is not a reason to do anything. Maybe to stay away from here, but not to come back."

"My dance studio could—"

"Okay," she interrupted me again, sighing. "Okay, fine."

"I'd rather just have a normal job and not have everybody all worked up every time I eat a piece of lasagna." I'd planned that part in advance; lasagna was my mother's favorite. If it was on a menu when she dined out, which was rare, she ordered it. We'd eaten almost exclusively Italian food while she was with me in New York. She refused to try anything else. "No need," she'd told me. "Don't mess with perfection." She had lasagna six times while in the city.

"I can't say I have ever understood that part, but that's fine with me if you want to come back, as long as it's for a good reason. Are you going to stay with us?" Now she sounded scared. This was not at all the response I'd expected. She hated that I lived in New York and was loath to tell people that I was a model, thinking it only a gateway to porn. A girl can't make money off her looks without the threat of porn.

"Do you not want me to move home?" I asked. "And yes, I guess I thought I'd stay with you. Can I not stay with you?"

"I just can't see it, Danielle. I just can't see it. You've been all over the place, living on your own, and now that I've been to New York, I know the difference. There's nothing in Pressville—just some place to live. I like livin' here, but that's mainly 'cause I haven't ever lived anywhere else. I don't care about all that, but I'd say it's going to be hard for you to forget everything you had in New York to tool around here day after day."

"I'll get a job, and then I can open my—"

"Sweetheart, nothing here is going to pay like the modeling stuff, and you can't just open a ballet school! You're gonna be makin' eight bucks an hour, answering somebody's phone or tagging dry cleaning. And that's a fact."

"Maybe Dad can get me a job at UPS," I suggested.

"Oh, Danielle, come on now. You're clearly in some sort of conflict, and I don't pretend to know what it is, but you're not going to work at UPS. Last time you were here, you said picking up the gallon milk jug hurt your wrist. Give me a break."

"It did hurt my wrist," I said. "It really hurt."

"Let that be a lesson in hurling heavy boxes for a living."

"Well, I think I'm depressed, so I need to come back."

"Why don't you move to Atlanta? At least there you won't be bored. I don't know what you'll do for work. You kinda pigeon-holed yourself into this life by refusing to finish school, but it is what it is. I didn't think this was a real future—not the kind that makes a life—but you wanted to do it, and now you've done it. I don't even know if they have models in Atlanta. Maybe they do stuff for the Varsity. I can't say I know a thing about it."

I rolled my eyes, because the Varsity was the only thing my mother knew about Atlanta. There was a fast-food place in town called the Varsity that sold greasy food and frosted-orange milkshakes, and if you mentioned Atlanta, then my mother mentioned the Varsity. I think she'd been there once. It must have been a very powerful experience.

"I think I might be cursed," I said in my pleading, distant way. I don't know what I wanted her to say, but I wanted her to say something to make me feel better. "I think that's the problem—a curse."

This got her attention more than anything else I'd said. My mother took curses seriously. "It's not a New York curse, then," she said. "They don't have stuff like that up there. It followed you from here. We get curses in the mountains."

"Why is that?" I asked.

"Bad dirt."

23

2019

I fell asleep on the couch. The girls were in their beds, which I assumed had been Jasper's doing. He did not bother to wake me when he got home. I could see his shoes and briefcase by the front door, neatly placed, marking his territory.

I'd started preferring it when he was gone a couple of years before. Earlier in the marriage, especially when the girls were very small, I'd cried every time he went on the road, but it became almost a treat after a time. Being that I had grown up in the house, I felt different when he wasn't there, more like a child myself. It was the teen years, before I left for New York, that I reimagined. I started buying clothes like those that I'd worn then. My shorts got shorter, the T-shirts either tighter or more likely to slip off my shoulders. I let my hair grow long again after wearing it at my chin for all four of my pregnancies. When I looked at the photos of us later, especially when the girls were so small, I look like I'm pretending to be something I saw in a magazine. We're all wearing pale-blue seersucker in one of the family portraits. I must have been about to completely dissolve when I arranged that. The wedding photos are less egregious. I look happy—I was. I was overcome with relief that someone like Jasper would make such a commitment to me. I'd found him and kept him. I considered it an achievement, as I'd not been able to keep anything else I found.

"Jas," I said, wandering timidly into our bedroom—my parents' bedroom. He stirred on the bed. "Jas?" I said again.

"What?"

"When did you get home?"

"I don't know. What time is it?" He sounded irritated.

I glanced at the clock. "Four."

"Around one. It was around one. The girls were on the couch. Can I go back to sleep now?"

"Sorry. Is Cady gone?"

"Is that the police lady?"

"Yeah."

"I have no idea. They were still out there when I got home."

"You didn't go down, did you? We're not supposed to go down there." I stood over the bed with my bare feet and thin, cotton shorts. I'd cranked the air-conditioning before we started the movie. The house felt like a meat locker.

"No. I'm going back to sleep." He rolled onto his stomach

with his head almost entirely under the covers. I took another step forward but didn't say anything else. I was hovering but paralyzed. There would be so much to tell Jasper when the time came.

I heard the girls in the kitchen around seven thirty in the morning. I had fallen asleep, a dank, muggy slumber during which my dreams tried to strangle me. Small snippets of the past—of things I'd failed to tell anyone, admit to myself, confess—were like strands of hair I couldn't get out of my eyes and then my mouth. They eventually got into my nose and began to choke me, taking over my sinuses with their thick persistence. They pressed on, much like I had. I still did.

The girls were at the back kitchen window overlooking the ravine. They had toast in their hands, the melted butter filling the rings of their fingertips, painting the crevices. "I wonder if they left the bones," Leigh said.

"No." Tessa shook her head. Her faint-brown hair, weightless and airy, moved around the collar of her shirt. "No, they took the bones. They just left their tents."

"They might come back to dig?" Rose looked excited. She'd had Froot Loops; there were remnants between her bottom teeth. "It rained last night," she said, as if this had anything to do with it.

"It was more thunder than rain," Jasper interjected. He was dumping sugar in his coffee. He made himself breakfast—eggs, sausages, etc.—and let the rest of us eat whatever we could find. I bought the groceries but somehow still felt I was excluded from his efforts. I bought enough for everyone; I don't know why he was so certain he was the only one who wanted any.

"It's like that in the summer," I said. The room had a faint buzz to it, coming from the floor. I felt like I couldn't hear anything too clearly. I turned on the fan over the stove, having to reach around Jasper, who was visibly annoyed by my arm grazing his. "Is it smoky in here?"

"No, that's outside." Jasper motioned with the plastic spatula. The rear of the house was precariously perched on the edge of the woods. Beams attached to the foundation reached twenty feet in some spots before they found earth, where they penetrated. I didn't know how deep the wood went, but the house didn't move. It hadn't in a hundred years. My mother used to comment on the stupidity of building something on land like that, like this. I blamed the angle for the accident. I blamed the land for my part in it. Bad dirt.

"It's cold out," Jasper said, more to the girls than to me. "That's mist, not smoke."

"Looks smoky," Pamela disagreed.

"It's not," Tessa said. She was still in charge. "It's fog."

"Exactly." I nodded at the window where they stood. "I should call Cady," I said to myself.

"Who?" Jasper asked.

"Police lady."

"Why?"

"Oh, I'm pretty sure I know who it is." The girls turned and looked at me in unison. "Pretty sure," I said again.

24

I got a job shooting a commercial for a fast-food restaurant, which was very outside my comfort zone. Normally, I put lotion on and wore angular clothing while pinching my waist with my hands or arching backward to make a skirt flair out in just the right way. I'd done commercial work, but as Claudia often said, I was too "country looking in that really sophisticated way that's so popular right now" for mainstream commercials. A fast-food commercial was about as mainstream as they came. It was for a bundle of money—and I wouldn't be wearing pants.

"You shouldn't do commercials like this, but I'm allowing it because they specifically wanted a fashion model, so...there," Claudia said. She preferred high fashion. No KFC or lying on a lawn chair in a bikini for a weed killer advertisement. She said once you started doing that, you might as well move to LA, because it was "over!"

I was to sit in a men's dress shirt, unbuttoned and draping off one shoulder, and devour a fully loaded hamburger on camera, pantsless. The director told me I could "just throw it up after" if I got too full. I told him I couldn't vomit on command. "And you call yourself a model!" He laughed, and so did everyone else on set, uproariously. I didn't throw up, and the shoot only took a few hours. I ate three full burgers. People cheered but made jokes behind my back that this would be my last job.

It was a good paycheck but mostly humiliating. I called Claudia as I was walking home from the set to tell her I was going back to Georgia. She'd put me on hold twice before taking my call, which I took to be a sign that I was making the right decision.

"Sorry!" she said breathlessly when she finally answered.

"I need to talk to you."

"Okay?"

"I'm coming in."

I was both embarrassed but also vengeful, feeling somehow that I would bring Claudia down a notch by telling her I didn't think modeling for the Lawton Agency in New York was the greatest thing in the world. But when I walked into the agency and over to her desk, I saw her looking pale and drawn, with her cane leaning up against the wall and marks on her arms from where she'd had her chemo treatments, and realized she probably didn't think it was the greatest thing in the world either. She frowned for a long time after I told her I was really leaving but didn't argue with me. Her hair had grown a little but was still very short. It was thick and worn in spiky, gelled spurts all over her head. I liked it and told her so.

"Oh, shut up," she said.

"I really am going to move home. I've made up my mind."

She dipped her chin and closed her eyes. "You've been saying that."

"No. I mean it. I'm gonna move to Atlanta, though. You know—city girl these days?"

"Well, Atlanta is not New York… Never mind. I don't approve, but I support. That's the luxury of being me: I'm not your mother. I can support what I don't approve of. Do you want to work in Atlanta?" she asked.

"Yeah, but I don't think you can be a full-time model there or—"

"No, you can't, or they'll try to send you back up here, because this is where all the good work is. But you do what you want. I know it's hard after a while. I do." She meant that it was hard for girls like me, who made great money but not life-changing, super-fame, million-dollar-contracts kind of money. We had to work, hustle, show up, and huff it all over town. Sure, we were making a living, but not more than a receptionist would make. I'd done okay, but I was never going to be on the cover of *Vogue*. We all knew that now.

Claudia went on. "My friend has an agency in Atlanta. You could work for her… I mean, work work, like in her office. I'm sure she'd send you out on stuff, because she's going to be lucky to have someone with your look at her disposal, but there just aren't enough jobs there for that to be all you did. That's the problem. You're going to have to work... You know, like your mama works."

"She doesn't work," I said.

"Okay. Well then, you're going to have to work like I have to work." She pointed at herself and made a little popping sound with her lips. "Her name's Grace. I just hope this isn't about a boy. And he is a boy, Dani."

"Who?" I asked.

"Good answer, and it doesn't matter. Just hear me out: You may feel like a kid now, and you sort of are, but you're making grown-up decisions. A boy has no place in grown-up decisions. You won't be able to come back and pick up where you started. This"—she made a circular motion with her hands—"will be over. We won't drop you or anything, but everyone will forget you and they'll move on, so there's no changing your mind. The longer you're gone, the deeper the grave. Don't think you can run back here and it will be like it was...like it's been."

I was sitting at Claudia's desk next to a chair full of Polaroids that were spilling off the edges and onto the floor. A whole collection of baby faces and pleading eyes with brains behind them that hadn't fully developed and that wouldn't fully understand what was happening to them.

"I just can't do this forever."

"No one does anything forever." She pointed at her head.

New York became freezing and winter-like in a matter of days. The city might have sensed something very meaningful was about to happen and decided to retreat into itself, not daring to confront the passing days with warmth and light as it had before. Now we were touched only with ice-cold metal gloves over skeleton fingers. I felt nothing. The city exploded, and all that was left was gray ash. I couldn't have been more ready to leave. I was just waiting out my lease and then I would go home—finally and permanently. I would be back in Pressville by Christmas.

Louisa came by Lawton one afternoon while I was there getting the rest of my cards. She asked if I wanted to go to a party in the Village with her.

"What?" I said, confused and irritated.

"There's a party in the Village."

"I heard where it was," I said.

"There, there," Claudia said. "Don't attack little Lou Lou. Be nice, Dani."

"Sorry," I sneered.

"Let's not get nasty," Claudia said with her gaze on her computer screen.

I again declined the invitation and left the agency feeling like I'd been excused when Louisa showed up.

I left a message on his family's answering machine but didn't hear back from Benji that day. I did, however, get a call from my sister Raquel later that night, when I was getting in bed to watch *Steel Magnolias*.

"Hey," I answered, thinking it was my mother calling.

"It's bad," Raquel said immediately. She had an urgent, whiny voice no matter what she was saying. She sounded especially prickly.

"Huh?"

"You know your boyfriend got arrested, right?"

"Again?"

She paused. "I don't know, but he got arrested, and now people are saying he got a girl pregnant last year in Wingham and that he hit her when she had a miscarriage 'cause he was saying she got an abortion, and that his brother's been stealing motorcycle parts and drugs from this dealer from Ridgemont and he's gonna have to go to jail for a long time."

"He got someone pregnant?" I didn't sound surprised. I sounded like I was already accusing her of lying.

"Yeah. Her dad, I guess… I'm not sure, but her dad is trying to sue him or something. Sue him so he goes to jail."

"I don't think you can do that. Where did you hear this?"

"I hear stuff about him all the time, Danielle. Everyone does."

"What else do you hear about him?" I was impatient and annoyed.

"I guess they stole a bunch of guns or something from their

neighbor's house last year, and he hooked up with one of the substitute teachers at our school. She got fired. I know you heard about that. Amber Staley. You know she got fired for having sex with him."

"That's gross," I said, as if Raquel needed to be reminded.

"The brother is even worse."

"Stop gossiping. You called to tell me rumors about Benji Law?" Now I sounded like I thought he was beneath our regard. "You know how Pressville is—I bet only a quarter of that's true. Are you telling Mom this stuff?"

"Oh, Mom knows. She just tells people you guys weren't together; you were just helping him find a place in New York."

"Wait, what?" I'd been prostrate this whole time but now sat up, got out of bed, and started pacing.

"Everyone knew he was up there with you," Raquel said. The twins were normally a little apathetic toward me. They stayed out of my business, and no matter how much I tried to impress them, they were not very interested. There was an age gap, and I didn't really line up with what they admired. They wanted to be cheer-leaders with platinum-blond hair, washboard abs, and boyfriends with lifted trucks and a boat at their disposal. Those were the things I'd wanted, too, until I realized there was a whole other world by which I could measure myself, different comparisons I could make between my life and other people's, a whole array of ways in which I wasn't as special or significant—ways I'd never even thought of to feel inadequate. Raquel and Janelle wanted the tightest ponytail at the Friday-night football game. A small part of me was jealous. That would have been enough for me, too, once upon a time.

"He wasn't," I said. "With me..."

"Well, I guess everyone's saying that he got some girl up there pregnant, too, and that's why he's home. He ran out on her too."

"I am not pregnant," I said. "I'm a model; I can't get pregnant. I mean, like I shouldn't, because of my figure or whatever."

"I don't know—somebody saw him at the women's clinic, so they were thinking that maybe you... Just sayin'."

"The women's clinic? In Pressville?" Everyone knew where the clinic was and what they did there. You could often find people praying outside or holding hands by the doorway. My mother would tsk every time we drove by; I never really knew who she was tsking at. "Why would he go to the women's clinic in Pressville if I was pregnant up here?"

"Maybe to get some pills or something. At least, that's what everybody's sayin'."

"Raquel, this makes no sense at all. You just told me he hit his last girlfriend because she got an abortion and that he's going to jail. You're goofy."

"Maybe vitamins or something for the baby!" She sounded excited.

"Well, I am not pregnant. I think I would know."

"Yeah, I guess Cady Benson told Mom you look normal and that you're smoking, so you're not knocked up."

I exhaled, leaving a hot mist on the mouth of my phone. "Okay. That makes sense now. Jesus Christ, Raquel."

"I'm just telling you. Mom says you shouldn't come home for Thanksgiving until this blows over and he either goes to jail for good or whatever."

I'd forgotten that I left a message for my mother earlier. I'd called the house to let everyone know I was coming for Thanksgiving. Sometimes I had time to fill, and so to fill it I made plans, mostly involving other people. Their confirmation and forced engagement with me helped alleviate some of my insecurities.

"So y'all just sit around and talk about me?"

"Not really, but he's, like, the talk of the town. So it's kinda hard not to talk about you. Everyone knows—"

"I don't care what everyone knows," I said angrily. "What would I do for Thanksgiving if y'all kicked me out? Seriously. Are you saying I can't come? Is that what Mom says?" Raquel was fifteen now and had her learner's permit. She sounded older, less convinced of my superiority. It was strange for me to be asking her permission for anything.

"Oh, come on, Danielle. This isn't the first time you've missed a holiday here. That one Christmas you were in Miami the whole time, butt-dialing us from nightclubs. I'm just telling you like it is. Mom's a mess."

"Sounds serious," I said. She pretended to laugh.

———

Because I couldn't get in touch with Benji for a few days, I started to think maybe he'd gotten arrested again or that he did get sued by that girl's dad. I kept leaving messages at his house but didn't hear back.

My mother and father, however, were available to talk, and talk they did. My mother said I needed to stay in New York for the holidays. "Just better this year." I could tell she'd been crying. "I literally think they might try to tar and feather you if you came home...or burn you at the stake. Whatever they do to witches. I know you'll see him if you come, and I just can't have that in my house. You have no idea who he really is, and I don't want him having anything to do with our family."

"I can't believe you sent Cady Benson over to spy on me, by the way." I wasn't working much and was spending more and more time in my apartment, half of it lying in bed. My sheets smelled like cigarette smoke, and I was wearing my pajamas until around five in the evening most days. I was usually able to avoid leaving until that time but would get hungry and tired of what I had on hand. It was very gray, and biting cold. When I looked out the single floor-to-ceiling window in my place, all I saw was trash blowing on the sidewalks under a lead sky. A few people were calling to see if I wanted to get coffee or food; I ignored everyone who didn't have a Georgia area code. "She showed up here out of the blue like a stalker," I said of Cady. "I thought she was gonna offer me some chicken!"

"I have been trying to get you to meet with her since the day you moved to New York. I did not send her to spy. She was doing me a favor by checking in on you."

"Well, whatever. My lease is up December fifteenth, and then I'll be home," I said. "I can stay away for Thanksgiving, even though I think that's ridiculous. I haven't done anything wrong."

"You've been lying to me and everyone else." She was matter-of-fact. I flinched for a moment, realizing it was the first time we'd spoken honestly about Benji. Normally, I did lie and didn't think much of it. I'd somehow admitted that I'd been seeing him, that he'd been here, and all because he didn't seem to be able to stay out of trouble back home.

"I lied because I knew you didn't want me to be happy," I said.

"Oh, Danielle. You sound like a child. You are a child. I have done so many things wrong in my life but nothing as wrong as letting you move up there on your own at seventeen. If I could take it back—"

"Just stop. You're making me feel like I'm some horrible disease you have."

"I don't mean to do that, sweetie, but I just can't help but think you would have made very different decisions for yourself if we'd kept you here, had you finish school. I don't know."

"Well, Benji Law is in Pressville, Mom. He's not some crazy New York modeling person. He's one of your own."

"He will never be one of my own. You should hear the stories, Danielle. You'd move into a convent if you heard this kid's history. And he's only sixteen! How has he had the time?"

"You just don't know him."

"And you don't either."

―――――

I spent the Thanksgiving holiday with Louisa and her parents instead. She was an only child—that wasn't difficult to tell—so they came to New York to wine and dine her in celebration of the holiday and her success. Louisa's mother had been to visit about six times in six months, but this was her father's first trek. I liked him immediately, as he also had a clueless-but-okay-to-be way about him that I associated with funny men who were smarter than they needed to feel. My own father was much like that. Spending time with Chuck Radcliffe made me miss my dad, who was apparently the only one in my family who was upset that I was not home for Thanksgiving. I asked my mother if she planned to set a place for me at the table anyway.

"What? Like I did when you missed Easter to go to Saint Bart's?" She had a point, even if she didn't know what Saint Bart's was.

Mr. and Mrs. Radcliffe took me and Louisa to Houston's in Midtown. I ordered a steak, and the rest of them had the Thanksgiving special made specifically for the occasion. Louisa's mother asked me if the agency was always on me to lose weight.

I put down my fork, which was heavily laden with macaroni and cheese, and asked why.

"Because they say stuff to Louisa about her weight all the time, and she's always been such a stick. I can't understand how they could possibly want her to be thinner."

"They just try to hammer it into you that you have to keep your measurements to work. It's just the way Claudia is. A lot of other models are on drugs or have to fast for every runway season or whatever. And a lot of them spend all their money and are flat broke all the time, living with photographers and whoever else. But Claudia won't have that. She makes you like a little business woman—at least, she did me. So she's always saying 'take care of this'"—I pointed up and down Louisa's chest, the only part of her body I could see, as we were sitting at the table—"'and even more important, this,'" I said, pointing to my own face. "She makes you think of it as an investment."

"Right," Louisa's mother said. She looked terrified. "I just don't want it to become a thing, if you know what I mean."

"I hope it won't," I said and then smiled at Louisa, who was picking at her corn bread with a teaspoon.

———

Even though I'd broken bread with her family and seemed to have made friends with her parents, Louisa didn't talk much around me. I heard she was a regular motormouth from everyone else, though.

"She's so quiet around me," I told Claudia one day when I was at the agency, borrowing a pair of roller skates. I had an audition for a soft drink commercial, in which I was going to have to skate with a sexy look on my face.

"Maybe something to hide," she answered. "Go practice." Claudia picked up her phone. "Hi, baby!" she said to the receiver. She turned to me and winked, reaching for my hand for a quick grasp and release. It was the second time in recent memory I left Lawton feeling strangely like I'd been asked to.

I went to Tompkins Square Park with the skates and my headphones. A young man with an old-fashioned camera took several pictures of me there, and I was on a sort of a high when I took a risk and skated home. When I was almost back, I saw that Louisa was entering the building. I rolled my eyes and thought of turning around and skating to Whole Foods before she noticed me, but I was too late—I'd been spotted. She was on the phone, so I figured I wouldn't have to avoid actually talking to her. I caught the tail end of her conversation as I approached, still on wheels, and heard her say, "I love you— Oh my gosh..." She hung up and quickly put the phone in her pocket. "Hi!" she said too enthusiastically. "Cool!" She pointed at my feet.

"Oh yeah, they're Claudia's. Or her cousin's or something."

When I got into my place, after removing the skates so I could take the stairs, I first looked around for Benji, which I still did sometimes.

I refused to change my mind about him, no matter what anyone in my family said—and we still talked, although not about much in particular. I hadn't had the nerve to ask him about his ex-girlfriend or the clinic or any of it. Mostly I just tried to get him to say he missed me.

I called his parents' house after plopping down on my bed. He picked up and sounded hurried. "You there?" he said like an excited question.

"It's Danielle," I told him.

"Oh… Hey." He sounded a little confused.

"So I'm thinking about coming home for Christmas," I said immediately. I'd already told him that twenty times. I guess I was just going to keep saying it until I got the response I wanted.

I could hear the television in the background—it sounded like *The Simpsons*. The Laws loved *The Simpsons*. I think they admired them. "Yeah," he said. I'd anticipated a stronger reaction. "That's cool."

"Do you want to go down to Atlanta for a little while?"

"Naw, I don't really like Atlanta."

I exhaled heavily into the phone. "Okay, I guess I'll come home and we won't see each other."

He took a second to respond. "If you're in Pressville, we're gonna see each other."

He sounded so distracted that I almost hung up, but a fleeting yet oppressive feeling of finality kept me from it. If I did hang up at that moment, it would be the last time I would talk to Benji.

"Maybe I can steal you away for a bit."

"I like bein' the victim of your crimes, Danielle." I could tell he was smiling when he said it, but it was the kind of smile a person gives you when they have to let you down.

"You're definitely living a life of crime these days, Mr. Law," I said.

"Naw. Don't believe a word of it. I'mma be a good boy from now on."

25

The first time Louisa ran away, it was treated with careful apathy. Claudia didn't want anyone pressuring her to return. "For all we know, she's overwhelmed. She was at the MTV Music Awards last week sitting next to Pharrell, okay? She's a fifteen-year-old kid from Kentucky." Claudia was telling me mostly, but others in the Lawton office were listening and adding their two cents. "She was in six cities last month. I know she's tired, and the mother went back to work, so she's not coming as much now." She turned to me. "Dani, I need you to keep an eye on her, okay?"

"Well, if she ran away, then I can't really, can I? And anyway, I leave in a couple of weeks." I'd made my announcements more and more loudly every time I was in, and it seemed to me everyone cared less and less. Claudia would look at me with distracted concern but move on quickly. I suppose, in a way, she felt bad when we'd been promised the world and were now working for slightly more than minimum wage.

"Do your best, *mon petit bisou*," Claudia said. I had learned that was one of her favorite ways of dismissing people.

I actually don't think anyone would have said she "ran away" if her parents hadn't been so adamant that that's what happened. They even called me; according to Claudia, I was one of the first people to be contacted, which surprised me. It was probably because of Thanksgiving, but I thought I was pretty obvious about how much I didn't like little Lou Lou. Her parents didn't see it that way and thought that my loneliness during the holidays and the way I'd been forced to help her get a place meant that I was someone they could trust, that I cared about their daughter, that I wasn't reeling with near-constant crippling jealousy.

Her cell phone was off, no one answered at her apartment— apparently Mr. and Mrs. Radcliffe had already sent someone from the agency over when they couldn't get a hold of me. I hadn't intentionally ignored them, but I'd had a busy week. Louisa had missed both a casting and a job—it was something quite heady, like Ralph Lauren or Dior; it was very specifically because of this that the agency began to worry that she really was missing.

I was not called to fill in for her with the photographer. A Danish girl named Stina, who was sixteen, took the job. No one could find Louisa for a solid four days. Her parents were convinced she was dead, abducted, or had been drugged and shipped to

Eastern Europe in a human trafficking ring. Claudia, however, although worried and a little angry about the job, thought she "ran away to Georgia to be with her boyfriend."

"I don't think she has a boyfriend," I said. I'd met Claudia for coffee so we could discuss my big move and also because I don't think she had anyone better to meet with that day. I was a time killer. Sometimes she'd send me a text to come by the agency, and when I got there, there was clearly no reason for it. She liked us milling around her desk, chattering away. She knew I wasn't that busy, so she called on me to be a stand-in for more important clients. She was glowing a pale lime green in the morning glare. I figured it was from her treatments. All she could talk about was Louisa and how no one had heard from her in almost a week, like that would also be the only thing on my mind.

"She does. Talks about him all the time."

"Okay, well, he's not from Georgia. She would have told me that." My latte was over-roasted and bitter.

"She doesn't tell you anything, sweetie. She thinks you are intimidating and that you don't like her."

At least she had that figured out, I thought.

"What?" I put my cup down, smelling distant dog feces. I looked for a culprit.

"Horse's mouth," she said, putting a finger to her lips. "She's been complaining about the pace lately. She said she wanted some downtime, so I think she turned off her phone and went to see lover boy." Claudia raised an eyebrow before looking at her own phone, clicking away, her index finger like a woodpecker. "She's stressed. All is forgiven. She's Louisa—Ralph Lauren will come calling again."

Claudia suggested I go to Paris for a week. "Lot of work there," she said. "So fucking cold here. I can't stand it."

"Just as cold in Paris," I told her. "And anyway, I told you I'm moving home."

"Well, you're not doing much here, my sweet. Why don't you go for a few days; then you can come back to New York, pack up, and leave. It can be your last hurrah before you become southern again." She waved her hand dismissively. The last time I'd gone abroad, I'd come back to New York owing the agency money. "I'd just like you away for a little bit. It will be good for you."

I tried not to read into what she'd said. I couldn't figure out if I thought there was anything to read into. We said our goodbyes before I tossed the rest of my latte in the trash.

A couple of hours later, Claudia called me and said she'd booked some fittings and had me staying in one of her friend's flats in Montmartre. I didn't remember telling her I was 100 percent on board with leaving town.

"You leave Wednesday. Let's just hope Louisa will come back."

I hung up, failing to see how me going to Paris had anything to do with Louisa.

My exit did, however, prompt Louisa to return. I saw her in the lobby of our building the next day. She almost ran when she saw me. "You're back," I said as she skittered away, muttering something about being late. I called Claudia, who, of course, already knew.

"She needed a break. Went to Mexico. Said she'd never do it again."

"Okay?" I felt like a small child with people talking over my head. Claudia then told me that Louisa had paid the remainder of her lease in my building and was moving to another place in Nolita with a roommate. She would be gone by the time I got back from Paris. I felt sorry for our building with both of us moving out. It was kind of a sad little place anyway, so dark and scared, shoved there between higher structures.

"So she's out of your hair now," Claudia said before we hung up. "She thought you were already in Paris."

"What?" I said.

"Never mind all that. I have to run, *mon petit bisou*."

To make matters worse, Louisa was at the agency when I stopped by before heading to the airport. She gave me an awkward hello and told me she was going to Miami for two weeks. She was bright and glowing a pale pink—her usual, softly captivating color. I asked what number sunscreen protection she was wearing. "It must really be working. I'd look like a catcher's mitt if I was out in the sun like that all the time." She was puzzled and murmured something about not having freckles. It felt like an insult; I had freckles. "Weren't you just in Mexico?" I asked as I picked up the rest of my stuff and went to leave the office.

"Quiet," Claudia barked after me.

"It rained the whole time we were there," Louisa offered softly as I walked away, and I heard Claudia tell her not to worry.

"You're perfect," she said. "Dani's just jealous."

I was in a profoundly agitated state during my flight and couldn't sleep. Not only was the Louisa thing bothering me—I'd called Benji the day before, and our conversation had been so stilted that I'd felt nearly sick to my stomach when we hung up. He was listening to Elliot Smith when he answered, which was curious because he only liked country music and the occasional heavy metal, thanks to Blake. He told me that he'd talk to me when I got back from Paris.

"That's when I'm moving home," I said. I sounded mad but had been hoping he would say something like he was excited to see me or that it was going to be great to have me close again.

"Cool. That'll be good." He might have been trying to sell me a bridge. I was almost shaking with disappointment.

It was absolutely freezing in Paris, but it had been a good idea to go. For brief moments, I didn't think about Benji at all. I worked from almost the second I stepped off the plane. I saw some familiar faces from the industry, who invited me to parties or a concert here and there, but I declined. I went back to the flat in Montmartre at night and sat in the cavernous window, staring at a small park where children played. They were messy kids, with ripped pants and hair that stood on end. They were unaware of me and of anyone else who might be watching. I wondered what it would be like to grow up in an apartment in Paris. This wasn't anything like my home in Pressville—my parents' enormous house, with its deteriorating woodwork and wide stairs, everything creaking in unison, separated from the rest of town, the state, the world by long, winding roads and endless tree cover. I think it was while watching the French children kicking the ball, during this moment of pleasant serenity, that I realized that Louisa's boyfriend from Georgia must be Benji.

I bit my lip, furious and dumbfounded, just as one of the little boys kicked a ball at another's face—fighting and crying followed in that order. Some adults became involved and ruined my interest in the scene. I went back into the flat after slamming the window shut. I decided I was hungry; that was why my hands were trembling.

I walked to a small café on the corner and ordered a glass of red wine, which they served me with a small bowl of olives. I took the pits out of my mouth with my fingers and stared at the streets rising and falling like waves of concrete memory that no one person could recall. It would take all the sinners and all the saints together to chisel the truth out of those stones. A collective anguish melted like butter between the cracks. It was a lot like home in that sense; there was no way to fix what happened. Trees were spreading like a fungus over the streets; I wondered how long they had been there and how much they had seen. Surely I was insignificant. Surely this pain that was settling into my sternum like a fissure paled in comparison to all that had taken place here, century after century of bloodshed and turmoil—at least, according to what high school history I'd absorbed at P-High—but I was unable to think about anything worse. There was nothing worse. Louisa. Her name cracked the bone that split the fissure. I heard one of the children crying again, and I was glad.

I sent Claudia a text. It would be afternoon in New York. Please just tell me. I want to know. Just tell me the truth.

I don't know anything, she wrote back. She doesn't say much about it. She knew exactly what I was talking about.

I left some money on the table and walked back up Rue Burq, back to the apartment. I was quaking with confused anger. I called Claudia's desk line and then her cell phone a few times, but she didn't answer. I wanted confirmation. I remembered something she'd said to my mother when they first met, when I initially came to New York to work. My mother asked if Claudia had children, because that was how my mother measured a person's worth. "Kids?" she'd asked after Claudia revealed that no, she was not married, but divorced with no children.

"I have hundreds of daughters," she told my mother. "All of my girls...my chicks. I take care of them. It's more than I can do—"

"Not really the same as having your own children," my mother answered sharply.

"No, I suppose it's not. It's not the same, but it's something."

I called Claudia's phone again and again. Why did she lie to me? I kept calling until Claudia finally picked up. "I'm at the doctor," she said, very sullen and quiet. "I can't talk right now."

"Why didn't you tell me that Louisa ran off with my boyfriend? Is that why you sent me here? I'm barely going to break even. Were you just trying to get me out of town so she would come back?"

"Dani…" She paused. "I have to go. I'm having tests run. Just go…work. Lord knows I need the money right now. Stop being so obsessed. Really. It's making you ugly."

26

I leased a place in Atlanta, sight unseen. Chantel braved the traffic and told me that the apartment was "really, really nice... Huge bathrooms, but I don't know why you need a place with two bathrooms." Chantel always found a way to ruin the moment.

It was actually someone's condo that they needed to sublet, a girl named Paige who was getting married. "You can live there as long as you want," she told me. "I don't ever really want to sell it, but Ryland has a place off West Wesley, so I can't go on living here, now can I?" She asked this giggling, perhaps thinking that I'd be impressed with Ryland's address. I had no idea who Ryland was, where West Wesley was, and even less interest in where young Paige would be living. She asked if I was married, to which I said no.

"Well, you'll meet a nice boy here."

"I have a boyfriend," I told her. "That's why I'm moving back. I'm a model in New York."

"Awesome!" She was patronizingly approving, and I knew she didn't really believe me...about the modeling. She also didn't care about the boyfriend; she was marrying Ryland with the house on West Wesley.

Benji was not my boyfriend, and it didn't sound like I was going to see him any time soon. He was going with his parents to West Virginia to visit his mother's sister for Christmas. I'd barely talked to him; my understanding was that he was in a lot of trouble about the drugs at the Shell station. I still hadn't asked about the girl and the baby or any of that. I was too scared he'd tell me it was true, and then how would I argue with my mother? I also hadn't said a word about Louisa. I willed it to be untrue by refusing to speak her name.

I was staying with my parents for Christmas and planning to move down to Atlanta after the holidays. It was very strange to be home with such finality. There were several errant comments about "when I left again" that weren't corrected but rather talked over hurriedly or rushed past once the remark had left a mouth. It was seen as a distinct failure on my part that I had not been able to "make it" in New York. That was what I heard my mother say to her friend Janet on the phone.

"Yes, Danielle's moving back. She couldn't cut it up there... No, the modeling didn't work out. You know leggy brunettes are a dime a dozen. It's expensive, and she wasn't working as much as she wanted to, and she got her own apartment; that ate up all the money, so…"

"Are there any more people getting arrested in Pressville?" I asked one evening over dinner. "You know they love to put people in jail here for gardening." It was like I blamed my mother for New York, for Benji, for the way I was home but no one seemed to care.

"'Gardening'? Is that what we're calling it now? My understanding is that a bathtub was involved." She picked up her iced tea and gulped, her plastic nails tapping the glass and her eyes like a blurred scrape across her face.

"They were dealing meth," Chantel said after putting her fork down on the table officiously. "Meth isn't a plant."

I rolled my eyes.

"He's got another girlfriend, anyway," Janelle said, like she had no idea this might destroy me. "Super pretty. She was here for a while, but I think maybe she left. She was hella pretty."

"Don't say that word," my mother corrected her. "That's not even a word."

"She's beautiful," Raquel added. Where the twins were concerned, if a person was pretty, then they were excused from almost all their failings. Strangely, I don't think either of them found me particularly attractive. If they did, they never said it. No one in my family acknowledged my looks. It was an unspoken assumption that sooner or later, whoever was paying me to look like me would come to their senses and see that I was just a Greer from Pressville, and what's so special about that? It seemed I had proven them right.

———

I met with Grace in Atlanta on the Wednesday morning before Christmas. Her office was closed, but she came in specifically to talk to me. She was elegant, with long legs and white-blond hair—clearly an answer to gray—and a navy-blue pantsuit.

"So you're washed up?" she asked me with a drawl.

"Gosh, I hope not," I said.

"Well, you're back here. Can't be good. You look fantastic anyway. You weren't working anymore? I find that hard to believe. Claudia must be losing her edge."

"I just wanted to move home," I said, and for a second I thought I would cry.

"Well, this isn't Pressville," she offered. "Claudia tells me there's a boy involved."

"Oh, Claudia," I said, then pressed my lips together decisively, hoping to halt this line of inquiry.

"I, too, had a promising career in New York," she said, looking me up and down. I was in four-hundred-dollar cargo pants and a merino-wool sweater tied in a large knot at my waist. "Not like yours, of course, but I was working. I didn't want to live up there, though, so I came back thinking I could go back and forth or just work here. It doesn't matter anymore. I do understand. Anyway, the girls here are subpar... Of course, every once in a while I find someone magical, but then they're gone and I'm only getting a small commission, but that doesn't matter. I'm doing my damnedest to build a men's department, but I don't have the eye for it, so maybe you can help with that. Yeah, I wanted to come home too. I missed my daddy." She was fishing through a stack of photos. "See this one?" She showed me a photo of some brooding teenager with long hair and a nose ring.

"I don't know about him," I said.

"Well, that's what I said, but I guess he's working a lot in Miami. But you know how they are down there."

"I worked in Miami," I told her.

"Yes..." She looked at me, then back at the stack. "I can't pick the boys. I just don't see it. Anyway, about the job—you can just come in on Monday mornings, and we'll set a schedule for the week. I'm going to send you on castings, too, so you may not be in the office all that much. I really can't say. I'm glad you're here." She smiled and wished me a Happy New Year. Things had been largely professional, and I wondered how we were going to manage our relationship if she was asking me to make coffee and then taking 15 percent of my jobs. "We have another girl here—sort of the same situation, but a failed actress—home from California. I'm afraid she's a bit of a dingbat, and I really can't be sure she'll show up for work every day. I don't know if it's pills or...

Anyway. Her name is Heather. And, Dani, I can't call you Dani... I want to, but they just won't get that here. You'll be Danielle Greer. Sorry," she said, not seeming sorry in the slightest. "Say goodbye to Dani."

My parents wanted to hear all about the meeting when I got home, and by my parents, I mean my parents and Chantel, who was almost ever present at the house. They were pleased that I had a "regular job," as they called it. "I think it's great," my mother said more than a few times. "It sounds like this Grace woman has done well for herself. Maybe since you don't want to model anymore, you can work on the other side...or however... I don't know what you call it."

"I'm still modeling," I sneered. "I just want to do something else. It doesn't mean that I got, like, fired from being a model or that I can't be a model or whatever. I just don't want to do only that anymore. I'm tired of pounding the pavement and being good at only one thing. Like I need to expand my résumé." We were on the couch. I was watching fashion television, hoping to catch a shot of myself on the runway or in a backstage vignette. I felt both glad I wasn't in New York and yet full of remorse that it didn't look like I'd ever be a model in New York City again.

"You want to expand your résumé, so you're working with models?" Chantel said. She always asked questions like she, herself, had singlehandedly invented question-asking. In her mind, they were all zingers—her stupid inquiries and bland commentary. I don't know what kind of response she expected; I didn't think she ever added anything meaningful to any conversation.

"I'm learning the business," I said to Chantel sharply. "It's either that or interior design."

"What do you know about interior design?" Chantel asked.

"Well, if you ever came to visit me in New York instead of always expecting me to spend my own money to come here, then you would see how stylishly I decorate. I have excellent taste. A lot of my friends asked me to help them with their apartments, and I have a good eye for vintage and antiques as well."

Everyone in the room shifted in their seats at the same time. I'd said the unspeakable. They'd never come to visit me in New York; I suppose they hadn't had much of an opportunity, being that I didn't live there as long as I'd hoped to, expected to, more or less been promised I would—but either way, they hadn't come. It was as if it was a joke from the beginning; no one took Claudia and Frank Dabney seriously but me.

My mother accompanied me the first two weeks of my stay and never returned, appearing to be relieved when she left for the airport. She'd gotten that out of the way. A lot of excuses were made as to why it wasn't a good time to come, or it was too expensive, or wasn't I working all the time anyway? The twins were keen on visiting, but my parents would not allow them to go unaccompanied by an adult. When I turned eighteen and said I was an adult, my mother replied, "Not that kind of adult."

My family simply wasn't interested in New York. "I don't really care to go back," I'd heard my mother say. "If I never see a loogie on the sidewalk again, it'll be too soon."

Chantel said she was saving her money for a trip to the Grand Canyon.

"You ever make it to Arizona?" I asked her during the puddle of uncomfortable silence into which we'd all stumbled.

"We're going in the spring," she answered crisply.

"With who?"

"Maybe Bobby," she replied. I gasped in both surprise and a little bit of excitement. We might get rid of her yet.

"Boyfriend?"

"No, she's my boss at the library. Short for Roberta."

Chantel was always letting me down. She may have been going on vacation with her boss, but she did have plans to move out of my parents' house, having completed four years at the community college in Darren, Georgia. She had a degree in communication studies, which to me sounded the same as saying she had a degree in talking. I thought this was strange for an excessively quiet person. She'd taken a job at the local Pressville newspaper, a bimonthly publication that contained stories about pig-roasting over a spit and the dangers of putting toothpicks all the way in your mouth. My parents, of course, couldn't have been prouder. I was on the cover of *Marie Claire*—albeit with two other girls—but Chantel had a feature about a local boy named Chuck who'd built a three-wheeled skateboard. That was it. The skateboard had three wheels. My parents were like balloons over it, floating in their excitement about her future as a "journalist!"

"Anyway, feel free to visit me in Atlanta. No plane ticket required."

The following morning, my mother pulled me aside and spoke more sincerely than I could remember. I could see chips in her nail polish, smell her Pantene hair spray leftover from the day before, detect the fine lines around her mouth that were not yet covered in the orange-hued foundation she would apply after breakfast. Her roots were dark with speckles of gray, and her eyes had a weary look to them that had nothing to do with a rough night's sleep. It was the way she was being forced to reckon with me. She'd lived so much of her life in a mirage of her own creation. I was like her nightmare, someone who could legitimately claim the attention she had apparently always been seeking. "I know someone your age doesn't think like this, but there can be things you do—or just one thing you do—in your life that can lead to years, maybe decades, of regret. I don't want you to look back and wonder what the hell you were thinking."

"Mom, I want to live in Atlanta. I'm not sad about leaving New York. I think it's time. I'm not Christy Turlington. I'm not going to be a model forever. I need to move on with my life."

"I'm not really talking about that," she said before hugging me in what felt like a final-scene-before-tragic-death kind of way. "Just don't make decisions based on other people. If you get married and have kids, then that's all you get to do, so now, when you don't have to...or... I just don't want you planting your fields with something that won't grow." She raised an eyebrow and turned her head. It was the first time I thought that my mother was really starting to look old. "And he's trouble, Danielle," she said over her shoulder. "Not the normal kind either. He'll be on *COPS* before too long, and you don't want to be on there with him."

I'd already started paying for the apartment in Atlanta but didn't move in until after New Year's. I'd had all my things in the dining room of my parents' house, where we usually put a small Christmas tree by the window but couldn't on account of the mess I'd made. My clothes and bags and all that had festooned my apartment in New York looked terribly out of place on Bell Road. For just an instant, I'd been so special, and now I was back in Georgia, with my cool clothes that I couldn't afford and would have no place to wear. I'd sold my furniture to my landlord when I left New York, so the only thing that came with me were odds and ends. I'd had only a couple of plates and a handful of pieces of silverware, which I put in my suitcase, surrounded by my sweaters. My mother gave me the strangest look when she saw me taking them out to be washed before I moved everything down to Atlanta. She simply couldn't understand a person who didn't need kitchen items. I told her I often ate peanut butter for dinner if no one invited me out, to which she said, "Now that's just sad. The kitchen's the heart of the home." I'd betrayed every-thing about my childhood in less than a year.

I remember her asking me if I ever got soup in New York, like that was something she would do. "You know the soup places...I saw a dozen when we were there. You could get chicken noodle soup when it's cold out." I'd not eaten chicken noodle soup once. I got lattes and cigarettes. I hadn't even known what a latte was before I moved there.

"Claudia says we shouldn't eat pasta," I'd responded.

"That's just absurd."

We piled everything into my mom's van and drove down to Atlanta to get me moved in. My mother had insisted on grabbing several things from the dollar store to "get me situated," as she called it. She got scouring pads and a toilet brush. She bought an industrial-size container of dish soap and little felt pads for the legs of my furniture. We'd argued over that because the apartment came furnished, so I was sure it already had the pads.

"But if it doesn't, you'll be blamed for scratches," my mother said. "Oh, this is nice," she said of a small plastic plant. "You could put this on the kitchen table." The plant reminded me of her, so much so that I almost laughed as she was holding it next to her face.

"I don't like fake plants," I said.

"Oh." She put it back on the metal shelf. "I thought it was sweet."

Paige's place smelled faintly of baby lotion and hibiscus. I thought of these as Paige's smells, and though pleasant, they needed to be destroyed. I set about lighting candles that I'd purchased at LaGuardia Airport in every room. My mother picked one up to get a closer look.

"Twenty-five dollars for a candle?" she said. "They had some good ones at the Dollar Tree. You could have a candle on every surface in here for the same price."

She stayed for another hour or so, faintly suggesting we go get dinner or go for a walk in my new neighborhood. "This isn't like New York, Mom," I said. "I can find my way around—and anyway, I start work in the morning, so I want to go to bed early." It was four o'clock in the afternoon.

"I thought we could fill up your refrigerator before I go." She seemed to be stalling.

"With what?"

"Food, Danielle."

"I'll probably just eat out." I was impatient to be alone. I wanted to put my things away and wash a set of sheets for the bed. Chantel had been right—the bathrooms were huge. I couldn't wait to take a shower in the one with the glass-looking tiles and pink cloud mat. I was given cause to wonder what I'd been doing all my life, living in my parents' house, with the one tub that was creaky and stained, and then in New York, where my bathroom had been a marvel of modern architecture with the way they were able to fit both a toilet and a sink in the same cramped room with the shower.

"I don't know where you're getting all of this money—how are you going to be able to eat out all the time? You have to get a car."

I ran my hand over my forehead and tried not to roll my eyes. "Mom…"

"Fine, fine. I'll go. But, Danielle," she said, "we cannot help you if you do drugs or whatever it is this boy is doing with his life. We cannot get you out of jail or, I don't even know… I feel like in New York, they would have just let you get away with things because of all the murders and terrible things happening there all the time, but Georgia is a death penalty state, and they put people in jail for drugs here."

"Mom!" I was smiling, though I wasn't sure why. It was as if I thought it was funny to be associated with something that was bothering her so much.

"It's very serious, Danielle. The brother is in jail, not juvenile detention or whatever it is the other kid was in. Jail."

"You sound like Dad. 'Sounds serious!'" I giggled nervously. "I'm not going to like do drugs or something."

"It's not even that you can't do drugs. You can't even be around drugs. You can go to jail just for being around them. And I don't know if you know this, but he had another girlfriend who—"

"Okay, okay." I pressed my hands on the slick white countertop. "That's enough. It's over, anyway."

She sighed. "I really hope so. Well then. I guess I'll go. I can get McDonald's on the way home." She seemed satisfied by that and picked up her purse. "It's nice to think you'll be just an hour and a half away. What a difference." She reached to hug me, a tight little squeeze that made me feel like I was being forgiven.

I began work that following day at Grace's office. "Hello," she said as I walked in in the morning. I'd taken the train to work and had to walk what felt like a mile.

I wondered if Grace had been drinking, the way she seemed to be flopping around in her chair and didn't seem to be able to focus her gaze on anything specific. Her hair was in a pile on top of her head, with several pens and pencils pushed through it. She was wearing a sweatshirt over a flannel button-up, with a miniskirt on the bottom that was too revealing for her age—for any age. "So we've got a bunch of model calls today," she told me. She was smoking a cigarette and letting the ash drop all over the floor. "Goddammit!" she cried out when she saw what she was doing. She put the butt out on her shoe, which had been removed for that purpose, and then put it back on. "I smoke here," she told me conspiratorially. "My husband doesn't even know I still smoke, because I only do it here. I'm one of the last who'll light up at my age, but I have to. It reminds me of being young and of not caring. You can smoke here too."

I'd been cutting back, but the invitation was accepted, and we spent most of the day in a haze of Virginia Slim and Parliament Light fog. I drank sparkling water the entire time, mainly because she kept looking up at me like she'd forgotten I was there—"Oh!

Oh, that's right"—then offering me a Pellegrino. She said she was ready to send out for lunch, which I thought at first was my job, that I was the one being sent out, but a young man came up from the first floor and took our order.

"You don't care, do you?" Grace asked me. "It's cold, or I'd suggest we go out."

"Oh, no," I said. I asked for the chicken salad.

"Same for me," she squawked, "but no fucking mayonnaise!" She threw her wallet down on the couch and rolled her eyes. The young man said that, to his knowledge, all the chicken salad at Highland Bakery had mayonnaise in it.

"In it or on it?" Grace asked.

"In it?" Phillip's upper lip was damp with nervous sweating.

"I just don't want mayonnaise on it. I can't afford the calories. Go!" She sent him scurrying out the door with a wave of her hand. When the food came, she ate the mayonnaise-laden chicken salad croissant with gusto and seemed to have forgotten entirely about the earlier conversation. I made a mental note to check the office bathroom for drugs.

At three in the afternoon, Grace announced that she was tired and going home. "Oh," I said. "I thought we had model calls at four."

"Can you do that? I'll pay you double. I have a headache, and I really need some of those insoles for my shoes. I have to go to the Walgreens." I noticed this about Grace. Almost every place had a "the" in front of it: "the Target," "the Dantanna's," "the Charlotte, North Carolina." I never asked why. I still didn't know why Claudia claimed to be French when she was clearly from Illinois or Ohio. I accepted these rattled women, and others, the way they came to me.

I wanted to ask if Grace could guarantee to remember that she said she'd pay me double, so I wrote a note to myself to email her my hours at the end of the day with a disclaimer that I expected to be paid twice my rate for the time after four o'clock: thirteen dollars an hour. I'd made several thousand dollars an hour at least a dozen times, but for some reason the discrepancy between then and now didn't bother me. I'd drunk my weight in Pellegrino, and I was home. In Georgia. Closer to Benji. I'd tried calling him the night before, but no one at the house answered. I knew they were back from West Virginia, because I'd seen his mom in her giant Lincoln sedan coming up Rampart the day before I moved into my new apartment, but I still hadn't seen Benji. If it was true that Blake was in the clink, then it made sense his family would be too busy to answer the phone. Too busy doing what, I wasn't sure, but I decided that was the reason I'd barely talked to him since I got home, and that was that.

Grace had mentioned another girl who worked there, but this phantom employee—Heather—never showed up that first day or week and was not brought up again. Grace's was clearly a real operation, though. She had several clients, a few of whom I was a little impressed by. She said every day at least one person was working. I didn't think that sounded like a lot, but she told me she was a "small office feeding bigger offices. If they're working here, then that means they weren't a great find. If I can ship them off somewhere else, then I still have my eye. I would have run across a ten-lane highway to get you in here," she told me. "But Claudia knows her stuff."

"It was Frank Dabney," I told her.

"Oh, well, that man can find a model anywhere. Anywhere!" I had to guess it was true. I'd been at the mall.

Heather Clack finally showed up after a few days. She was taller than me, with short, blond hair cut razor sharp at her chin. "So what are you even doing here?" she asked like an accusation.

"Oh," I said, startled. "I moved home. I was ready to move back home."

"Why? You won't make any money here. It's not New York."

"I know. That's why I took this job."

"This is a shit job. She's like Darth Vader. Seriously." She nodded toward Grace, who was painting her nails while standing over her desk with a cup of yellow tea balanced on top of her keyboard.

"She's fine," I said knowingly. "Believe me, I've met some really strange people over the years." I felt the need to exert my experience. Heather Clack didn't know anything.

"Well, wait till she staples your bra to the wall."

"I'm not wearing a bra," I said.

It came to light that Heather had been on a cruise with

a professional football player, hence her absence. She dated ambitiously and wanted everyone to know it.

"Grace tells me you're a lesbian," she said.

"Oh, well, I just told her something like that so she wouldn't ask. I don't like to talk about my personal life."

"I do," Heather said. "I don't care what anyone thinks. I almost did porn. I don't care."

"Great." I nodded. I would not share with my mother that the other girl in the office had almost done porn.

I kept a running list of things I would tell Benji about the new job, Atlanta, and the rest. I was always preparing to talk to him, thinking of witty ways in which I would describe people, things, my misadventures. I finally got him on the phone the Friday of my first week of work.

"I have to get a car," I said as soon as he answered. Gone were my clever stories and laundry list of anecdotes to share. I was nervous to actually be speaking to him. I'd ramped things up so much in my mind that I could hardly form a sentence.

"Okay, girl." Benji sounded older, cooler, more sure of himself. I had to guess that his troubles had weighed on him. "Let's jump right in."

"I've been calling and calling. I'm in Atlanta now. I have my own place."

"Cool."

I'd been hoping for more. "You can stay here any time you

want. It has two bathrooms." I squeezed my eyes shut, annoyed at myself for saying that.

"I do love a bathroom."

"Are you okay? I heard your brother is still in trouble."

"Oh, yeah, he'll be fine. S'okay." He didn't say more.

I squirmed on the couch uncomfortably, trying to think of something else to ask him. "Do you think you can help me get a car? I need one...like...now."

"I do like cars."

"Can you come this weekend?"

"I don't know, Danielle. I mean—how'rya gonna pay for it, or...?"

"I have some money from when I sold my furniture in New York."

"Okay, but a car's, like, thousands of dollars."

"It's cool. I have a real job now."

"I guess I can come down."

"Tomorrow? Tonight?"

"Yeah, I can come down."

"Wait, what?" I sat upright, my leg shooting straight out in front of me. "Like, now?" I asked.

"Yeah, I can come now."

"Oh my gosh, Benji!"

"Well, don't get too excited. I'm not there yet, but yeah, I'll come down."

I set about cleaning, though there was little to clean. The floors were perfectly swept and shined. I couldn't find a single crumb to vacuum. With nothing to wipe or tidy, I took a quick shower, then applied all my tonics and lotions—things I had spent hundreds of dollars on in New York because I'd been told by other girls that I needed them—and sat back down on the couch with a magazine. I knew a lot of the models in the pictures within, some of them well, others only in passing. I was excluded from them now, never having really belonged anyway. I decided to hide the magazine in case Benji thought the other models were prettier than me or realized that he'd never seen me in a magazine, and here I claimed to be working all the time.

It was two hours before he arrived. I had explained to him how to get to my apartment and gave him the building code without hesitation, believing this was just the beginning of him visiting me, that this would be the new normal—Benji coming down on his bike at eight on a Friday night and staying with me for the weekend. I was congratulating myself on making the best decision of my life by moving back to Georgia when I heard him knock on the door.

I don't think he was expecting my reaction. I practically threw myself at him, wrapping my legs around his waist and burying my face in his neck. "Whoa, tiger," he said, laughing. "It's good to see you too." He smelled like the cold and the road. His jacket had burnt patches on the shoulders. He was glowing, though; the icy air gave him a shimmer that had me lying to myself all over again.

"Oh my God," I whispered into his neck. "I thought I'd never see you again."

"Now, don't be silly. I'm here."

———

When I left the next morning to go for a run, he was still asleep. I had more skip in my step than I'd had in months. All of a sudden, my memories of Paris were pleasant—fanciful, even. I was smiling as I dodged a puddle here and a crack in the sidewalk there. Atlanta was hilly and winding, like Pressville, only concrete and poked through with buildings. It was small compared to New York, but green and thick the way Georgia is, creating hidden crevices that are wrapped in knotted patches of a busy, flourishing snarl. My ponytail swished merrily between my shoulder blades as I pounded about, so grateful for my new life. If Benji got tired of Atlanta, he could go back to Pressville but be back here in as long as it took me to do a load of laundry.

When I got back to the apartment, Benji was lying on my couch with the fashion magazine I'd hidden in his hands. "It's Louisa," he said, smiling with a sublime crinkle at the corners of his eyes. I'd almost forgotten she existed.

27

I blared the *Evita* soundtrack from my kitchen stereo. Jasper had picked up a small unit from the electronics store, claiming I was the last person alive who wanted a CD player in their house. I set it on the counter and purchased CDs, which were increasingly hard to come by. *Evita* was my favorite—not the one with Madonna, but the original. I listened to it over and over and over, especially on days when I was feeling particularly nostalgic. Sometimes I sang along—"Another Suitcase in Another Hall" was my favorite. Sometimes I could listen to it twelve or thirteen times in a row without a break. It was one of those days. I watched out the back window, humming to myself.

There had been little progress on the bones. The girls were either pressing me to go outside and explore the back—"You know... Near...the area, you know,"—or they were terrified and wouldn't leave the second floor of the house. A couple of times,

I caught Leigh standing by the window in the back hallway. She'd angle herself so as not to be seen from the outside, then turn and face fully forward, then jerk herself back into hiding. It was a conversation with an unknown observer, one who might have been waiting down the steep hill.

"Should we clear all those leaves out of there?" Jasper asked me the week after they found the remains. "I mean, God knows what else is out there. It's probably three feet thick."

"At least," I said. "They've been collecting there for a hundred years." I was going to tell him that we never found anything back there when I'd been a kid. It was his blood that made the omens come true, the curse that had long waited to find me. When I'd been the girls' age, we played hide-and-seek at night. We jumped on moss trampolines and climbed trees with low limbs. I had no bad memories from my time in the woods. Jasper mixed with me, and now we had bones. I could blame him if I tried, and I did try.

Jasper took two days off work to settle the girls and supervise the police presence on the property. I was grateful he was there, because my nerves were shot. Every time I went to the bathroom by the kitchen, I found myself standing in front of the small window mounted awkwardly on the wall right next to the toilet. My own mother had placed a sheer curtain there, saying that no one lived behind us and therefore there was no reason for privacy. I had a pull-down blackout shade over that window. Maybe I knew all along what was out there, waiting to be discovered. Hiding in three feet of leaves with her anklet and her perfect clavicle.

All I did was wait. Cady would call sooner or later and confirm. She kept saying she would need to talk to the girls, but we didn't get any formal requests. I checked the news; Pressville had a paper and a website of its own, but there was also the county weekly news. There hadn't been anything other than the initial report that human remains were found on a local homeowner's property. Cady said she would not be sharing a lot with the press. I might have laughed at that statement some years before. There was no press, even if it was Pressville, but this time when she said it, I knew why. It was better if they didn't advertise how poorly they'd handled things before.

After two days of walking around like a priest called upon to bless the house, Jasper said he was going back to work. "It'll probably be unsolved," he suggested. We were getting ready for bed. I'd brought my kitchen stereo upstairs and was on the seventeenth run of "Another Suitcase." I had it plugged into the bathroom wall, with the small speakers resting precariously on the edge of the counter. My mother had loved the porcelain faucet handles. I couldn't look at them without thinking that I shouldn't be living in her house. She'd abandoned it—the house, her life, every bit of our childhood, which had been slowly fading from within. We'd all been mostly grown when it happened, anyway. The accident. They were out of the house by the end of that year. She and my father told me it was mine when I was ready. I suppose that was why I married Jasper. I needed someone to live with in the house. My sisters had been horribly offended by the gesture, feeling cheated out of having an enormous Victorian to take care of and pay taxes on, but it was clear to all of us—if not precisely then, but later—that I had been given the house as compensation for my losses. My mother, as much as she tried not to understand what had been taken from me, wanted me to have it. It was the only thing that mattered to her, and then she needed it to go away.

"Did the detective call the kids?" Jasper asked upon returning from work.

"No," I said. I was chopping carrots. I nearly got my finger and jumped back from the kitchen counter.

"I thought she said she was going to—"

"Jasper, you ask me this every day. She hasn't called—about that or anything else. I'm not going to track her down. If they don't need to talk to us, then they won't. They're little kids. She probably knows they won't be able to tell her anything useful. And she's not going to call them. She'll call me and I'll arrange it."

"It's just strange. I mean, it's behind our house. I'd think they'd be communicating with us more." He was in his suit with the tie pulled loose from his Adam's apple, moving around the kitchen purposelessly but with great fanfare.

"I don't know," I said about the police. "I'm sure it's going to take a while to confirm her identity."

"So you think it's—"

"No," I said sharply. "No, I don't know why I said that."

"It would make sense." He opened the refrigerator, what he did when he didn't want to leave the room but had run out of things to say. "Y'all had pizza?" He pointed at the Ziploc bag with leftover slices.

"Yeah, on Friday."

"I have to leave again on Monday." His eyes wandered aimlessly around the refrigerator shelves before he closed the door and turned to look at me. "Danielle, what are you going to do if it's her? And the police want to talk to you? Like, really talk to you?"

28

Benji went home, then came back sporadically over the next month. He'd stay for a few days, then say he had to go back to Weatherby or to see his brother. When he was in town, he drove my car while I was at work, purchased in haste right off the lot after my return to Georgia. My father wanted us to "really search" for the perfect deal, but I told him I couldn't take a cab to work every day. "That's, like, all the money I make," I whined. He said if we shopped around, we could find a good low-mileage car in great condition, but I didn't want to shop around, so I bought a beat-up Infiniti SUV with over a hundred and fifty thousand miles on its odometer. Benji thought the car was too big and in terrible condition. He worked on its engine and cleaned it while I was at the office, a task that seemed to bring him profound joy.

One morning when I arrived at the office, Heather was already at her desk—odd, as she was normally at least twenty minutes late. Grace couldn't remember what time she'd told us to be at work and so didn't know to care when Heather came rolling in at ten.

"Who's that guy you have living with you?" she asked me as I sat down after plopping my pack of cigarettes on my desk. I kept telling myself I was going to quit, but Benji was like a chimney, and one of our favorite things to do was sit on my balcony and puff away.

"My boyfriend," I said.

"Looks like the kid from *The Terminator*," she said.

"I don't know what you're talking about." I picked up my phone and pretended to focus on something there.

Later that day, Heather took it upon herself to tell Grace that I had some "boy" living with me. We were in the office; I had a Pellegrino and Heather a KitKat. Grace was putting callous cream on her heels and setting appointments.

"A boy?" Grace asked. "Well, Claudia called, and you have to go to New York, so leave your boy here for a weekend."

"No, he's like a real boy," Heather went on.

"Pinocchio," Grace said before hiccupping loudly. "Oh, for fuck's sake, why do I always get the hiccups when I chew gum?' She slammed her hand down on the desk. "Let's get sushi for lunch. I'm buying."

We walked to the sushi restaurant in the building next door and sat down. Grace insisted we have cocktails and so ordered us stiff martinis. "God, I love drinking during the day," she said to the server, who was a young, intimidated man with a food-stained tie.

"Anyway," Heather said. "So *Terminator* boy, is that what brought you back to Georgia?"

"Leave her alone," Grace said, taking a long pull from her drink. "I need her to make money this weekend. See"—Grace turned her attention to me—"you'll get me some money that I'll have to turn right back over to you so I can pay you for sitting with your feet up on the desk all day, but I guess that's life in this business. God, this business." She waved a hand in front of her face.

"I'll leave her alone when I know the dirt." Heather nodded, then began fiddling with her plastic chopsticks.

"She'll tell us if she wants to," Grace said, patting the table decisively.

We ate our sushi quickly and went back to the office. I put my headphones on and clicked around on the computer, pretending to work. I looked at my cell phone, which I'd left in the office when we went to lunch, and saw that I had twelve missed calls from Benji and seven from my mother.

I told Grace I had to leave immediately. "I have a family emergency." I ran out of the office and called Benji as soon as I got outside. He was calm but serious. Apparently, my mother had come down to Atlanta with Chantel; they were going to surprise me with some food and housewarming gifts from Marshalls. When they'd knocked on my door—innocently, they claimed—Benji opened it.

Benji was working on my car that day, so I had to take a cab back to the apartment, shaking and biting my lip the whole time. I had blood running from my mouth down to my chin by the time I arrived. I ran up the stairs of my building and saw Chantel in the hallway. She was crying. "Oh, come on!" I snapped at her. She looked down, wiping her nose and eyes, but did not respond. When I got inside the apartment, I found Benji standing half-naked in my living room, talking to my mother's stricken face. I grabbed a paper towel from the roll on the counter and tried to stop my lip from bleeding all over my clothes.

"Danielle!" my mother said upon seeing me. I could see her foundation line around her chin. She went from orange to blotchy red. We stood staring at one another like if we could just get past this moment, I might be cured.

My mother pointed her index finger at my chest and got her arm pumping. "Get over here right now, young lady! I don't care how old you are, you're gonna hear it from me, and you're gonna hear it right now! Both of you!" I thought for a moment she was talking about me and Chantel, but it was Benji.

"Mom," I said, scanning the room. Benji was putting on one of my sweatshirts and a pair of jeans. His hair was disheveled, but he looked more irritated than anything.

"I saw his bike in the parking lot. I didn't even have to come inside to know what was going on. I'd know that death trap anywhere. Good God, son, I can't believe you'd drive that thing on the freeway all the way down here. You're lucky to be alive. And you"—my mother turned to me with her finger still pointed like a gun—"you'll be lucky if you don't end up in jail!"

"He's not in trouble anymore," I said quickly, as if I'd rehearsed defending myself in this way a hundred times.

"He's a drug dealer, Danielle. And he has another girlfriend. Another little toothpick girl who goes around with him on his motorcycle." She looked back at Benji. Her hands were shaking. "He's using you when she's not in town."

"And he has to go back to jail, Danielle," Chantel said angrily. She'd decided to come in my apartment, braving potential contamination. "He got busted for a bunch of stuff, not just the weed at the Shell station. Everyone knows they've been selling meth." Now she was talking like she was pleased, other people's downfalls being one of her hobbies.

"People make mistakes." I wasn't sure what else to say.

"Yeah, and you're making one right now, young lady. What is he even doing here?" my mother asked. "Did you get kicked out of your house?" She was talking to Benji while looking at me.

"No," he said, clearly pissed off. "I don't get—"

"It's okay, Benji," I said. "No, he didn't get kicked out of anywhere. He's here because we're in love and getting married."

"Oh, Danielle," my mother said. "Oh, Danielle, what are you talking about? This isn't right. You're not pregnant, are you?"

"What? No."

"Yeah, she lived in New York; she knows what to do if that happens," Chantel said.

"You know this surprise-visit bullshit?" I said. "I don't buy it at all. You came down here to spy on me. Who told you?" Now I pointed my finger at Chantel. She looked dowdier and more smug than usual.

"No one told me a thing," my mother said.

"You lie."

"No, Danielle—you do." Her voice cracked. "You've been lying for a while now, so you're in no place to be saying anything to anyone." Her eyes were red and watery. She had clearly dressed up for the occasion of spending the day with me in the city. Her hair was bigger than normal, done in a wave over the top of her head. Her face was made up like a beauty-pageant contestant. She was wearing hoop earrings and the tennis bracelet my father had bought her at Penney's. Upon seeing that she'd brought her good bag, I started to cry. I'd been trying so hard for so long. Everything had been such effort—the modeling and making friends in New York, trying to keep Benji to myself, lying to my family. I didn't think anyone could properly appreciate how exhausted I was. Benji tried to walk over to me, but my mother stopped him. "Hold it right there. This stops now. Today. I mean it." She put her hand up to Benji, and he obeyed. "I want you to stay away from my daughter."

"Mom." I wiped my face and stared at her in disbelief.

"We don't do drugs and drop out of school and get arrested...
no!" She was emphatic.

"Danielle did drop out of school," Chantel offered.

"Not so she could work at a gas station!" My mother's voice
was pitched. "And, Danielle—you don't even know the half of it. He
beat up his girlfriend and knocked some guy unconscious who is
still in the hospital. He is absolutely going back to jail. The guy has
brain damage, Danielle. He and his brother used a baseball bat."

Benji was shaking his head and looking around, but he didn't
say anything. He moved like he was about to speak, but Chantel
blurted out, "He's got another girlfriend, Danielle. It's embarrassing."

I could say anything about the drugs and the fighting and
school, but I didn't know what to say about the other girlfriend,
about Louisa. I thought that Benji had even tried to mention her
a few times, but I ignored it, changed the subject, assured myself
that I was the chosen one. I'd watched a movie one night when
Benji was back home where a woman was having an affair with
a married man. I kept thinking how stupid she was to share her
man with someone else. I was convinced I wasn't sharing, though.
He was young, and Louisa was beautiful and pushy. I knew it was
her who kept things going, who flew into Georgia to see him, who
made him participate. He came to me by choice, because he loved
me, because I was important.

"This," I said angrily, "is the most important thing in my life
right now. Ever."

"Oh, stop it, Danielle!" My mother's face was flashing red from beneath her foundation. "Just stop it." She turned again to Benji, who had his hands in his pockets and an oddly serene look on his face.

"He isn't some thing I shuffle around where I want him to go," I began.

"Obviously," Chantel said crossly.

"I don't even know what to do about this. He has to go home, right now," my mother said. "We can drive him, but then the bike's gonna be down here. You could probably fit it in the back of that monstrosity you're driving, so maybe you can take it back to Pressville at some point. I don't really know what to do. He has to get out of here now." She turned to him. "My daughter is not going to jail with you."

"Ma'am—" Benji began.

"I am not asking," my mother said sternly. "Danielle, you stay here or you... I don't know. Jesus, what would Cady Benson say about this?"

"What?" I shouted. That was the final straw. "Who cares about her? Are you serious? We don't even know them. And I have to go to New York this weekend," I told her sharply. I looked at Benji. "I'm sorry. I have a job up there. Grace is insisting. It's really good money—"

"Good. Go. Go now, for God's sake. Jesus. And I care about Cady Benson. I really put myself out there so you could be friends with her, and now this."

"Yeah, what the hell was that about you feeding her dying dad? Mrs. Charity over here." I was scowling and sounded angrier than I was, even though I was mad. My mother had gone on do-gooder streaks before. She made pies for the Habitat for Humanity crew working down the road in Culver and kept stray animals in our basement after the shelter flooded. I could remember one Christmas when she made us give her all our socks so she could donate them to the sock drive in Putney. Nothing lasted very long but she was fiercely committed, if only for brief periods.

"You were alone in New York City, and she's a police officer!" A gray cast passed over her face.

"She doesn't know about this," I said. "Not that I have anything to hide."

"She wouldn't believe it if I told her. And no, maybe you don't, but he does."

I was only half listening and pushed my way through the kitchen to reach for Benji, but my mother halted me with a chop of her arm. "No, absolutely not. Get in the car, Benji. There's probably a warrant out for him right now. Danielle—you just have no idea..."

Benji went with Chantel after a few moments of standing off rather dramatically with my mother. His face was stern and his breath tight. She was sweating; I could see her makeup running a little when I got close to her. It was only February and still cold; it was her worry that was heating her so, like an oven of distress set to broil. "You stay here or go back to work or whatever, but do not contact that boy again. This is done. There's probably drugs in the apartment now."

"What about his bike?" I said.

"Forget about the bike. I'm going to get your father to come down with his truck. You are not to have another thing to do with him, do you hear me? Jesus, we should never have let you go to New York." She shook her head. "You were far too young for a place like that. Messed with your head. I don't even recognize you. What could you possibly be thinking—and, Danielle, Chantel is right. He has another little girlfriend. He is just using you for... Well, I don't even want to say. And he's probably selling drugs down here. You're too stupid to see that, but he's coming down here to sell drugs. I'd bet the farm." She walked out of my apartment with a bang of the door, and it was only then that I noticed she'd brought me flowers. They were lying in their paper wrapping on my kitchen table. It was a beautiful bouquet.

29

Cady came to the house, as I had anticipated she would. "I'm sure you know why I'm here." Same snug button-up and wide-ankle trousers. Her gun belt was visible this time, no blazer over the top. Her badge was fastened to the side of the belt and also perfectly visible at its slight tilt. She hadn't bothered with the belt the last time she came to the door. I had to suppose today would be different.

"You want to talk to the girls?" I opened the front door wider. "Why's it always raining when you're around?"

"No," she said, resting her thumbs in the belt that had commanded all my attention. I couldn't stop staring at her waist. "We believe we've identified the body."

"Are bones a body?" I asked, not insincerely.

"Yes. Human remains." She took an audible breath and waited.

"Okay." I nodded, trying not to hear the sound of Benji's

motorcycle on the turn. It had such a roar to it. I could still vibrate down to the roots of my teeth if I wasn't careful. He always got going too fast on Bell Road. He liked a good lean and a downturn with his leg, making a triangle with the bike for balance. I'd hung on with a death grip, my insides in a swirl that shot straight down from my head. I closed my eyes and didn't open them again until I heard Cady Benson talking.

"...Louisa Radcliffe..." There was more said, but I'd heard all I needed to.

I could feel my head nodding. My mouth was clenched shut, kept that way with heavy wire I'd had running through my skull for almost twenty years. Louisa Radcliffe.

"Obviously, we're still waiting, but there is some—"

"Lou Lou."

Cady stopped talking abruptly. I wondered if I'd said something. I didn't think I'd spoken, but she looked surprised and like she was trying to figure how to address something delicate that had passed between us. "We don't know that yet, but that's why I wanted to talk to you. She was reported missing around that time, and—"

"They called her Lou Lou. Or...whatever—Claudia called her that sometimes." I reached for the door handle. "They've been looking for her forever." I moved like I was going to close the door. "Or I guess they gave up."

Cady put her hand out to stop it from shutting. "This is an ongoing investigation. We have not officially identified the body yet, but the dates add up. I'm going to need to talk to you, your parents…"

"Oh," I said, stepping back again. "So you know it's her, or you don't?"

"Preliminarily, we do. We are waiting on one more lab."

I heard Pamela call my name. She was complaining about Rose, who had apparently used her hairbrush without asking.

"What if it's not her?'

"It's her, Danielle."

30

I called Grace the evening after my mother kicked Benji out of my apartment and told her I could go to New York and that I would be back in the office the following week.

"Who is this?" was Grace's first response. She texted me a couple of hours later asking if I stole her sunglasses. I didn't respond.

It was strange to be back so soon. I'd been certain I would never model in New York again, and yet here I was a couple of months later. I saw Claudia at the fitting, where the first thing she said to me was that Louisa was out of town with her boyfriend. "You switched places," she said slyly.

"That's not her boyfriend," I said. The shame was set to kill me slowly, death by a thousand cuts of quiet indignity.

My father had gone down to Atlanta and got Benji's motorcycle the day after my mother showed up unannounced. I saw him in the parking lot as I was taking out the trash. He smiled at me and waved from his truck, but when I tried to approach him, he rolled down the window and said he was in a big hurry.

"Can't talk, Danielle. I have to be at work by noon, so I need to get back on the road. Don't worry." He smiled again, only this time it was a sadder smile. I saw Benji's prized possession rattling around in the bed of my dad's truck as he pulled out of the lot and felt strangely sorry for it. I didn't talk to Benji for several days after my mother skirted him away in her minivan. No one answered the phone at the Law house when I called. I'd sent him an email asking about Louisa, but he didn't respond. I told myself he didn't email much, which was true, but I knew he checked it. They had a computer and internet at the Shell.

I'd tried asking Chantel if she'd seen him. She told me to call a psychotherapist.

"He's a junior in high school, Danielle. Get over it."

I finally got him on the phone before I left New York. I'd only been there a few days, but it felt like an eternity. The job Grace had lined up for me was for a catalog and required a lot of pinning fabrics and messing with the part in my hair.

He picked up after the third ring. I'd been just about certain it was going to go to the answering machine again—Benji's sister's voice telling me to leave a message. "Hello?"

"It's Danielle."

"Oh, hey." I could hear a faucet running and a TV in the background.

I waited, but he said nothing. "So…" I waited again.

"What's goin' on?"

"You haven't called me," I said.

The sink stopped running. I could still hear the TV. "I just thought I needed to leave you alone or whatever…" he said.

"Benji, please." I was rubbing my eyes and pulling at the ends of my hair. I saw that I'd smudged my eye makeup and was annoyed—another hour in the chair getting that fixed.

Benji sighed, his breath hitting the phone. It was a sad breath, the kind that indicates the person breathing is trying their hardest not to confirm that the rumors are true. "Danielle, I don't know what to say."

"Are you with Louisa now? Were you just coming down to see me when she wasn't around?"

"I'm not with anybody," he said impatiently. "I was never with you, Danielle. I'm not…like…'with people'. I'm just some kid from Pressville."

"Stop saying my name over and over." It was really the way he kept saying "with" that was bothering me and not my name. That, and his constant reference to being a kid from Pressville, like I didn't know where he was from.

"Sorry. Okay."

"Were you fucking her in my apartment in New York?"

"What? No." I could tell he was moving. His footsteps echoed on the Laws' buckled flooring. There was the faint sound of a hinge creaking and the television booming completely muffled. I figured he was in the hallway where the bedrooms sat. He and Blake shared a filthy bathroom. I could remember the first time going to their house and seeing the mold ring in the toilet and the mildew-covered shower curtain with rusted hooks holding it to a plastic rod. The bath mat had crusted edges, and none of the towels looked like they'd been washed in a month. The Laws' kitchen had a similar grimy layer. I was never very comfortable eating there. The forks and knives sat in a naked drawer that was filled with food crumbs and sometimes a few small hairs that I tried not to notice. That was not how I grew up. Not how Louisa grew up. She was pretending too.

"So you fucked her in the guy from Seattle's apartment?"

"Huh?"

I rolled my eyes, more at myself than Benji. There was an edge to me that I couldn't file down, a jagged nail that finds a place to get caught—over and over again, like the whole world was made of dangling threads.

"We don't fuck, Danielle." There he was with that tone and my name again. "We're friends, and she's not obsessed with controlling me like you. I don't really want to talk to you anymore, Danielle. I'm gettin' tired of feeling bad all the time, like I don't think I did anything wrong. You're not my mom or something. It's fun when we hang out, but you always need something from me."

There was a click, and I thought for a second he'd hung up

on me. My eyes went wide, the most furious hammer of sorrow smashing down on me at a bad angle, leaving my head stuck at ass level for the rest of my life.

"You there?" he said.

"Yes." I was crying now. All I could think about was how awful I must look. I was glad I was alone, but I would have to go back into the shoot any second and try to be presentable again. I figured I could say my dog died or something.

"Awwww, Danielle. I don't want to make you cry. See, this makes me feel real bad. Danielle?"

"Sorry," I said. "I'm sorry, Benji. I don't know what I was thinking. I don't know why…"

"It's fine. Like, see, that's the thing—I still want to see you all the time and hang out and talk and all that, but I'm not real serious or anything. I don't know how to be serious about this stuff. I don't want to make you cry. I really don't. I'm just not gonna always do what you want. I can't."

"But you're doing what Louisa wants."

"She doesn't want anything 'cept someone to have fun with. She doesn't even know what she wants. She's not like you."

"Will I ever see you again?" was all I could think to say.

"You can see me any time you want."

He shouldn't have said that. That really was the wrong thing to say.

3 1

2019

I was in Cady's office. She'd closed the door behind her. We were not in one of those interrogation rooms like I'd seen in movies but a regular office with a chipped and peeling desk, an old phone the color of Dijon mustard, and several empty foam coffee cups scattered about. "Sorry for the mess," she said as she sat down. She tended to something on her computer, then turned to me.

"Is there anything you want to tell me?"

"I'm sorry?"

"This is an active investigation, Danielle."

"Okay." I wasn't sure what she wanted me to say. "It's Louisa, isn't it?"

"It is Louisa. The dental records are a match. It took a while to get them, but yes. It's her. Is there anything you want to tell me?"

32

I flew home to Georgia without telling anyone I was coming and took a painfully expensive cab ride to my parents' house. I'd left my rambling wreck at my apartment and would have been happy to never see it or Paige's place ever again. I didn't even thank the cab driver, who was confused about where we were and probably wondering if it was worth it to drive off the edge of the world like that for a few extra bills. I thought to suggest he go down to the movie theater parking lot, because sometimes people took cabs from the bar that was next to the theater, but I didn't feel like talking, so I slammed the door in his face and walked up the front steps to my parents' house.

"Hello!" I yelled upon entering. It was about seven at night and still dark. March had not brought on any evening light as of yet. "Hello!"

My mother came out of the kitchen. "Jesus, you scared me. What are you doing home? Are you okay?"

"Like you would care," I said.

"I do care." She was holding a batter-covered spoon. A drop fell on the floor. She noticed it but did nothing. I was reminded of Grace with her cigarette ash. "You just didn't tell us you were coming home." She was in her robe with her night cream already applied. She put extra at the corners where she had crow's-feet. I could see it caked there, melting into the crevices, leaving a white residue—like hardened frosting.

"Do I have to tell you I'm coming? Am I not welcome here?"

"I just didn't know you were coming," she repeated. It had already been established that I wasn't welcome. "I figured you'd go back to your place."

"Well, I'm here, and I'm not leaving."

"Okay." She shrugged. "I'm making a cake, so…" She turned on her heel, noticing the batter on the floor, and went back into the kitchen.

"Don't act happy to see me or anything!" I called after her.

She came back to the hallway entrance to face me where I still stood in the foyer. "I am happy to see you, Danielle."

"You didn't even hug me."

"Okay." She put the spoon down on the counter in the kitchen after a moment of deliberation as to what to do and hurried over to me. I was crying now, suddenly aware of it and trying to stop the flow. "What's wrong?" she asked, reaching out.

"Benji's run off with some other girl."

"Oh God," she said, annoyed and even less welcoming. "Danielle, please."

"What? You don't care now that it's because of Benji? That doesn't matter? If it's him, then you don't care. I get it."

"I do care, but I also don't want you to waste another second of your life pining after…after some redneck kid! You just got back from New York, for God's sake! And Paris before that! I have never been to Paris and will probably never get to go. Do you know how many people would love to see all these places, once—just once— before they die, and you're there and everywhere else all the time, jetting off with all this money, getting to live in New York City. We live in Pressville, Georgia! There's not even a Target here. Come on, Danielle! Can't you just enjoy your life? He is not that important… He's sixteen years old!"

"I don't want to enjoy it," I said.

"No, I don't think you do." She finally hugged me with certainty. We stood there together for a long time until my father came downstairs, wet from his shower and surprised to see me.

"Oh, hey, Danielle," he said. "I didn't know you were coming home. What's wrong?"

"No one loves me." I was weeping.

When we were kids, my dad used to say that the weeping willows on Lake Murphree missed their children, so they cried. Their seeds were scattered to the wind, some ending up at the bottom of the lake, never to be seen nor heard from again. The trees grew straight up into the air, their branches shooting out to the sides like helicopter wings, until the day their seeds left and never came back. Then they collapsed with grief. I was a willow; my baby was gone, going to grow in someone else's soil.

"I love you," my father said. "I love you so much, Danielle."

"We're not enough," my mother answered.

Chantel was with a friend that night—unusual for her—and the twins were at the neighbor's, so my parents and I had the house to ourselves. My mother had been making the cake for a party with her book club friends but said she could make another one and allowed my father and me to eat the batter with spoons. "What if we get salmonella?" he asked, sticking his finger in the mix.

"You're going to have to die eventually... That's as good a way as any," my mother answered. We watched a movie on television, complaining about the number of commercial breaks, and went to bed around eleven. I couldn't sleep and heard Chantel come in at midnight. I could tell she was having a snack in the kitchen. The sound of cracker-crunching reverberated off the walls of the downstairs and through the vents up into my bedroom. I rolled around in my bed, wondering what Benji was doing. I was so close to him, but I didn't know how to reach him. In every fantasy I entertained, he kept disappearing without a moment's notice.

The following morning I was in a slightly better mood. The

trees on the ridge were blooming early because of a warm spell, their buds like small grains of rice about to be split, then unfurled, revealing secrets they'd kept all winter while they played dead, scared-possum trees. Everything else woke up with them, too, and the gully to the back of the house vomited noise with the flutter of every type of wing, the scurry of every type of foot, and the scattering of every type of peace I could not find. It would go cold again, and all this would cease, backpedal, retreat—but for a moment, it felt like I was going to make it after all.

My revelations were interrupted when I came upon Chantel in the kitchen. Gone were the crackers from the night before. She was fixing a sandwich. "What are you doing here?" I asked. Her face indicated she had been thinking something similar about me.

"I come here for lunch," she said.

"Oh. Is this closer to the library than your place?" I asked.

"No, I don't work at the library anymore. I work for the paper."

"Oh, that's right. Where are their offices?"

"Oh, come on, Danielle," she said. "You know you don't care." She sat down at the table with what looked like a BLT and began to eat.

"Is there more bacon?" I asked.

"Nope," she said before opening a magazine that my mother had left and turning the pages slowly.

"God, I hate this place sometimes," I said before going up to my room. Gone was the sheen of the morning, and in its place was

Chantel. I don't know why we didn't get along better. She always did seem out to get me, with her aggressively plain outlook.

I called Benji's house, but no one answered. I knew I shouldn't be trying to get in touch with him, but I had convinced myself that I just wanted to finalize things, tie it up and ship it off. I wanted to feel better about everything, and for that reason, I was going to need to see him. Having made the decision that it was best if Benji and I got together at least one more time, I needed a car. I wasn't going to be able to invite him over to the house; I honestly thought if I did that, my mother would ask me to leave and never come back.

I went to my parents' room to find my mother organizing her closet. She turned to look at me. "Can I borrow your car?" I asked.

"For what?" she said. "And where's your car, anyway?"

"It's back at the apartment. I hate driving it. It's too big, and... I don't know. I just wanted to come home." She wouldn't understand that the apartment, the car, everything in Atlanta had been tainted now. When she and Chantel showed up with their guns blazing, they had cast a spell over the new life I was trying to make there.

"You're going to have to go get it at some point. Anyway. Where are you going?" She laid a sweater on the bed in front of her. "Do you want this?" she asked. It was a gold color, with large pockets on the front and what looked like some sort of ruffle on the back.

"No, I don't think so," I said.

"Where are you going?" she asked again.

"I don't know...just out."

"Don't go within a mile of that Law boy, Danielle. Just don't."

I didn't answer but picked the sweater up off the bed. "Have you ever even worn this?"

"I wear it all the time," she said. "Or I used to. You haven't really been around, so..."

"No, I guess not."

I took her keys and drove to Arby's, where I got a Jamocha milkshake and a Beef 'n Cheddar. I was in the middle of telling the girl who took my order over the speaker system in the drive-through that they didn't have Arby's in New York when she cut me off and told me my total. "Thanks," I said, pulling forward.

I ate my sandwich in the parking lot with the windows down. It was chilly, but I liked the sound of the birds. I was within a mile of the Shell station but couldn't be sure if Benji was there. I drove by, with the van's sun visor pulled low in a half-baked attempt to remain undetected. Benji's and Blake's motorcycles were parked out front. I didn't see Blake; I figured he was still in jail. I pulled in the parking lot and found a spot away from the pumps. A couple of seconds later, I saw Benji walking around with a cigarette in his mouth. He turned around at the sound of the van and saw me. I opened the door and got out, taking a few steps toward him. He smiled at first, then made a curious face that was somewhere between troubled and amused. I thought he might laugh, but he walked over with very serious steps instead.

"Hey," he said, like I was someone he knew from playing ball. "You're home?"

"Surprised?" I asked. I wanted to reach out and pull him close to me, but instead I stood still and waited.

"Yeah," he said before stomping his cigarette out on the ground. "Can we go somewhere?"

"I don't know, Danielle."

"What? You scared he'll tell Louisa?" I nodded at the guy behind the register, who'd come outside and was watching us with a squint. I felt conspicuous and small inside my mother's van. I was trying to be funny. He did not laugh.

"It's just not a good idea anymore," he said, looking around. "When did you even get here? I didn't know you were coming home."

"So that's it? Because it's hard?"

He frowned. "It's not hard," he said with a little edge, like maybe he was making fun of me. "It's... I just..." He paused again. "I just don't want to anymore." He looked at me close. There was something new here, something between us that was leaking out like a thick syrup all over our feet, making it hard to walk. The stench of disapproval was around our heads, slowly flowing down our necks like hair.

"Okay," I said, touching my mouth. "Okay." I walked the few steps back to my mother's minivan and got in. Benji did not try to follow and said nothing more to me. I could barely get the car in gear to back up, I was so dumbfounded, but I managed. He turned around and walked inside the gas station. His head was low, the hair at the base of his neck a little shaggy. I knew I would never touch his neck again. I could tell by the way the ripple left my skin. I was plain and blank; there was no longer a rock in my stream to direct my flow. I went down without interruption.

I drove straight home, having nowhere else to go. When I got there, I went out to our back deck, which was nothing more than a few pieces of weathered wood and latticework that none of us ever visited. There was a single plastic lawn chair there for a person to sit but otherwise nothing except the remnants of old dirt, disintegrating gumballs from the sweet gum tree to the porch's left, and some splintered pieces of wood that had come up from years, lack of use, and the weather. It was a lonely place to sit, but I had the ridge for company. It had always been there, lurking like a shy friend who can't make the first move. Too steep for us to have really played there, it had served as a reminder of what all of Pressville must once have looked like, land on a decline. What goes up, must come down—including moods. I didn't think I would ever feel right again. I watched a solitary bird, brown with a gray breast, make his way from limb to limb with only a small flutter of his wings. His head jerked from left to right, up and down, like the top of a pen being clicked over and over. There was simply nothing else to do. I would have to watch the birds.

After a while, I heard movement inside the house. My mother

had still been upstairs when I got home and hadn't come down when I walked through the kitchen to get to the back porch. I heard my father remove his boots at the front door like he always did. My mother liked a clean house; she, like my grandmother, was not very outdoorsy and preferred to keep what was out out and what was in wiped down. I think that was why the deck was so neglected—my mother had no interest in watching the birds. She entered the kitchen, muttering in frustration like she always did when tending to things in the house, which all needed more tending than she was able to give. My dad talked to my mother for a bit. I could hear small tidbits of their conversation, which included my father telling my mother that he'd seen her van at the Arby's "right across from the Shell where the Law kids are always running around... Did Danielle go over there and see that kid?"

I breathed heavily. I stood and opened the door to the kitchen but did not step inside. "It's over!" I stood next to the door with my hand on the knob.

My father looked at me. He was next to my mother, by the refrigerator. Their expressions were weary. "Okay," he said.

"Yeah, that's exactly what I said."

33

2019

Leigh was the first to say she was having nightmares. Rose quickly followed suit, and then the rest of the girls. "Really bad," Rose said. "It's because of the dead body."

"Right, but the body is not there anymore," I said. They were doing a weeklong ballet camp, though none of them had expressed any interest in ballet. We were in the car, en route.

Tessa was the most excited to be doing something, even if it was ballet. She admitted to me that she felt neglected because she was one of the kids in her class who didn't do "activities." I suppose she thought ballet camp would mean she no longer fit into that category—a neglected child with no activities. I told her I was sorry that I was lazy. The ballet camp had been Jasper's idea. His mother had also expressed some concern that the girls didn't do anything. I wasn't sure what they were supposed to do, exactly.

I'd had my turn signal on for at least five minutes. "What's that sound?" It was Leigh.

"It's footsteps," Rose whispered. I glanced in the rearview. She was pale, wan, alert.

"What?"

"That's the girl walking in our house."

"What is?" I was getting annoyed. We were behind a landscaping truck that was taking its time making the tight right turn. "Good Lord, get outta the way!" I hissed at the back bumper. "Come on."

"Are we going to be late?" Tessa asked.

"She's walking on her high heels. Tick tock, tick tock," Leigh said.

"Stop!" I turned to look over my shoulder. "What are you even talking about?"

"It's that thing!" Tessa was sitting in the passenger seat and pointed at the steering wheel.

"Oh." I flicked the signal bar back to its home position. "Sorry... But what are you talking about, the dead girl in the house?"

"The girl. Who died," Rose whispered forcefully.

"She's not in our house," I said.

"But she was."

We pulled up at the community center parking lot. There was a small line of cars weaving in and out of cones. "Girls..." I said, not sure if I should park and walk them in.

"Mom." Leigh sounded frustrated. She'd grabbed her bag and had her hand on the door handle. "Let us out."

"Just a second—wait," I said, tapping the brake a little too heavily. I'd stopped halfway between the drop-off zone and the lot. Someone behind me honked. "Okay, okay." I held up my hand.

"Can we get out?" Pamela was right behind Leigh. She'd packed her own lunch. I'd tried not to oversee the process, but I was pretty sure all that was in there was Nilla Wafers and string cheese.

"There is no one in our house," I said firmly.

"No, I know she's not there now," Leigh said, "but she was. Before she died." She spoke as if trying to explain oxygenation to a first grader. "She was there before she got killed."

"No," I said. The person behind me honked again before accelerating around my van with a roar. It was Cricket Matthews. I'd apologize later; she was always a bit of a hothead, anyway. "No, there was never anyone in the house." My mind rolled over itself and onto Benji, who could fill my head even this long after. It was because of the violent death. My mother said that a violent death makes spirits more pernicious. You grow more troubled over time instead of less; the thought of them becomes increasingly wicked. That was why she and my father wanted to move out of the house. I could remember her pleading face.

"It won't bother you," my mother said to me. She was talking about the spirits. "They're not after you."

She'd changed the day of the accident—irrevocably. She said

a lot of strange things after Benji died on Bell Road: some made me mad, some were mildly comforting, some were incoherent. "They'll leave you alone now," she told me right after it happened, like we were glad to be rid of Benji. Finally. As though I, too, would be relieved; she certainly appeared to be. My one true love was nothing more than a thorn in her side, some fractious issue she kept having to deal with, over and over, and now he was gone. "They'll leave you alone now," she repeated.

But it wasn't that—this expectation that I agreed he'd been nothing but trouble. She should have said he'll leave you alone. It dawned on me only now, in the parking lot at ballet camp. She should have said he'll leave you alone. It was an important detail.

34

I told Grace I was sick and would be gone for another week. She didn't seem to care and said she might close the office for a few days anyway so that she could cleanse her aura.

I didn't hear from anyone that Louisa was in Pressville. Rather, I felt it. One morning I woke up and knew that she had arrived. The air had changed. Every clatter from a dropped fork in the kitchen; every slap from a sandal on the hollow, wooden steps; every motor on the road had an eerie power to it that had not been there before. I was hearing as if through amplifiers.

I didn't leave the house much, so even after a few days of firmly believing that his motorcycle was heavier on the road—I couldn't possibly say whether any of the motorcycles I heard were Benji's, but I was convinced that there was one, one very specific bike that was tearing into the asphalt with malicious fury. There were two people on it. I knew the sound of two people. I waited by the front window sometimes, hoping to catch a glimpse of them, or maybe to prove to myself that Louisa was not in Pressville and that all was not lost. I never saw him. I would say that later with certainty. No. I did not see him on Bell Road.

"Have you seen Benji?" I asked Chantel, because I knew she nearly hated me and would want me to know upsetting information that might cause me pain. She was out and about each day with her job and her endless errands. She did seem to have friends too; I recognized some of the names from school but had to wonder who everyone else she talked about was. I had a hard time imagining people moving to Pressville and then striking up a friendship with Chantel, of all people. They did things like go to the bookstore together and have girls' night, during which they painted wineglasses and ate cheese platters from the grocery store.

"I don't think he dates, 'cause he's, like, a high school dropout with an illegal motorcycle who's wanted by the police." Chantel paused for effect. "But yeah, there was some girl here with him for a while. I don't think she lives here, though—or I don't really know. He's on that bike all the time. She was with him. I've seen them." She was matter-of-fact about it, and I knew it brought her great pleasure. She was home for lunch again. I thought to ask her why she was eating my parents out of house and home just to save money when she knew full well they didn't have any either.

"Yeah," I answered. We looked at one another but did not speak about it again. Chantel came for dinner that night too. I'd noticed a pattern—Sundays and Tuesdays and almost every other day for lunch. She was too frequently at the house. It didn't seem healthy.

My mother would sometimes make a remark about Chantel to no one in particular. "I do wish she'd date and not count on me and Dad to be her dinner company." Then she'd look down and away, realizing perhaps that I was the only one listening and that she could say the same about me now.

Dinner was always some strange combination that spoke of the Great Depression or the Dust Bowl—some flaccid-looking sausages and plain noodles with canned peas on the side. I tried not to turn my nose up at the spreads while my father would remark, "Delicious!" and have three helpings.

It was over these dinners that I made some casual remarks about going back to New York instead of Atlanta, to which my mother sighed exasperatedly. "You just moved to Atlanta. You hardly even worked for that woman and now you're going to quit and move again?"

"Todd says I can stay with him in the city. I would save money," I said.

"Who's Todd? The actor from England? Well, he's just about as useless as an eleventh toe, isn't he?" My mother rolled her eyes. "You have a real job in Atlanta. I think that's better, don't you? You can't just stay here or stay in New York or... You have to work wherever you live."

A strong, punitive silence fell over the table, and I put my fork down loudly. "I'm really sorry," I said, but even as the words came out of my mouth, I knew they weren't true.

"We know you are, sweetie," my father said, reaching over to pat my back.

I didn't leave Pressville immediately, and I should have. All that followed could have been avoided if I'd just gone back the next day or even the day after that. I received a message from Claudia that evening. She wanted to know if I was going to see Louisa while she was in town. I wrote back, I'm in Georgia. What do you mean?

A few minutes passed, and she replied, She's in Georgia with him. She's there now.

Claudia was making sure I wasn't surprised if I ran into Louisa. Her text came well after office hours and probably after some pensive drinking with her boyfriend—a Bosnian power broker turned chef named Igor. She wanted me to know what I was in for. I assumed Louisa confided in her; we all did. I responded, Thanks...I promise I won't kill her.

I couldn't sleep that night again and went downstairs at two a.m. to watch television. My mother was awake and at the kitchen table with a magazine and some Cheez-Its in a small bowl. She smiled when she saw me. "I always wake up about this time," she said. My mother loved magazines and had quite a collection. We all grew up perusing them from time to time. Thoughts of my mother always include a periodical.

"I don't," I said. "I'm afraid I'm going to do something stupid."

"Oh, well, that's nothing to be afraid of..." She laughed a little.

"No—really stupid."

"Well, don't, please. Your father and I don't want any more to answer for."

"You won't have to answer for anything," I said.

"We always do, Danielle. We're your parents."

35

2019

There was wind that day. Not a breeze, but wind. The trees bent, their thin branches like the threads of a pom-pom being shaken in enthusiastic anticipation. I shivered while looking out the front window.

"If you're cold, turn the air-conditioning off," Jasper said. I hadn't heard him come in over the whir of the unit. We had one in our bedroom too. Jasper said I was obsessed with air-conditioning. He liked to accuse me of being obsessed with things. It was clearly something he saw as a weakness. He was taking a few more days off because of the body. And the investigation, which he thought might continue, grow, morph. *Morph* was the word he used.

We'd had a conversation about it the night before. Our first real conversation. Jasper didn't go in for a proper discourse often. He liked to talk around things so he could think about business and home repairs. It was like I'd married my childhood. He wasn't my father; he was a shadow of the inner workings of our house, the thing slinking in and out of the room when my family was together. Most of adulthood, as I understood it so far, was pretending to care deeply about inanimate objects and worrying about your children and their ability to purchase inanimate objects in the future. That was what Jasper went in for—this type of adulthood. I was on the fringes. Now I was the shadow bouncing in and out of the rooms of our reality. Sometimes when I looked at the girls, I thought I was one of them. I could hardly claim ownership of anything, especially not with Jasper around. I'd granted him precious authority because I never felt worthy of making it out alive.

Jasper's sensitivity to the situation reminded me of how we originally met, what had brought us together. I had been having a good year and taking classes at the University of Georgia. It was some time after the accident. My parents were in the midst of renting the house out and buying a place a little outside of town, much smaller and with only one bathroom. It had a carport, though, which everyone thought was a vast improvement; no more parking in the rain.

It took me a while of doing courses online at the library, but I got my GED and was able to get into UGA. My mother said it was a miracle; I proved her right by doing a whole bunch of miraculously normal things like getting my associate's degree and meeting a fraternity boy. Jasper was there, in my merchandising course, wearing his hat backward with his burgeoning beer belly tipping over the edge of his frayed khaki shorts. He looked every bit what I should have

243

always wanted. It was like the modeling, New York, Benji—none of it ever happened. I could be a college girl from Pressville and have a boyfriend in Sigma Chi. And that was what I did. Jasper was never quite sure about the missing time in my life; I told him I'd modeled for "about five years" but not much else about why I was older and in undergraduate classes. He was on the six-year plan and making up for some missteps during his freshman year when we met. We looked through my modeling portfolio just once during those early years. He was impressed but mostly curious. It didn't seem to him it could be the same person. For me, it wasn't.

Now, with Cady Benson breathing down our necks and a stack of bones removed from the ridge, he was certain it hadn't been the same person. I could tell by the way he looked at me. He was trying to figure out how much he didn't know. I'd been hiding behind my apparent laziness and apathy for most of our marriage. I had long ago decided never to really care about anything again.

"I'm fine," I said. I wasn't talking about the air-conditioning unit but turned it off anyway. It was a habit to have it blasting.

"They called your parents," Jasper said. He was pretending to fold his clothes. He moved one oxford around while he laid the other on the bed.

"Those go on hangers," I said of his shirts. I was trying to ignore what he'd said about my parents. I didn't talk to them much. My mother was an expert at being unapproachably cheerful and passive with me. I asked Chantel if she thought Mom had changed.

She said I never really knew Mom. It was the final insult. I told Chantel she was a child who had always wanted our mom to love her more. I believed what I said.

"Because they're saying this had to do with the accident." Jasper wasn't going to let up.

I walked to the closet to get him a few hangers, annoyed that he'd ignored my comment. "I know that, Jasper. I've talked to Cady Benson."

"Right, but there are other people involved. It's not just Cady Benson. This isn't personal, Danielle. You always act like—"

"I don't always act like anything. She's the one who came to the house and she's the head of the police here, so that's all I'm saying."

"But they've got people here from the FBI and God knows what else. Your mom said they've had people at the house a few times."

I was trying to remain calm and look busy. I went to my underwear drawer and riffled through the rather uninspiring collection within. I made no effort when it came to lingerie, nighties, any of it. I thought if Jasper needed a little kick in the pants, he could look at some of my old modeling stuff. I'd done a hundred shoots in my underwear. I was done with all that.

"What do you want me to say, Jasper? You're...like...accusing me or something."

"I'm not accusing you of anything. I'm just wondering if there's something you need to tell me. Do I need to get the girls out of here?"

"What?" I dropped my hands to my thighs.

The kids were downstairs. They'd had the TV on, but now the house was quiet, peculiarly so, but I hadn't heard the front door open. We always went in and out the front—never the back, and never the basement. The stairs were too treacherous; they'd always been that way. "What do you mean, 'get them out of here'?"

"Danielle, someone is going to be arrested." Jasper leaned forward like he was addressing his clothing. "They were warning your parents."

I blinked, feeling strangely detached from this conversation and anyone it was about. "I certainly hope so."

"Danielle."

"Jasper." I flipped the air-conditioning back on.

"Is that really necessary?"

"I like it." I ran my hand over the vent.

"Well, I'm freezing. Can you go do your thing in the living room?"

I could only vaguely remember Jasper ever being in a really good mood. It had been before the girls. The crippling responsibility of five females to care for had diminished his ability to do anything joyfully. He was happy when they were born, but then each day after that was marred with the weight of their cost, the worry we would fail them, both the prestige of having so many people dependent on you and the commitment to pay for four future weddings—and of course, before that, their hormones and boyfriends, which were still distantly waiting for us, like the weddings. Jasper referenced paying for his daughters' weddings all the time. I suggested more than once that they might not marry or want a wedding. He was incredulous. What could I be thinking?

I'd introduced nothing but trouble, Jasper's sloped shoulders seemed to say. Danielle—the weight around his neck. He only took nibbles of responsibility for fathering the girls; the rest of the time, he lamented being so harnessed by duty. They were all my idea. That was true; Jasper had been ambivalent about children. That might actually have been his entire personality—ambivalence, followed by endless duty.

"I'm not going to be arrested, Jasper." I said after a long silence had rolled between us like a marble that would become lodged and forgotten in some dark corner of the room. "What do you think I did?" I asked the question while facing the vanity mirror. I could see him in its reflection. He sighed heavily like I'd asked him to plunge the toilet.

"It just sounds like they think something." Now he was pensive. He'd stopped folding his shirts. "Your mom says there's been a development."

"She's always on about something, isn't she?" I looked at Jasper in the mirror again.

It was Louisa. We all knew it was Louisa.

I didn't know what that had to do with my mother.

36

I'd seen Benji the day before on Forte Drive. I was in my mother's minivan again and both jerked my head to see him better and tried to duck in embarrassment. He'd been alone on his motorcycle, which was a relief. I don't know what I would have done if I'd seen Louisa with him.

And then I did see them—together, finally—at the Shell the following day. I figured Benji must have stopped by there to get some cash. Blake kept all the money they made and paid Benji only occasionally. I'd told Benji it wasn't a good arrangement and that he couldn't possibly know how much he was supposed to be making, but he said he didn't care while looking at me with mild disgust. "Money's not everything to me, Danielle." He said things like that often. Preoccupation with money was something I thought I'd inherited from my parents, but it might have grown from within me, an errant seed planted when I met Frank Dabney.

A girl should never be told she's that pretty—so pretty it's going to pay the bills.

With Blake in jail, though, who knows what he was doing there. Maybe it was God's way of making sure I knew, of making sure I couldn't lie to myself anymore, of making sure I saw it with my own two eyes. And I did. She looked just like me—on the back of the bike, wearing his sister's helmet.

For years, I would wonder what I could have done differently, how I could have changed the outcome. I think it's here that I should have done something else, anything other than what I did—which was nothing. I didn't call him, confront him, call Louisa, show up at the Laws' house, go back to my apartment in Atlanta—nothing. I sat in my parents' house, staring at the walls. My mother kept asking me if I was going to "pack up," meaning, When are you leaving?

"I'm waiting," I said every time.

"For what?"

"I don't know."

"Danielle."

The conversations all went like this. Round and round.

"You done enough feeling sorry for yourself today?" she asked over dinner one night.

"Not sure. You know I do a lot of feeling sorry for myself in Atlanta too? Would you prefer I did it there?"

"Why's that, sugar?" My father was getting sweeter with each passing day. He was worried, and the way he expressed it was to grow gentler. I was a pumpkin, sugar, honey, sweet girl—all sorts of things he only called me when his concern got the better of him. He'd done this in the beginning of the modeling adventure too. "That's some picture, little bit," he said of me in a thong and string-bikini top showing all the underside of my breasts.

"Well, at least you're getting paid in Atlanta," my mother said decisively. She was eager. I'd become a drain on the mood.

"I'm gonna stay a little longer." I pushed a piece of macaroni with my fork. My mother had made pasta salad to go with the barbecue sandwiches.

"You are." Her eyes widened; it was not a question. The twins were at cheer practice, having shown almost no interest in me since I'd arrived. Chantel had a date. My parents had been inordinately pleased to announce that she would not be coming for dinner so she could "go to Red Lobster with Tuck."

"Just a few more days."

"Why?" My mother put her own fork down.

"I just want a few more days." My breath was shallow. "I just—"

"This isn't about that kid, is it?" My mother leaned forward heavily. Her elbows slid on the table. "Danielle…is this about that kid?"

"No, but he's got… It's a long story. It's nothing. I think they're doing construction on my building or something. It's loud."

"Danielle." My mother stood up. Her chair screeched loudly

and tipped back before slamming down on the floor. "You are not staying here longer so you can sit around and pine after some sixteen-year-old drug dealer. I'm not going to allow that. I'll drive you back to Atlanta myself, but—I cannot for the life of me understand why you'd want to sit around here and sulk. Over a high school dropout."

"Okay," my father said, also standing. "Okay, then." I figured we were done with dinner, though I'd eaten very little. "Danielle, if you want to stay home because you just want to be home, then I understand—"

"No." My mother was as furious as the day she and Chantel had shown up in Atlanta. "No. You cannot stay here. I know he's got a new girlfriend or whatever it is, but you cannot stay here. It's done, and you are leaving. That's final. This is ridiculous! God, what I would do to make that kid go away, I can't even tell you." She stormed over to the sink with her dish and let it clatter in the drain. "I've had enough!" She walked out of the kitchen and stomped up the stairs. I heard the bedroom door slam; the entire house rattled along with the hinges.

My dad was silent. I thought he might be about to make a joke about things being serious, but he remained grim. "Danielle, she is right. This kid is bad news; you'll end up in trouble." He paused. "It's embarrassing, really." It was so unlike him to say something like that.

"Well, I'm sorry I embarrassed you."

"You didn't embarrass me." He left it at that. He was not talking about my mother either.

My dad and I cleaned up the kitchen together with the television going in the background. "I'll leave Friday." I spoke as if to an empty room. I think I was assuring myself that I was going to do the right thing.

I don't know if leaving any earlier would have changed things, but I do know if I hadn't been home brooding so much, the accident on Bell Road wouldn't have happened. It was caused by my listlessness and my waiting. You can't drive fast on Bell Road, and you can't wait for something to happen. It will happen.

37

2019

My mother called and asked if I wanted to go to lunch.

"Are you okay?" I hadn't said yes or no yet.

"I'm fine, but I want to talk to you."

I exhaled into the receiver.

"You know what this is about, Danielle."

"I didn't do anything," I said. I felt fifteen years old, lying about breaking the globe on the mantel. I hadn't broken it, but no one believed me. I ended up having to use my allowance money—paltry, to say the least—to pay for its replacement. I never could figure out why my parents wanted a globe; they certainly weren't interested in going anywhere. "I'm not worried about this," I said.

"You should be."

"Mom…"

Now my mother exhaled. "I know you didn't do anything, but there is new information, and I am concerned. The new information… I think we should meet before they identify the body."

"They think it's Louisa," I said. "She went missing about that time."

"Right."

"You remember that, right? The model girl from Kentucky. She was here, then she left, and no one knew what happened to her."

"I remember."

The girls were at the neighbor's house, a family with three daughters. I had to drive them because there was no way to walk anywhere, especially not on Bell Road. We considered anyone who lived in Fisher Forest to be a neighbor. It was the only neighborhood within a mile, and a small one at that. Our house was so isolated that it turned boring and stale by midsummer, sometimes by midweek during the school year. I'd never been good at occupying children. I leaned on the television and food. The older they got, the more interested in the woods they'd become, but that was now over. They would not explore the ravine again; bones will do that to you.

I hadn't realized I wasn't answering my mother. I'd been thinking about Fisher Forest and how normal it seemed to live there. My mother's family's house on Bell Road was an outlier, an oddity in Pressville. I hadn't particularly liked growing up there, and now I was raising my children in the same fugue-like state somewhere between town and the wilderness, halfway up a steep hill that led nowhere in either direction. "What?" I said. My mother was talking quickly, hurriedly, urgently.

"I'm wondering... What I'm wondering is..."

"Mom, spit it out. Jeez."

"What I'm wondering is—you see, maybe that girl was on the motorcycle. With Benji."

"But she left. Everyone said she left. Anyway, there were people who saw him riding that day. He was alone." We'd been through this. There was an investigation then, a long one. It was like torture. I could remember shaking violently when the police first showed up. The fire trucks arrived shortly after. It was blue lights first; that, I remember clearly. We heard it, then the fire; then they evacuated us because it had been dry. They were worried about the house. It wasn't Cady Benson then. She came later, but it was an accident. There was nothing to investigate at the time other than how the bike went off the road. She wasn't that kind of detective. I did wonder how she'd ended up running the case. It made my mother nervous; I do remember that. My mother wrung her hands about Cady Benson looking into the accident.

"Danielle..." My mother was urgent again. "Are you listening to me?"

"I am," I lied. A car came down the hill in front of the house. A lot of the time, we could smell brakes or even tire tread being left behind. If you were going down, it tilted to the left; if you were going up, you leaned right.

"I think maybe she was on the motorcycle."

"Yes." I wasn't sure what I was agreeing to.

"Can you come over?"

"Mom—why do I need to come over? I don't know anything more about it." I was irritated, having enjoyed my solitary confinement in the quiet house. I had nothing to do and nowhere to go. Jasper was at work and the girls up the street. It was unusual to be this alone.

"I'm worried they're listening on the phone."

"Who?" I almost shouted. "Come on, this is Pressville! They are not listening on the phone—and Cady Benson already told me it's Louisa. Anyway, I have to go get the girls in a little bit."

"Where are they? The girls." My mother sounded like a wood chipper. Her voice was staccato and vicious, louder than normal. She had become quieter as she'd gotten older, a kind of wallflower grandmother who occasionally visited with the kids, bringing them hair bows and coloring books and asking them about their teachers. They didn't know the Deb I'd grown up with. I considered it a loss for them, but she had changed after the accident. Her whirling-dervish style was supplanted with a nervous intensity that, although seemingly calm, put everyone else around her on edge. She changed, and then my parents moved; that was what followed the accident. My mother had always been Deb Greer who lived in the giant old house on Bell Road. Then she became a lady who lived on Fullham. Sometimes I longed to be a lady who lived on Fullham, but I was now the Greer who lived in the giant old house on Bell Road.

"At the Hoffmans.'"

"Oh." My mother had never liked the Hoffmans. "I've never liked the girls playing over there."

"They hardly ever play over there," I said.

"Can we meet somewhere?"

"Mom, please. I have a headache. I don't want to meet anywhere. I'm going to hang up now. Don't worry."

"Danielle!"

I nearly dropped the phone. "What is it?" My hands and under-arms were sweaty. I thought of standing in front of the window unit for a while. "What is it?"

"Danielle, you need to prepare yourself. I think Jasper and the kids should go stay with his family for a while. I don't think they should be there."

I could hear my pulse, throbbing in my ears. "I don't know what you're talking about."

"I think you need to be prepared."

38

2004

Claudia emailed me two nights before I was set to go back to Atlanta. I'd told Grace I would be in the following week. My mother said she'd never heard of any job where a person could just come and go as they pleased and that I should be counting my lucky stars.

Louisa is gone again. No trace. Is she still in Georgia? Can you call the boy? Can you go over there? Have you seen her?

The last few messages I'd received from Claudia before this had been almost friendly—kind, even. She and I had never had a particularly warm relationship. It was probably me. For some reason, that wasn't what I thought I was supposed to do; I thought I was supposed to be snarky and tough around her, and if she was going to be nice, she did it with such an artificial flair that I never took too seriously.

"No" was all I wrote back.

A friend, Millie Malcom, who was also with my agency, had called me a couple of days earlier to tell me there were rumors that Claudia was sick again. "Like the same kind of sick or...?" I asked. I was in my room, going through my high school yearbooks. There were only three because I'd skipped out on the last year. When I looked at my junior year photo, I wondered who could have seen anything special in me at all. I was gangly, awkward, slouched, and naive. I don't know why I thought I had to have an edge. My complete lack of sophistication had been part of the original appeal, though you could never have convinced me of that.

"It spread," Millie answered. She was more or less warning me. "She's in bad shape. I'm not sure when you last saw her, but it's not good. They're saying she's going to step down." Millie was someone I'd come through the ranks with. She grew up on a ranch in Texas. She wore cowboy hats to castings and only ate red meat, citing its health benefits. I wanted to be like her when I grew up, even though I was older. She never seemed as affected by the oddities of her lifestyle. She could put it on and take it off. I was not the same. Frank Dabney had defined me before I'd even had a chance to make up my mind about who I wanted to be.

"That's sad," I said. I meant it. I couldn't imagine Claudia not booking models, talking about booking models, thinking about it, tapping away at her computer, shouting in her fake accent across the office's polished floors. She didn't have another dimension; she was only Claudia from Lawton. That was the saddest part, to have no more to you than a thing you did for money. It was the tree I'd been barking up too.

"And anyway, I don't know if you heard, but Louisa Radcliffe is missing again," Millie interrupted my thoughts. "Vanished."

"She wasn't missing before. She went to Mexico. But yes, I heard."

"No, like no one's heard from her in ten days or something. Her parents are in New York. The police were at her apartment."

"She was just here," I said.

"Right, but I guess that kid…or the boyfriend, or—"

"Yeah, she's seeing a guy here."

"Right." Millie knew. Everyone did. "I guess he said she left."

"Sounds serious," I said, closing the yearbook. I'd been lying on my stomach on the bed and now pushed myself up and off. I looked around my room, feeling both that a million years had passed since I'd left home for the first time and like it was yesterday that I thought Pressville was all there was to know about the world.

"So, what have you been doing?" Millie asked, also ready to change the subject.

"Oh, I don't know. I've been home for a while. I was in Paris before. I got really burnt out and I kept thinking, is this it? Like I couldn't imagine doing this for much longer. You know—I get really lonely in New York, and it's all about making money and trying so hard all the time, and I don't know what happened." I was pacing on the dull beige carpet. "I like being home, I guess.

I'm working for this woman in Atlanta, but the money's not the same."

"Yeah, I get lonely up here, too, sometimes, but I don't think about it. I guess I don't care if I'm lonely. It's just work. I'm eventually gonna move back home, but I like doing this for now. It won't last forever. Here today, gone tomorrow, so why not do it while I can? I know what you mean, though. During a slow week, I get pretty depressed, and I just want to go home...live the simple life."

"Well, at least you know what you want. I don't know what I want; I just know I don't wanna hustle around the city, making sure my bikini wax is up to date for all eternity. Whatever..." I trailed off. Millie was notoriously positive. I had the impression that all people from Texas were like that. It's flatter there. Maybe the hills make us moody in other parts of the world—a person can't see straight for the life of them.

"Don't worry about your boyfriend, Dani. I don't want to say what's not my business, but breakups are hard, and you'll get over it. I always think that's the answer—the next thing. Oh, when this is done, I'll be a wife or a mom or whatever, so if things don't pop off, then I'm just devastated, mainly 'cause there's all this time to fill again, but it's okay. It's going to be okay. I just wanted to warn you about Claudia. You should know. She's not good. And anyway, at least you're not missing. Louisa's parents are really freaking out."

"Right, too bad she's missing all the time." I should have said something about Claudia, but I was too worried about myself and Louisa to care about cancer.

The next day, at around the same time as Millie's phone call had been, we heard a crash on Bell Road. It was one in the afternoon. I was putting a bunch of my old toiletries in a travel case, disposing of what was almost empty and making a pile for Raquel and Janelle to go through. They liked makeup and didn't have access to anything good at the Pressville drugstore.

I had heard the motorcycle up the road; I knew it was Benji's. His had a special racket, some loose part or old piston. I didn't know the lingo and didn't care to. I felt a wave of longing that immediately turned sour when the screech came before the pounding. A tree snapped. There was a whirring and a series of clatters after that shook the house. I could smell smoke. Later, the police—Cady Benson especially—would ask me over and over if I'd heard any voices.

"No," I kept saying. "I didn't hear anyone. Just screeching."

The fire started immediately, and that had been the biggest concern. There was no hope for the driver of the motorcycle, but the fire would spread, and spread quickly. We hadn't had rain. I only heard people saying these things around me, from the window of my bedroom, later when we were standing in the kitchen, on the front porch, in the eyebrow driveway. At the time of the crash, I had no idea what was going on. I was alone—alone with the wreckage, with the sound of metal hitting a tree I'd looked at almost every day of my life, alone with an exploding gas tank, alone with a poor soul who'd been ripped out of his life by a bend in the road and a tilt of his wrists.

I didn't come downstairs at first. It immediately felt as though I'd done something wrong. Instead, I stayed in my bedroom, standing by the window. Because of where the house sits, solitary, on a steep curve, there were no heroes running down the slope; there was no one around at all. Eventually, a passing motorist who made his way up Bell a couple of minutes later saw the wreck, pulled over, and called the police. The time between the crash and everything that came next felt expanded, stretched to the point of breaking.

"He's dead!" It was Jenks O'Riordan. I saw him running to our front door. Sirens grew gradually louder and then closer, as if being summoned by the flames. "Help!" I could hear yelling. "Help! There's been a wreck! I think he's dead!" Suddenly, there were more people, more voices, more dismay.

I could hear my mother's hurried footsteps downstairs. I hadn't known she was home. Normally, I knew when the van pulled up in front. Her brakes squeaked; it was like an announcement every time she returned to the house. She was at the front door, and then Jenks was inside.

The fire roared up the hill rather than down it. It went back toward the road, returning to its source, retracing its steps. Of course I knew it was Benji. The second it happened, I knew it was Benji. There was nothing in the moment, only emptiness and finality. It occurred to me that I'd almost been expecting it. My mind drifted to how my sadness would change. I could stop thinking he'd left me for someone else. Now he'd just left. I put my hand in my mouth—all of it except the thumb—and began to cry. It was a silent choking. Nothing was released; I swallowed every last bit of it.

"Danielle!" Someone was yelling my name. My father was at work, but it was a man's voice. "Danielle!" It was Jenks O'Riordan again. I didn't think he knew who I was.

"Danielle!" There were other voices now. I'd heard other car doors slamming. People had pulled over. The sirens came next, low and wailing. I remember going downstairs, but it must have been much later. The fire truck was outside, pulled off the road; it appeared to be dangling. They had the hoses out. I could hear trees snapping and someone calling to keep it away from the motorcycle.

"It's the Law kid!" people were hollering.

"It's the Law kid. It's Benji Law!"

"Somebody's gotta call the parents!"

More cars stopped. I stood in the foyer and then by the front window in the living room.

"He didn't make it. There's no way!"

"Never wore a helmet."

"Helmet wouldn't have helped this."

"I'm sure it's one of those Law kids, but I don't know which one."

"Danielle." It was my mother. She was approaching me from behind.

"What happened?" I said before turning to see her.

"I don't know, but there's a fire, and we have to get out of here."

"I can see there's a fire." The fire was moving the opposite direction of the house. It made no sense for us to leave, to go outside where we'd be more exposed.

"The fire department wants us out of the house in case of wind."

"It's not windy." It actually looked like it was going to rain. It often looked that way where our house sat on Bell Road. We were in front of a ridge that shot straight up in front of us. Only a piece of the sky could be seen from the front window. If a cloud took over that space, you'd think we were in for it.

"Danielle, there's no way he lived."

I looked at her, finding this a strange thing to have said. "Wouldn't you be happy if he didn't." It was a cool blade of a statement, a razor to what was left between us. Her eyelids flickered before she told me again that we needed to leave the house and go stand on the other side of the road. I wasn't wearing shoes. I can remember thinking I should put on shoes, but I didn't.

Chantel arrived some twenty minutes later. Someone had called her to tell her what happened. The twins were at the park with friends. My mom was not concerned about them. "Janice Wing is with them. Haley's mom. They're fine. It's better they're not here." I think she was talking to me. I felt something between us, the blade on its side, growing thicker and wider.

Chantel ran to my mother first, like my mother would need comfort; someone dying on your property is an unbearable hardship. I stood next to them like I was waiting to take their order.

"It's Benji," I had said finally as Chantel had continued to ignore me while caressing my mother's arm, which was blotchy with feeling and blood. Chantel looked at me but said nothing. She looked back at my mother, who closed her eyes.

"Where's the van?" I asked.

"I parked down the hill." My mother did not look at me when she answered. We had a small leaf-covered gravel drive that went down to the house's basement entrance—an immovable overhead door with a handle so rusted it looked bloody. If my dad had his work truck, he parked it down there even though it could be hard to back it up the small hill. My mother never parked there. It was an anomaly. Everything about this day was singular, unusual, distinct.

"Sorry, Danielle," Chantel said. She reached for my arm now, which was pale, bloodless, and limp by my side.

39

S o as you know, Louisa Radcliffe was reported missing by her parents June ninth, 2004. Now, there were rumors that she was here in Pressville. With Benji Law." Cady Rae Benson paused, moving her lips around her teeth in a clench. "You were also in Pressville at the time."

"Yes," I said. Benji had died June 13. The date was otherwise unremarkable.

"Benji was interviewed at the time. He said she had been in Pressville but left. There were no records of her leaving on a flight. He said she drove back to New York in a rental car with a friend—he didn't know the girl's name. We did not, at the time, take the parents' claims all that seriously because they'd filed a missing person's report on her before when she went on a vacation to Mexico. We figured she was with him in Pressville but didn't want her parents to know. I regret that we were not more invested, but it had only been a few days since her parents had talked to her, so we decided to wait. She was never seen or heard from again, and as you know, Benjamin Law died in a fatal motorcycle accident a few days after we last spoke to him."

I nodded. Of course I knew all this.

"You were never questioned because there was no reason to believe you were involved—in—"

"No," I said. Cady had asked to meet at the house. I told Jasper to come home from work so he could be with the girls. I had a terrible feeling. That was what I kept saying to him: "I have this terrible feeling. I'd like you to be here."

"I am aware that you were involved with Mr. Law at some time, previous to the accident."

"I was." I nodded, feeling every bit eleven years old and in the pediatrician's office to discuss my first period. I had my hands clasped in front of me and was sitting erect and attentive. "For a brief time."

"But you did not have a relationship with Ms. Radcliffe?"

"I'm sorry." My inflection was wrong, and it sounded like I was actually apologizing.

"So you did not—"

"What do you mean by 'relationship'? I knew her. She lived in my building in New York, and we have the same agent. We had. I don't model anymore."

"And she's dead," Cady said.

"Yes. Claudia died."

"So did Louisa Radcliffe."

"So sad," I said. I knew how I sounded, disingenuous and distant. "Her parents never gave up."

"No. They're here now. With the body."

I looked up sharply.

"Yes, they arrived last night."

"Do they want to talk to me?" I heard a car out front. Jasper had the uncanny knack of returning too soon. He would say he was going somewhere and would be gone for a certain amount of time and then come back much earlier than I expected him. It was indicative of other aspects of his personality. He never did things quite the way he thought he would. He had riddled his life with unreachable expectations of his own making. He wanted four children, probably not four daughters but four children, who then appeared to cause him nothing but stress and grief with their endless needs and talking. He wanted to go somewhere for two hours but stayed only one. He wanted to have a beautiful wife but married someone who used to be beautiful and who had no interest in it anymore.

"No. They don't want to talk to you," Cady said. "And I would not recommend that you try to contact them."

"Why?" There was a knock on the door. I wasn't expecting anyone, and Jasper wouldn't knock. My stomach buzzed with discomfort.

"Because this is an active investigation."

"Danielle?" It was my mother's voice. "Danielle?"

"I'm in here." I didn't go to stand. "With Cady Benson."

My mother was disheveled, pulled down and weary. She wasn't wearing any makeup with the exception of a thick line of eyeliner on her bottom lid. She sometimes did this, thinking this single stroke of effort would save her face.

"Oh," she said.

"I parked down your hill there," Cady said, motioning to the side of the house. "Does anyone park there?"

"No. Never," my mother said. Her eyes were moving back and forth between me and Cady. "No," she said again, needlessly. "I mean, I don't live here anymore, so…"

"I have some photos of the scene when the bike flipped, when Benjamin Law died here, and there's a van parked down there. Your car, right, Mrs. Greer? A Chrysler minivan."

"You can call me Deb, Cady." My mother's face was tense and deeply wrinkled around the mouth.

Cady Benson said nothing. She continued staring at my mother in a morbidly contented way, like my mother had just admitted she was the one who walked on the new rug with shit on her shoe and that was why the room smelled so bad. "So you were parked there that day?"

"I had some things to unload."

"Mom?" I'd made no effort to speak. The word came out like an exhale. It was almost as though I was asking her if it was true.

40

2004

There was a funeral for Benji, marred by the missing person investigation. Louisa Radcliffe's parents had hired a private investigator, a man named Arnold Mahon, who came to our house a number of times the weeks following Benji's death. My mother would only talk to him on the front porch, never inviting him inside. When Cady Benson showed up, Deb was gracious and coddling. She'd bring out cookies and offer lemonade, sitting very closely to Cady, who always looked uncomfortable but willing.

I did not go to Benji's funeral. Apparently, his mother wailed and beat her fists on the ground, refusing to accept what had happened. Benji's father identified his body. His mother was not fit for the task.

No one from my family attended. My father said that was shameful, but my mother insisted on our absence. "It wouldn't be right." Even through his shame, my father agreed.

According to Janelle and Raquel, all anyone could talk about was how Benji died right in front of my house, and wasn't that an omen or something?

"It's the curse of Bell Road," Janelle offered.

"No, it's not," my mother snapped back. "Stop saying stuff like that. You'll make something out of nothing. And stop calling him 'that kid,'" she added with some sympathy—for whom, I wasn't sure. "Benjamin."

"Benji," I corrected the room. I remember us standing in the kitchen. We were always standing in the kitchen. When the house was mine, I could be found almost exclusively in the front room with my air conditioner. I liked to look at Bell Road, not the ravine.

All I'd wanted to say was that I was going to stay a little longer. Somehow this provoked a family meeting, wherein we were going to decide if our house was cursed and who had invited the curse into our lives.

"You should not stay. Can you give us a break, please?" my mother said viciously. "Really. Give us a break."

"Deb," my father corrected her. "Let's be careful how we talk to each other."

"We can't leave the house," my mother said, whacking an egg against the side of a bowl on the counter. Several pieces of the shell fell into the batter. She didn't remove them and began whisking vigorously. "We're prisoners here."

"But I want to go to the funeral," I'd said stupidly.

"No." It was my father who was definitive. "This is not your time, Danielle. This is time for his family. Your mother is right. You need to get back to work."

"Sounds serious," I said.

"Well..." he said. "Yes, it is." He didn't laugh. He didn't even smile.

And so I went. I left the following day. My father's only concern was whether my car would start, having sat for so long in the garage at my apartment building.

My parents were visibly relieved to see me standing by the front door with my bags. I wondered if I would ever feel comfortable in their house again.

Claudia called, not to say she was sorry about what happened to the love of my life but to tell me that everyone in New York was worried sick over Louisa. No one cared that Benji died. It seemed like no one even knew that.

"Her parents hired a PI. They're moneybags. She's not in Mexico. They flew someone there, and nothing. Her parents are going to Georgia. They're gonna see if she's still there. Hiding out."

Instead of pining over Louisa, I kept reminding her that Benji had died. He wasn't missing; he died. "The accident happened right in front of my house," I said.

"Well—I've heard people in Atlanta are horrible drivers" was all she could think to say back. After the second or third phone call like this, she told me, rather abruptly, that she was going to leave the business. She dropped that last part on me like maybe Louisa disappearing was her reason for throwing in the towel, and maybe that she didn't really want to keep chatting with me, being that she wasn't going to be a model booker anymore.

Millie Malcom told me the agency hosted a retirement party for her at one of our favorite clubs with a totally inappropriate red carpet and paparazzi. "You know she's retiring because she's dying, right? And they were serving vodka Red Bulls? And the DJ kept playing 'Come On Eileen.' Her name isn't Eileen. It was so bizarre. You should be glad you weren't there." Millie said Claudia was very emotional the whole night and burst into tears several times, holding everyone's hands and stumbling about. She drank too much and practically had to be carried out of the party.

I started back at Grace's office, but the mood was subdued and more like grunt work than the circus vibe I'd had there before. I was actually asked to make copies, call girls about their bookings, and organize a filing cabinet. One afternoon, completely out of the blue, Grace told me Claudia was going to be in town. I had been trying not to cry as I filled out the stock sheet for the man who'd shown up to refill our supplies. He reminded me of Benji. He smelled like gasoline and cigarettes and said "we'll see" just like Benji did.

"She is?" I nearly dropped my pencil and the paper I was writing on.

Claudia never left New York unless it was to go to the Hamptons or Europe, and even only certain places there. Everything else was beneath her. "Details," she'd say when someone mentioned an uninspired locale.

"Yes. She's been down before. We have fun," Grace said, pulling her glasses to the end of her nose and drawing her brows together. "I can't see this line here. What's the rate? Can you please come look?"

———

Claudia did indeed show up the following day. She came straight from her flight to the office, where she kissed Grace on both cheeks and said something about the guest bedroom.

"You can take the primary," Grace said. "Tim and I sleep in the basement now. We're too lazy to go all the way up at the end of the day anymore." Grace looked at me, then at Claudia like she might be reminding her of who I was.

"My Dani," Claudia said, walking over with her arms outstretched. She smelled like wine, and her eyes were dreamy and glassed over. "My Dani. Oh, I had high hopes for this one, Grace."

"Has anyone seen my mascara?" Grace asked the room. Heather was wearing headphones and didn't even look up when Claudia came in.

"Sorry to disappoint," I said, reaching to hug Claudia. She reciprocated but also pulled back. It left me with an odd sensation. I'd heard a hundred times that Claudia had been completely beside herself about the Louisa thing. Louisa was still missing. Apparently, she was crying so much at her retirement party because of Louisa and not because she was dying of cancer and couldn't book Prada anymore. A few of the younger girls at the party had even been wearing T-shirts that said FIND LOUISA with one of her photos from a Calvin Klein campaign emblazoned across the front. I saw photos from the event; they had tied the shirts in little knots so they could better show their flat stomachs while conveying the depths of their concern. I cried when I saw the pictures—for Benji. Not Claudia or Louisa, but Benji. It was as if he didn't exist, had never existed. In this world, he was entirely superfluous.

"So," Claudia said, running her hand through her hair, "I was contacted. Or the police contacted me because they wanted to search my emails or...I don't really know, but I haven't told you yet because I'm so afraid to let you down, but..." She stopped and took a deep breath. "So there's that email where I say 'Don't kill anyone,' and I guess that sounds strange to them. They're looking into it. I don't know..." She slowly closed her eyes like she was about to fall asleep. "I really don't know. Maybe it was a text. I can't remember. They've gone through my phone too."

"What are you talking about?" I looked at her hands. She still had the bandages from her chemo ports. I winced, remembering when she'd had the small plastic capsules in her veins at our lunches. She tried to cover them with her jacket sleeves or by putting her hands in her lap, but they were hard to ignore. Nothing can happen with your hands; they are the most impossible thing to keep secret.

"Louisa," she said. "Louisa Radcliffe." Now there was an element of impatience, impatience and something else like blame. "There's some woman on the case. A new girl is on the case," Claudia corrected herself. "At least, she sounds like a girl. She's here. I…"

My chest felt like it was caving inward; my heart was like an anvil being dropped over and over on my sternum. "You're here to talk to Cady?" I said.

"Yes!" Claudia looked pleased. "That's her name. Cady Jo or something. Anyway, she called to say they were going to go through emails and asked my permission since I was Louisa's booker at the time of her disappearance…and that she wanted to talk to me."

"Cady Rae Benson?" I asked, as if there was another Cady who might want to go through Claudia's phone, looking for information about Louisa.

"I had to sign something about my email account and phone number, but that's in there—I told you not to kill Louisa. Of course, I was joking, but now Louisa has been gone for several weeks, and they are wondering what the hell happened to her, so… I've been waiting to tell you. I don't know why. Something's not right." Claudia looked away. "Yes, not a good thing… I should have said something to you earlier. It meant nothing. Of course I didn't think you'd kill anyone. So silly, really, but I am going to see her. She said she would come up to New York because she says she used to live there or something, but I'm here. I'd do anything to help Louisa. Anything. I wanted to tell you, and Grace... I do love Grace!" The two women cackled like witches, delighting in the fun they would have while Claudia told Cady Rae Benson that I didn't kill Louisa Radcliffe.

"Anyway," she said before picking up her bags and saying she was heading to Grace's house, triumphantly and with the intention of ending the conversation with me. She walked out of Grace's office without looking back. She'd been so out of place there, anyway—like an unpleasant smell an entire room of people is trying to pretend they don't notice.

41

I have to bring you in," Cady told me at the door. "We're not going to cuff you or anything," she promised. Her eyes darted around, taking in the house. The girls were on the first few steps, with Jasper behind them. His face was stricken. All I could think was that I had done this to him. He had wanted a normal life. He wanted to be a dad with gripes and a six-pack on the weekend. His parents were very traditional and thought life was made up of commitments and complaining about them. That, and a college degree, was true happiness. I had factored awkwardly into their plans for their only son. I fit, but not really. I know I had always been a bit of a conundrum for them; my relationship with the girls, the mysterious modeling background, my connection to this kid who had died in front of my family's house. All of it had served to cool their fervor for me. I sat on the edge of their conversations and was remembered only peripherally at holidays.

Oh yes, the girl Jasper married…from up north. She's fine…a little odd.

"Let's go upstairs," Jasper said somberly to the girls.

"Am I being arrested?" I said. I felt nothing, only resignation. Of course I knew I hadn't done anything wrong, but it was time to pay the piper. I can't explain why I was so willing, so unable to defend myself. I think I already knew what happened, but I wasn't letting myself get it into focus. I left it as a blur in the corner, out of good light and just enough off-center, fuzzed out by a glare and crooked, so as to make me squint. I must have thought I could fix something by being compliant, by pretending I didn't have a clue.

Cady pressed her lips together. "No. I am not arresting you, but we are bringing you in for questioning. Formally. You don't have to come, but if you don't, I will go get a warrant and come back and arrest you." I thought she might be about to say she was sorry, but she didn't. I knew she'd married but had no kids. I was only aware of her and her husband having several dogs, and my mother telling me—years earlier—that she had not been able to conceive. I don't know how my mother would have known that. Her obsession with Cady Benson had faded after she'd left the NYPD to take care of her family. She was no longer going to be of service to us, and with that, my mother went back to disliking chicken restaurants.

"I'll go," I said, looking over my shoulder. The girls were lingering on the stairs, taking their time. Jasper drew his eyebrows together and watched me. "Sorry, Jasper," I said. "I'm sorry."

42

I called my parents' house later that evening, having spent the day at my desk, fidgeting and worrying about Claudia. Where the hell was Louisa, anyway? I wished she would just show up so everyone would stop talking about her.

"Hey," I said when my mother answered. "Hey" was one of her pet peeves. She'd told me she found it irritating when I called without anything to say.

"Don't call and expect me to talk." She'd been prickly since the accident. We all were, but my mother's mood was the sharpest, having been filed by shock, tragedy, and the constant stares around Pressville. We were the talk of the town; our house on Bell Road had become a place where terrible things happen.

"Right in front of their house."

"Of all the turns, it had to happen there… You know the daughter was seeing him."

"I think he was leaving their place. He always gunned it—he could have got going pretty good."

"Just awful. He was always speeding... Surprised it didn't happen sooner."

"That's a bad turn right there at the Greers' place. Real bad turn."

I swallowed and started to talk. "So..." I was going to tell my mom about Claudia showing up. I was nervous about it, this errant comment I'd made. I wasn't sure what I should do.

There was an unusual amount of movement in the background. Doors were slamming, I could hear drawers being opened and closed, things being dropped on the ground.

"What are you doing?" I asked.

"We rented a place."

"What?"

"We RENTED A PLACE." She was emphatic, pretending the reason I'd asked her to repeat herself was that I didn't hear her.

"What do you mean? Where?"

"On Potter. We're going to sell the house." If my mother had told me she just drank a bottle of fabric softener, I would have been less surprised.

"What?" I knew I'd raised my voice.

"Stop yelling and saying 'what' over and over again. I don't want to live here anymore. Not after what's happened." She was so matter-of-fact it sounded like the decision had been made years ago and that she'd told me a hundred times.

"What about me?" I said.

"What about you? Danielle, you're almost nineteen years old. You're an adult. I would think you would want us to get rid of the place too. It amazes me that you have any desire to set foot in Pressville, Georgia, ever again. Really."

"They still haven't found Louisa," I said.

"Who's Louisa?"

"Mom, come on. You know who Louisa is. The girl who went missing."

"Well, she's not here. And didn't you tell me she liked to run off to Mexico, on drugs and all that? I'm sure she'll turn up, but she's not here. They're not even looking for her here anymore. It's been all about Benji Law. Story of my life—Benji Law."

"Well, I wanted him to be the story of my life," I said.

"Okay, Danielle. I'm getting off the phone."

"Wait! When are you moving? And they are still looking for her, Mom. That's what I was going to tell you."

"End of the month, then we'll list the house."

"I want the house." The instant the words left my mouth, I could feel the wheels begin to turn. They'd been stuck, rusted to the track, immovable, but now they were sparking, metal on metal, and a puff of black smoke exploded from a pipe overhead. I'd set another thing in motion. It was a knack I had.

"No you don't."

"I do."

"How will you pay for it?"

"Isn't it paid for?" I asked.

"Yes, but we want to sell it. So you'd have to buy it, and then there's tax and insurance and all of that."

"I pay a shit ton of rent down here."

"Please don't argue with me, Danielle. You can't buy the house. And anyway, you don't want to live here. It's in constant need of maintenance, and Pressville is not the place for you anymore." She took a breath. "I left some flowers at the Laws' the other day, just left them on their stoop. They let the brother out of jail so he could go."

I'd been sick over not going to the funeral. I thought I'd let him down, that Benji had an eye on the service and thought he'd been right about me all along, that I didn't really care about him—I'd just wanted a toy. That was the reason I gave for being left behind, that I wasn't as doting, committed as Louisa. It was absurd, but it was how I got through the day. "Please don't sell my childhood home right after my boyfriend died," I said, sounding angry. I figured some of these unbearable feelings had to be my mother's fault.

"He wasn't your boyfriend. He was dating the missing girl. And don't use that as an excuse. For anything." She was incensed, seething. Before I could say anything else, she hung up.

I sat down on my sleek bed in my sleek apartment in my sleek clothes and wept. I'd been holding it mostly together since the accident, a lot of sniffling and wiping at my eyes, but no deluge. I hadn't allowed myself until now. I looked out at the small terrace where Benji and I had sat so many nights—but then, it wasn't so many nights, when I really thought about it. I'd stretched it in my memory, made it more significant. He was up in Pressville with Louisa half the time, all the time. It hadn't mattered to him a bit, sitting on the balcony with me, smoking Marlboro after Marlboro. He was just wasting time.

When we'd been in New York, it was different. Before Louisa showed up and he lost his way. Our place had an alley view. He asked me why I even bothered having windows; we did not sit on the fire escape there. We lay in bed in New York. It was a conspicuous detail. He didn't want to lie in bed all day in Atlanta. We'd sat next to each other, in opposing deck chairs, and then he left.

It was a crystalline evening, pale blue and vibrant. All my memories were caught at the tips of my fingers, like Chinese finger traps trying to reset the joints I'd knocked loose. The tremors would be long felt, rattling my steps from this moment until I could finally forget. I did not think I would ever forget the way he made me feel. And then he died. Everything that happened in between was part of the thread yanking at my fingers. I would not be able to grasp whatever it was that was just on the outside, no matter how hard they pulled on me.

A couple of days later, I was out jogging on Dresden, wearing headphones and lost in the jerking motion of my knees and ankles as I pounded the pavement, when I heard screeching tires behind me. I stopped running and turned right before I was knocked off my feet by a man who'd been walking to my right, in my blind spot. "Sorry," he said as we lay on the ground in a crumble. A motorcycle had skipped the curb and smashed into a trash can. "I thought it was going to hit you." He was around thirty, maybe older, with nice eyes and a strong build.

"Thank you," I said before getting up and starting to run again. I don't know if he wanted anything from me for saving my life. I didn't turn around to watch as a few cars stopped to check on the motorcyclist. His bike was still revving from its position on its side next to the can. He was lying partially underneath it and not really moving. I ran all the way back to my place at a quick clip, where I spent the next hour trying to figure out why I didn't care if he was hurt.

I didn't stay in Atlanta much longer after that. I went to college and stopped pretending I was done growing up; I became seventeen again, the age I'd been when I flipped my lid. I remember closing the door on the apartment in Atlanta for the last time. It was different from when I left New York, but oddly the same.

When I left New York, I knew that I would not come back with a certainty I hadn't had before. I looked around my apartment, thinking I should feel something more profound. All I saw when I looked at the oversize room and the bed frame I was leaving was a place I had never belonged. It was all this trying to belong, I decided, that had been the culprit. I belonged at home in Pressville, where I could feel trapped, useless, like I'd done nothing with my life. I had those same feelings at modeling calls for second-rate runway shows, but it was like no one agreed with me. At least at home, people would agree I really hadn't amounted to much.

43

2019

We were in a formal interview room this time. Cady had parked in the back of the building and brought me through a series of clicking doors. She was all business and didn't pretend to be interested in the girls or my mother like she'd done previously. I thought about how disappointed she must be to be back in Pressville, having wanted to be a cop at the NYPD. Jasper reminded me—I suppose after he did some research—that she had been a detective in New York and that that was pretty heady.

"Okay," I remember saying in response. "I know she was. I saw her when I was there."

"I'm just letting you know. I wouldn't try to pull anything with her."

"I don't try to pull anything with anyone." We'd had so many conversations like this. His perennial nervous twitching around me since they'd found Louisa's body. It was like he knew things would never be the same, even though I kept telling him I'd had nothing to do with it.

Cady set keys on the table and pulled up a chair across from me. "Tell me what we're missing here, Danielle."

"I don't know." I was wearing a flowered skirt and tank top without a bra. I looked like I was trying to be a teenage hippie. I had beaded sandals on my feet and my sunglasses on my head like a headband. I kept twirling my hair in my left hand.

"So Louisa Radcliffe was reported missing, Benjamin Law died; she was never seen again until her remains were discovered on your property some fourteen years later. What don't I get?"

I looked at her sharply. "I'm really not sure. I don't get it either."

"I don't believe that. Your mother was home the day of the accident."

"No she wasn't," I said.

"She was there when the police arrived. They took photos of the scene. Her van is parked in the gravel drive, and she was on the porch when the fire department arrived and asked everyone to evacuate the premises. It's in the reports. All of them."

"I don't really know what that has to do with anything. I was upstairs when it happened. I was in my bedroom. And what does that have to do with Louisa?"

"Louisa's body has been there a long time, Danielle. Did it not occur to you that she might have died around when Benji did?"

"Oh," I said. "See, that's kind of the weird thing." I had decided to speak freely. My skin had loosened, allowing all the burning oil I'd held within it for the last fifteen years to seep out. When it was released, it was like a truth serum. "I don't think I ever grew up. From that day forward, I've stayed the same person. I'm still Dani in New York with all my modeling problems, and Claudia's not dead, and Benji didn't crash his bike on Bell Road, and Louisa didn't exist. She never stole him from me. So when they found her, and y'all told me it was her, all I could think was that all of my thinking finally worked. She was gone, and I could have Benji again."

Cady's face was serene, contemplative, but not judging. "Danielle, the detail we were waiting for was her age when she died."

"Okay." My voice was flat, lifeless, barren.

"She was fifteen."

I nodded faintly.

"We're assuming she died the same day as Benji. In the accident."

"Yes." I didn't know what else to say.

"We investigated him at the time. Benji," Cady explained. "As you know, he was a suspect in her disappearance, but being that he died, there was very little to go on. We swept his home, yard, every inch of the gas station. We didn't find a hair from her head except—"

"In his bedroom."

"Yes. I suppose I always assumed he did something to her," Cady said. "I assumed we would eventually find out he'd killed her, hidden her somewhere, and then ended up dead himself. I might have even thought he drove off the road intentionally. I might have thought he killed himself. The guilt." She was in jeans on this day; it was the first time I'd seen her in anything but business slacks. I determined that she was actually very attractive, hardened by time, but pretty nonetheless. Her face was not as round, more chiseled and direct—leading me somewhere. "But that's not what happened, is it?" she said.

"I don't know what happened to her," I said. "Maybe she fell down the hill."

"Why was she at your house?"

"She wasn't," I said. "Or if she was, I didn't know."

"Why was your mother parked in the gravel that day?" Cady tapped her fingers on the desk.

I rubbed my eye a little too vigorously. All morning, something had been lingering in the corner, blurring my vision and making me itch. It watered and became more irritated than it had been. I tried squeezing it shut to see if that would curb the discomfort.

"Are you okay?" Cady asked me. I remember her being so bubbly and inanely optimistic when I met her in New York. All that was gone. I had to suppose losing her father and having to come back here had taken the wind out of her sails. Or maybe it was just me. She was done trying with me.

"I have something in my eye. I don't know why my mother was parked there."

"Was Louisa Radcliffe in your house that day?"

"What? No." These seemed the most preposterous questions to ask. "She was never at my house. I hated her."

"I know that."

I exhaled loudly.

"Did your mother ever meet Louisa Radcliffe?"

Now I closed my eyes for a different reason; I was trying to wake myself up from heavy, oppressive sleep. "My mother didn't know anyone. I don't understand why you keep asking me about her."

"You don't?"

I let my eyes dart around the room, something I associated with dishonesty in others. "I don't," I said after what must have seemed like some deliberation. I was genuinely confused.

"She's in the next room," Cady said.

"What?" My mouth twitched. "Why?"

"Because we found remains of a girl who died on her property—"

"Right, but that's my house now." I don't know why I was explaining.

"Louisa died fifteen years ago. That was your parents' house at the time."

"What are you saying?"

"Did you or your mother have something to do with her death?"

"Cady," I said, scolding.

"Danielle."

"I can't believe you're asking me this."

We sat in silence for some time. I was not provoked to speak, finding that I was more comfortable staring blankly at the space just next to Cady Rae Benson's face. I was trying to remember that day more clearly, trying to figure out why she would be asking me about my mother. I wondered which one of us had been a liar for the last fifteen years.

44

The skid marks had been on the other side of the road. The initial responding officer, some kid from Doe Falls who'd worked on the force for only a few years, noticed it. That was why Cady Benson was called. There were tread marks on the right and left sides of the road, not from the bike but from a vehicle with four wheels.

"People skid on Bell all the time."

"Those have been there for years."

I don't know who they told about how common skid marks were on Bell Road, but it seemed to satisfy the kid from Doe Falls. Cady Benson complied, but she kept notes in her head, where discerning people keep notes. The rest of us either forget or shout; both serve to completely evaporate meaning.

It was true, though. People did skid on Bell. We heard them. My mother's weren't the only tire tracks on either side of the double yellow line. But my mother never parked in the gravel drive that led to our basement—never. And she'd had a leaf stuck to her sock when she came in the house. It was the one detail I kept to myself for fifteen years—the leaf on her ankle. It was brown, dead, dry with the texture of old newspaper, the color of milk chocolate. She dusted it off when she saw me looking at her feet.

"She was a lot further down the hill. I almost didn't see her down there. I didn't see her on the motorcycle. I really didn't. I thought he was alone. She was dead. I know she was dead. I didn't leave her. I couldn't have helped her."

My mother had rolled Louisa Radcliffe farther down the ravine and thrown a rotted-out, hollow log on top of her, along with whatever leaves she could toss like a cat covering its mess in the litter box. Louisa was the reason they had moved, not Benji. My mother knew she was there, and so she had to leave.

"I swerved in front of him. That was it. We didn't collide. I didn't hit him. I swerved. It scared him, and he went off the road. That was it. The motorcycle hit the tree. I could see that she took the hit the worst. Her head slammed backwards; it nearly came off her neck, and there was this crack. I could hear it over the bike. The tree did it. I didn't hit him; the tree did. That's what caused the fire. They got thrown because of the tree; you know we cut it down after that. It was a huge oak. We cut it down. I didn't kill him. I just swerved." She spoke so matter-of-factly. Her face was very alert, her posture erect, and her chin appeared to be rolling along a track from left to right. I might have thought she was addressing a room full of interested people who'd shown up to hear how she killed Benji Law on a Thursday afternoon. "It wasn't an accident." She said this more to Cady. "I meant to scare him. It was an impulse, but I can't pretend that I didn't want to do it. My hand didn't slip. I wasn't trying to miss a squirrel. I've talked to myself about it a thousand times. I meant to do it. It was an angry swerve, and I wanted him to wreck his fucking bike." She still spoke serenely, like none of this was troubling her. Her admissions rolled off her tongue, not like she'd been holding them there, captive and trembling, but like it was only a matter of time before she said them so obviously.

I sat in the room with my mother and Cady. My father had been called to the station as well, but he was in the lobby, waiting. It was barely a lobby, anyway, just a small room with three plastic chairs crammed next to a high counter with all manner of laminated notices taped to it. I could imagine his placid and confused face, hearing my mother speak freely for the first time since that day. He wouldn't understand. He was never going to understand this about Deb. I don't think he even knew why he was there.

Cady had talked to each of us separately and, I suppose, determined that I really didn't know what happened to Louisa. I'd like to believe she knew that all along, mostly because it would have been so strange for me to come back and live in that house if I'd known.

"So you knew Louisa Radcliffe was on the motorcycle and that she'd been ejected, and that—"

"She was dead, yes." My mother nodded. She was wearing her eyeliner in a thick, uneven stripe on each lid. She had press-on nails that were hanging on by a thread. At one point, one of them appeared to dangle from her ring finger. She adjusted it, and it was appropriately situated again at the nail bed, looking perfectly placed and perfectly plastic. "She was dead. Yes." She seemed to be confirming this for herself.

"And you left her there." Cady Benson sat back in her seat. I could see now what a serious person she was. I could see how she might have been a detective in New York City, and maybe she really did run into the Twin Towers. I hadn't asked her about that.

"I left her there." My mother nodded again, took a breath, rolled her shoulders back, and sat up straighter. "I did. And I never told anyone."

"You were aware there was a missing person investigation involving Ms. Radcliffe, am I correct?"

"I was. But it wasn't really here, you know."

Cady Benson closed one eye pensively, tilting her head to the side. "No. It was here. We papered the streets."

"What streets?" my mother said. "Bell Road? Are there streets here?" She sounded painfully chipper. "I didn't know we had mean streets in Pressville." It almost sounded like she was going to laugh.

"There was a national campaign to find her."

"I don't really watch TV," my mother lied.

"Why did you move the body?" Cady said. "If you didn't hit

them, and he swerved of his own volition, why did you move the body?"

"Because she looked so sad lying there... And all I could think about was Danielle and how that might have been her. I might have killed Danielle. I thought—I thought I'd really gone and done it. But it wasn't. It wasn't my girl. I didn't mess up that bad. It was just that I didn't... It wasn't Danielle. I couldn't think straight because I was so relieved. I didn't know he had anyone on the bike with him; it might have been Danielle, and then what would I have done?"

"We canvassed back there a few times," Cady admitted to me. When we spoke in a separate room, she reminded me of the person I'd met in New York so many years ago. She was less stingy with her words, more willing and softer. I'd come to find I was almost afraid of her; it wasn't the investigation. I knew I hadn't done anything wrong, not in a long time. It was her. She had such a steely demeanor with me, so calculating and condemning. I can't say I wasn't impressed with the way she made me feel; I hadn't thought she had it in her. But she relented, and I was able to breathe. I was able to grieve—mostly the loss of my mother, who would never be the same, not for me.

But it was as though I had traded loyalties. I, too, was talking to Cady Rae Benson like it was Old Home Week, this pesky distraction finally out of our way so we could communicate honestly. My mother in the other room, silently contemplating her fate while I talked to the chicken restaurant girl about the dead body in the yard.

"When they gave you the house and moved, I always knew why, but we couldn't find anything. Mahon and I went out there in the middle of the night a few times. With flashlights. You hadn't moved in yet," Cady said.

"Took me a minute." The truth was, I hadn't wanted to move in alone. I'd waited until Jasper was ready. I asked Chantel, and then later the twins, if they wanted to live there with me, but no one was interested. My mother left most of the furniture. It was too large to move to their rental, and then to the new house with the carport.

"I was surprised you were coming back."

"I'm still surprised I came back." I paused, the comfort of being vindicated riddled with guilt over my mother. My father would have to bear the weight of her mistakes; I had already decided that she would not be blamed for mine. All that I had done—this profound misstep with Benji that had so marred my reputation, my thinking, my decisions—would now be thought of as the logical conclusion of my mother's poor character. They'd all suspected it, what with those boobs and that hair and the makeup. They should have known. She was always a suspect; they just didn't know for what crime. "I didn't know, though."

"No, I don't think you did. That's what I'm trying to say. When they moved, I knew somethin' was off." Cady looked at me. "But I'm sorry to do this. We do have to charge her."

"Of course," I said. And then, just as immediately as I felt I'd been absolved, I remembered that that jerk of the wheel, her small moment of impulse, the unique compulsion of emotion had been because of me, because I wouldn't leave. I wanted to stay and wallow, seed in their soil, let my roots get under their foundation, bury myself in their yard. "Of course you do." I paused. "I know you do."

When I left Cady's office, I found my dad sitting in the station lobby, petting one of two enormous Labrador retrievers who were circling his feet and taking turns rubbing their snouts on his jeans.

"Danielle!" He was smiling broadly and seemingly unaware of all that awaited him behind the steel door to the inner station. He was still quarantined in the front. "These are Cady Benson's dogs."

"She's arresting Mom," I said.

His face dropped. "For what?" He went on petting the darker of the two dogs.

"She admitted that she caused the accident and that she knew Louisa Radcliffe was on the motorcycle and that she died. Mom rolled her down the hill and hid her. For fifteen years."

"Oh." My father was disappointed, and by this particularly soft, humble, reflective reaction to the news, I knew that he wasn't angry with her. "Oh, that's terrible, isn't it?"

"Cady Benson is going to come and talk to you." My hair was in a high ponytail, ebullient and ridiculous for the occasion. I looked like a cheerleader, something I'd never been. "Where are Janelle and Raquel?" I don't know why I asked. They were both living in Atlanta. I suppose I thought they would come home because of the revelatory development, even if they didn't know about it yet.

"I suppose they're home. Do they know?"

"No. She's only just admitted it."

"Why would she do that?" he asked. This, too, had an eerie cheeriness that I couldn't reconcile with what was happening.

"She didn't know Louisa was on the motorcycle when she did it."

"Did what?" His eyes were glassy and his lip trembling, but still he continued to pet the Lab, who had no idea that the earth had just split open to swallow us all.

"I guess she played chicken with him and he flinched. It killed him. At least, that's what she said."

"She's never played chicken in her life." He was certain. I looked at his thin legs, bent at a sharp angle to accommodate the small chair. His jeans were a faded, outdated acid wash settling around him like a tissue paper tablecloth.

"I don't mean that she was actually playing chicken, Dad." I was about to explain when Cady Benson came through the door, allowing it to slam behind her. She acknowledged the elderly woman behind the desk, whom we'd been ignoring, and gave my father a half-hearted smile.

"What are you gonna do to her?" my dad asked Cady. "She's an old woman now."

"It doesn't really matter," I said, as if being called to defend Cady Benson and the Pressville Police Department.

"It will be up to a judge, I'm afraid," Cady said, ignoring me. "There is no statute of limitations on murder, but that's not what this is. So we will have to see."

My father looked at me very closely. He was blinking rapidly, I think to keep something internal he worried might leak from his eyes if he left them open too long. He wanted to narrow his accusation's chance for escape. But he didn't. "You couldn't just leave and forget that boy, could you?"

I was still to blame.

45

Louisa's mother wrote me a letter. I hadn't received many letters in my life—I'm not the kind of person you dedicated prose to. I'd kept some from Benji, who wrote me mostly little notes, scribbles of his affection. I hid them under the flat cushion at the bottom of my jewelry box, not wanting Jasper to know that any of that held any interest for me still. I only looked at them once or twice every few years. His handwriting was nearly illegible and a lot of his grammar woeful, but it reminded me of him trying so hard. He really had wanted to please me. In my recollections, I am younger and smaller than Benji. He is but a token of what I was trying to find, some innocence that could not be recaptured no matter how many devious ways I tried to locate it amid a crumbling tower of my self-worth. I hadn't known I would need to decide how I felt about myself at some point. I had always depended on the kindness of strangers. I was too young, and then not young enough for what I did.

I knew what the letter was before I opened it. There was no return address, and I didn't recognize the handwriting on the front, but I knew what it was. Her name was Linda. Linda and Louisa. Linda Radcliffe.

I don't know what to believe. I want to believe that you didn't know, but then I wonder how she could have been there, the whole time, under your noses without you knowing. She told me you were angry at her because of her relationship with Benjamin, but I couldn't understand it. You were older and had been living in New York and you were so aloof about everything. Louisa would rather have come home and lived in her high school bedroom, but you were so sure of yourself there. I couldn't imagine that you cared about Benji. I still don't understand it. I'm not sure I ever will, but I know it's because of that that she is dead. We knew a long time ago that she was gone. I knew it the day of the accident. I could feel that she left. What I cannot, will not, forgive you for is that if you knew she was there, why didn't you tell us? I know why she lied—because she didn't want to leave him, but you could have told Claudia, you could have told us, you could have told someone. I don't know if anything would have changed, but we wouldn't have spent almost fifteen years wondering what happened to her. I've been told you have daughters of your own. I have to believe you can understand how this has affected our lives, not just her death but the fact that we didn't know. There was so much fanfare, a ridiculous amount of fanfare over her in the beginning, and then when she disappeared, it was like she had never existed. I trusted you—I don't know why, but I did. I just need you to know that I trusted you. For whatever that's worth now, I did not think you were lying. I wish I'd tried harder to talk to you about what might have happened to her, but apparently you're saying you didn't know. I'll go to my own grave not sure if that's true.

I did not show Jasper the letter, although I could tell he'd read it. There was an errant smudge on the left side of the paper that appeared rather suddenly one day. To his credit, he handled Louisa's discovery quite well. Having always been averse to conflict, he did not shy away from his responsibility to explain to the girls what happened. My mother was charged, but with only a fraction of what she might have been at another time and place in history. There was a sea of empathy trying to drown her. I even thought Louisa's parents were strangely calm, not forgiving but removed from their angst. I suppose one mother to another, or maybe it was the opposite of that, maybe what she'd done was so foreign and inexplicable to them that they saw no reason to pursue her. She was beneath them. They wouldn't have done what she did. That's what Jasper's mother kept saying.

"I couldn't have done that. Just couldn't."

"No," Jasper would say as I sat silently. I wanted everyone to understand that she didn't mean to.

"It was an accident," I would occasionally murmur.

"What's that?" Jasper's mother was inconsolable. I'd brought dishonor to their family. She started spending more time at the house, with the girls, up in Pressville, thinking her influence was needed after all that we'd learned. She joined us for dinner, without Jasper's father, at least once a week, then insisted on spending the night due to the length of the drive to get back home. She ate all my yogurt and wore her reading glasses at the tip of her nose so that she had to look down to see. I'd not had a very strong opinion of her before my mother went to jail. I thought she'd done a commendable job raising Jasper, who had only mildly concerning personality flaws and didn't seem to have done anything particularly scandalous or even interesting in his thirty-six years of life. The more time I spent with her, especially under such scrutinizing circumstances, the more I saw how disappointed she was for Jasper, who she thought was nothing if not upstanding, and here I was—dragging him through the mud with something I'd done so long ago. The ripple effect. I'm still rippling. He is too. We live with our feet in the sand while the tide pulls out. We sink deeper and deeper, up to our ankles, and then slowly we're up to our shins, knees, thighs. I was unaware the effect my tide would have on my family. I suppose that is the privilege of inexperience. It is too difficult to imagine what could happen, so you don't.

"This is not what happens," Jasper's mother assured me one morning when we went to get doughnuts from the grocery store— her suggestion, my treat. She reveled in asserting that we should do something and then counting on me fully to do it. It was as though she hadn't existed before and was suddenly here, in place of my own mother, who had never suggested we get my daughters doughnuts on a Saturday morning.

"What's that?" I asked. I was driving with her in the passenger seat of my minivan.

"Part of me wants to excuse your mother, you know—that's just what happens. But leaving a girl to die at the bottom of a hill in the woods is not what happens. I'm disturbed."

"Oh." I pulled into the grocery store parking lot. "Do you want me just to go in or—"

"What am I? The dog? I'll go in. It was my idea. I want to get the girls' favorites."

"Okay."

"No," she said as we trekked across the barren, nearly empty parking lot with its jutting light poles and cracked parking barriers. "No, that's not a normal response."

"Normal response to what?" I said. "Sometimes they don't have just plain glazed here. At least, not in the cabinet. They'll have them in a four-pack, but not in the cabinet." We were walking very quickly. I assumed it was because of anger and not the warm morning. I could already feel the asphalt's heat under my flip-flops.

"The girls want sprinkles," she corrected me.

"Okay."

"It's not a normal thing to kill a kid on his motorcycle and leave his girlfriend in the woods."

It had been almost a month since my mother had made her startled confession at the police station. She remained startled thereafter, even while she was formally charged and then incarcerated. She couldn't wear eyeliner or fake nails anymore and looked surprisingly younger because of it. She would not be in jail long, the lawyer assured us. The statute of limitations had run out on all the offenses, some time ago in fact. There was initial buzz about murder, but the lawyer told us she could not be charged with murder. She didn't have the requisite mindset, he'd explained. Cady Rae had said much the same. She scoffed when my father asked about murder.

"Why are we talking about this?" I asked Jasper's mother angrily. I'd slowed our jaunt a little. We were standing in a pool of unrelenting sun that was giving me a blinding headache with its enthusiasm for the day, which already felt long and irritating. I'd woken up tired and to the sound of the girls arguing. Jasper had something he needed to do involving the hardware store and being outside for hours, unreachable and covered in earth detritus.

"I think you need to tell the girls—your girls—that this is very wrong, that you are very disappointed and upset with your mother, that you'll never speak to her again after what she's done."

We were now standing in front of the sliding entry doors, which were opening and closing because of our presence. Neither of us moved. "I'll tell them what I want to tell them. You don't even know my mother. She took me to New York when I was only seventeen and made it happen for me. She's a lot tougher than you are. You and your people from down south." I was trembling, clenching, roaring with irritation.

"Danielle, she hid a dead body behind your house. You have to tell the girls that you are never going to speak to her again. Jasper says you haven't told them that, that you're giving it time, but you can't do that. This is wrong. This wasn't some 'accident,' as you like to call it—you and your father. Your other sisters don't have children; they don't need to answer for this, but you do, for your girls."

The door kept opening and closing, and with it waves of air-conditioning smacked our front sides, then evaporated around us. "I know," I said. I think I was talking about how my sisters didn't have kids. They would eventually. Maybe not Chantel, who could not possibly have a sexual relationship with her husband. From what I could tell, they mostly played board games and complained about traffic—in Deering, of all places, which was even smaller and less overrun with traffic than Pressville. "Chantel wants kids," I said more to myself. "So do the twins." We went into the store and walked toward the bakery department.

"When are you going to tell your girls that your mother is bad people and that you're not going to see her anymore?"

I blinked slowly. "I don't think I'm going to tell them that."

"You have to, Danielle." She hadn't raised her voice but was speaking more viciously. "You have to." A small bit of spittle escaped her mouth and landed on the floor next to my foot. We both saw, then ignored it.

"I don't know what I have to do," I said. "But it's my fault, so I'm not going to tell my kids we can't talk to their grandmother anymore. Unless, of course, you keep this up." I think I'd conjured a little Deb in that moment, the Deb of old, the one I'd ruined. One false move on Bell Road and three people never came back. I hadn't seen my mother since it happened, not the Deb Greer I grew up with.

"What's wrong?" Jasper's mother asked. She was talking to me, I think repeating herself over and over about me publicly condemning my mother.

I realized I'd been standing there with my mouth open for some time. "What?" I said.

"Are you gonna faint or something? All I'm saying is that your daughters need to be told." She'd missed my comment about us ditching a grandmother.

"I'll still love her," I said, standing next to the pastry case. "I'll still love her no matter what I say."

"Who?" Jasper's mother was struggling with the tongs.

"My mother."

She raised an eyebrow, perhaps reminding herself why she'd always thought I was a bad match for Jasper, and she had. I was too old to be in college, and what was with the modeling lingerie in my teens? She hadn't approved; she had tolerated. It was the theme of her life, this tolerance. "He's not going to love her," she said. I knew she'd been wanting to mention this. Jasper was on her side; the Greers were bad news. She'd probably told him a hundred times before. Her sudden significance irritated me more than her urgent reproach of my mother. Why was she always around now? It had only been a month, and I could feel the pillow over my face.

"I'm going to love her because she loved me."

"I don't love everyone who's loved me," she said.

"No." I thought about Benji. "I guess some people don't."

We went home with a pack of glazed and four with sprinkles.

46

I went to the county correctional facility on the day they were releasing my mother. I had not, as requested by Jasper's mom, denounced Deb or anyone else to my children. I actually spoke more affectionately of her, like one might of a relative with drug problems who had once been so lovely.

My father was to pick her up, but I waited for her in the lobby, planning to speak to her before he arrived. It was just like in the movies. They gave her her clothes and a small bag with her belongings inside. She'd only been there about a month and a half. It was a blip on the radar screen, but it mattered because of what it represented—this thing she'd done, that I'd made her do.

"I'm sorry," I said when she saw me. There were people milling about, but like all things in and around Pressville, Georgia, it was not particularly busy.

"No," she said, and for a second I thought she was going to

argue with me. This teenage insistence that everything and everyone be against me reared its ugly head, and I tensed. "I'm sorry," she said. It was said plainly. My mother didn't say hardly anything plainly; it was how I knew she meant it.

I'd talked to Cady Benson the day before. She took my call after having me on hold for close to ten minutes. I thought maybe it was a power play. I hadn't responded to her the last few times she'd reached out. I couldn't figure out what to say. She had this irritatingly sympathetic tone in her voice, like she was so riddled with guilt over finally finding out what happened to Louisa Radcliffe after all this time and that it had something to do with my family— not me, but my family—that she felt sorry for me. I honestly thought she'd been feeling sorry for me for most of my life, first with the babysitting and then with the modeling—which she must have thought was such a scam, so embarrassing and desperate— and then the accident, and my mother. I must have seemed such a sad figure to her, especially when I came back to Pressville with my tidy husband in tow, living in the family home, this melancholy bundle of bad decisions and sorrow. To think we'd pitied her and her family's chicken restaurant.

"Hi," Cady said after the long hold, during which I listened to some excellent early-nineties love songs. "Sorry for that. We're having my mother moved into a home in Wayneston. I've been trying to get the details sorted out for a month, at least. I just needed to finish that."

313

"Sorry," I said. "About your mom."

"People get old," she said. "What can I do ya for? I've tried calling a few times."

"I know. So much on my mind."

"I understand."

"So you're letting her out?"

"I don't have anything to do with it anymore, but yes, they are releasing her—not without stipulations, I understand, but there's really nothing left to do at this point."

"What's done is done."

"That's right. Kind of that way every day, isn't it? Things are done pretty quick."

"Do you think she's a bad person?"

"No. I think she pulled the wheel of her car in front of that kid to be a jerk, and he went off the road because it's a bad road, and that's what happened. Now, why she would hide that poor girl down there in a ditch is another thing."

"She didn't know she was there," I said. "Not at first... I mean... you know, when she jerked the wheel."

"I believe that."

"What am I supposed to do?"

"What do you mean?" I could hear the creak of her seat, which I knew to be an old-fashioned rectangular-backed roller on a wheeled T-frame.

"I don't know what to do about this."

"There isn't anything to do, Danielle. It's already happened. It happened a long time ago."

"But I have to do something."

"Imagine if she was your daughter and not your mother. What would you do?"

"Go on loving her." My answer was automatic. "I'd think she was wrong, did a bad thing, but that I had to love her. I sound like I think I'm Jesus or something."

"I don't know about that, but I think you just answered your question."

Reading Group Guide

1. Danielle is quite young and inexperienced when she leaves her home for New York City. Do you think she is brave to do so or impulsive? Do you think she is too young?

2. How is life different in a small town versus a big city, and which do you prefer? Does Danielle act differently when she's in Pressville versus when she's in New York?

3. Why do you think Danielle is so eager to leave her hometown? What pressures does her mother put on her, both in Georgia and in New York?

4. How is Danielle affected by the way her mother sees the world? How do our parents and other family influence our perspectives as we age?

5. Danielle describes her mother as two people: "that woman, and someone else I feel like I've never met." Have you ever felt that way about a parent or someone close to you? Have you thought about the lives they lived and the people they were before you came along?

6. Does Danielle have a healthy relationship with money as a teenager? What do you consider to be a healthy relationship when it comes to money and spending habits? Has your relationship with money changed over the years?

7. Young Danielle is extremely uncomfortable in her own skin and very insecure. Do you think this feeling is normal for every teenager, or is it heightened in her case from her exposure to the modeling industry at such a young age?

8. What is the allure of the so-called "bad boy," and why do you think Danielle was so drawn to Benji?

9. What was your first love like, if you had one? Did you act differently with that person than any subsequent partners?

10. Danielle's mother greatly disapproves of her relationship with Benji. How do you think this affected the events of the novel? Is her mom right to get involved in the relationship? Do you have

experience with a loved one not approving of your partner or of your choices in life?

11. Danielle believes that in the fifteen years since the accident, she hasn't changed as a person. Do you think this is true? How does grief or trauma affect a person, especially when experienced at a young age?

12. If someone you love does something terrible, can you forgive them? Does it depend on your relationship to that person or what they did?

13. Danielle feels she is to blame for her mother's actions. Do you think she's to blame at all? Can you be responsible for someone else's choices?

Acknowledgments

I would like to thank Erin and Alyssa; you make dreams come true. Tish Goff for her profound insight and meaningful conversation; Mom, Dad, Rone, and Weez for being my family—I won the ovarian lottery. And finally Johan, Hol, and Con; you are my life.

ABOUT THE AUTHOR

Lo Patrick's first novel, *The Floating Girls*, was a finalist for the Townsend Prize for Fiction and a *Reader's Digest* Editors' Pick. She lives in Georgia with her husband and two children.